COWBOY

Cowboy

L.B. DUNBAR

BUSY
BEAN
CAFE

HeartEyes
Press

Editor: Melissa Shank

Editor: Jenny Sims/Editing4Indies

Proofread: Karen Fischer

For the patience and grace needed in 2020.
And milk, cheese, and ice cream.

1

IT ONLY TAKES ONCE

SCARLETT

If you told me earlier this evening I'd have a hot, hunky silver fox buried to the hilt deep inside me, I'd have told you that you were crazy. Hell, if you told me it would have happened even a month ago, I'd have said *never*.

However, I'm losing my mind over a man I met only hours ago.

"So, my friends over there. They dared me to come buy you a drink." He was all charming and nervous-sweet, and I just couldn't seem to say no. Then again, I'd been on my third beer at the local establishment called The Gin Mill, a place famous for their Vermont beer selection. My friend and I were celebrating my new status.

Single.

Sort of.

I grunt as his hips flex between my spread thighs, and my hands clutch at his broad back. I'd never done anything like this before, and I don't expect to ever do it again, but there is no denying how I feel at the moment.

Liberated.

Satisfied.

With his lips on my neck, and his thick shaft balls deep, the man over me means freedom and a bit of recklessness. However, I would not be under him without the approval of my friend.

Rita Kaplan had been my college roommate, and her nod at the bar encouraged me to speak up when this sweet-talking stranger asked to buy me a drink.

"I'll see your hello and raise you a take me to bed, partner."

Probably not what Rita had expected me to say, but she knew I needed this. I'd had a day a week back—a day of all days—but I am not thinking about that at the moment. With the musky scent of sex between us and sticky skin holding us together, this beautiful male specimen surges into me over and over again.

Bull is his name. Bull Eaton.

Earlier, the Eaton name sounded vaguely familiar, but I quickly dismissed it. In my line of work, the names all run together after a while. *Line of work I used to be in*, I reminded myself, when we met only hours ago.

Bull is living up to his name in size, girth, and stamina, but he's also got an anxious charm about him. His midnight blue eyes shifted over to his friends as his large, thick hands slipped into the back pockets of his jeans after he approached me. He rocked on the heels of his boots as he said hello, and his smile did swirly-twirly things to my insides. I did not attribute that sensation to the number of beers I'd drunk, but the slow curl of his lips and the crook at one corner. The silver scruff on his cheeks helped. I'm forty-two, and having a man my age, hitting on me no less, did something for my shattered ego.

And he's still doing something to me.

"So deep," he groans. I've never been so full in my life. My eyes roll back, and my ankles cross over his solid thighs, heels digging at the firm globes of his backside.

"Sweetheart," he huffs. The word stammers as he rocks into me, taking me to another world. Our position might be mission-ary, but nothing perfunctory is happening here other than the stars I'm seeing from the orgasms this man has given me. He's working on my third, and I just don't know if I can get there.

As if reading my thoughts, he shifts, dragging himself upward so his hard length rubs at my pleasure point in a new way, and I'm gasping for air again.

"Bull," I moan.

When he followed me to my rental at the Green Rocks resort, I didn't know if he'd really take me up on my offer or if he'd just intended to escort me home.

"You cannot go wrong with this swanky man," Rita had encouraged, and I felt like a heel leaving my friend behind. *"Honey, this is the purpose of this night."* I needed to lose myself with someone hot, willing, and available. Rita trusted him, which was good enough for me. I promised her we'd find her a man next time.

Bull's hand cups my lower cheeks, lifting me to adjust the angle and rub his thickness against my clit better. "Gonna give me another one." It's not a question or a warning. It's a tender command. He's already been more than generous with me. His fingers. His mouth. He wants this orgasm as much as I do, and I have a strong suspicion Bull Eaton could own my heart and soul if I let myself get carried away.

However, before we even got in his truck, we made an agreement with that first kiss outside The Gin Mill.

"Just one night, sweetheart. That's all we need to sort ourselves out."

I needed sorting. God, I needed so much sorting. But for tonight, I only needed Bull.

"I can't . . . I don't think . . . I've never . . . so many." I don't make any sense, and he chuckles even harder as he's moving me against him, sliding himself in and out of me.

"You will, sweetheart. You'll see."

My arms stretch over my head, reaching for the headboard behind me. I never had a headboard like this before, and it is an investment I seriously need to consider in the future. For now, I curl my fingers around the wrought-iron bars and hold on as Bull works his magic. My toes curl. My back arches.

"Bull . . . I . . . *ermygawd.*" I'm breaking free again, coming apart at the seams as he balances over me, letting me ride this one out with him inside me. He's on his knees, hitching my lower body up his thighs, handling me like a prize and taking me for a winning. He's moving faster than before, and I'm just dust in the wind, floating outside myself and letting him have his way with me.

"So fucking beautiful," he stammers, and I smile to myself. He's been saying it over and over, and I'll say it again, he's just so sweet. Even though I've worked in the public eye, I'm not used to genuine compliments like he's given me.

You taste like honey.

You feel like home.

Who says such a thing? I reach out for his chest, coasting my hands over the firmness of his pecs.

"Love your hands on me," he grunts, thrusting into me, and then he hisses, clutches my hips, and holds me to him. I look down where we're joined as if I can see what's actually happening. Instead, I feel it. I feel him, and it's amazing. The pulse. The pump. He pulls back and slams forward once more, finishing himself inside me.

Thank God for condoms and the pill.

He releases my trembling legs and falls over me, balancing on his hands as his chest heaves.

"Sweetheart, once will not be enough with you." I bite my lip in response, perhaps a little too pleased that he wants me again. "I'm not as young as I used to be, so give me twenty minutes."

With him still attached to me, our eyes meet, and an additional jolt seizes inside me.

"What was that?" I laugh.

"Aftershocks." He smiles, one side of his mouth crooking up in a tease. "You rocked me to my core."

We both chuckle and then he leans forward to kiss me. It isn't quick and brief. He isn't rushing to pull out of me. He isn't leaving me for his side of the bed. He's taking his time to kiss me, slow and steady, like he's grateful for what we just did when I'm the one wanting to thank him.

Emotions wrestle inside me and I fight the tears prickling at the corners of my eyes.

No more tears, Scarlett Russell. After this night, you're going to be just fine.

Bull sucks at my lower lip, tugging it as he retreats. Deep blue eyes stare down at me, looking at me like he really sees me. It's a bit unnerving, but I also like that's he's trying to see me, like he wants to know me.

If I only knew myself. I'm no longer certain who I am, or what I want.

"Twenty minutes, sweetheart?" His eyes ask permission, just like he did earlier. Before he kissed me. Before he followed me inside this rental. Before we did anything. He asked if it was okay with me, and I just couldn't say no. He could ask me anything, and I'd never turn him down.

"Twenty minutes," I whisper. "And not a second longer."

That wins me another tender smile and a quiet chuckle before his lips return to mine, kissing me like he'd never deny me anything.

HOW IT STARTED

BULL

"No more women." I stare into my beer, the thick head still visible as the waitress at The Gin Mill just served us.

"You aren't serious?" My younger brother Canyon laughs at me. He's shaking his head with a deep chuckle. "You're a damn hopeless romantic. How's that going to work for you?"

"I think you just mean hopeless period," I retort. One week ago, I had my final date from that stupid app my brother and his best friend signed me up on. DatingDairy dot com is just what it implies—a spot for men of my profession to meet women willing to date, mate, and marry dairy farmers. However, I've already been down the aisle a few times, and I am no longer interested in the endgame. Marriage is obviously not for me. And that date was my last as it was a disaster.

Canyon is a fine one to talk about romantics. He's always writing love songs in that old leather notebook of his. It might be strange to be best friends with my younger brother by three years but growing up on a farm makes tight-knit families or ferocious enemies. Working together day in and day out, we've had our share of fights, but at our core, friendship is more important than anything. And seeing as I might be living the rest of my life with only my brothers and father, I better get along with them.

"Well, if it isn't the Perpetual Proposer? Mr. Bovine King himself." My spine bristles at the sassy male tenor coming from behind me. Canyon looks over his shoulder, but I don't need to look up to know Redd Bottom is the one to make his remarks.

"Evenin', Redd. I'd ask how it's hanging, but I'm assuming short," Canyon states, holding up his thumb and forefinger only an inch apart. We might all be near forty, but when it comes to Redd and his sidekick Dillard Barnes, we are all still teens at heart. The thing about men who peaked in high school is they stay in that frame of mind for the rest of their lives, and Dillard and Redd remain eternal juveniles.

The Bottom family owns land adjacent to ours, and they've been wanting to do joint business with us, sharing fields between their sheep and our cows. My family isn't interested. Every cattleman despises sheep farmers because sheep can really tear up a field. Redd is an ignorant ass.

I snort into my beer as Canyon keeps his eyes on Redd behind me. Canyon glares daggers at Redd, and I finally turn to face a man who loves to compete with me. Formerly in football. Bowling league. Ax throwing. You name it, and Redd loves to *try* to best me, but I'm not called Bull just because it's my name. My skin has grown thick over the years.

"Redd," I address him.

"Come out to the Mill to find new tail?" he teases. "Or are you counting how many you can run off instead?" He slaps my back as if his cruel joke is hilarious, but I turn away from him. Fighting ignorance isn't worth it to me, and I want to just sit here and wallow in my beer this evening.

My youngest brother, Blade, is also at the table with us, and he shifts off his stool, standing to his full height beside me.

"Sit down," I mutter to Blade. We don't need any trouble tonight, and Blade likes to scrap. He's one mistake away from

7

asking Redd to step outside, but I give my brother an arched eyebrow. *Redd isn't worth it.*

"Be seeing you around the barnyard," Redd teases. "That's unless you bring the cows home first." He chuckles heartily as though he's just said the funniest thing. I ignore the fact I know what his joke means. Again, just want to sit here and drink a beer and not remember my horrible history with women.

"I fucking hate that guy," Blade admits once Redd walks away.

"His name is so appropriate," Clayton Parker huffs. Clayton works on our farm and rounds out our foursome of friends. "Redd Bottom. He's an ass."

Canyon snorts in agreement, and I slowly smile, letting Redd's remarks roll off me. My thick skin needs to be thicker some nights.

"He doesn't know anything," Clayton adds, meeting my eyes, offering me sympathy. But Redd knows a thing or two about me as do most people in this community. I have a bad habit of getting engaged but not married.

"Fuck him. You need to get laid," Blade adds. "And I don't mean fuck him to get laid. I mean, find a woman to fuck to get laid."

"We know what you mean," Canyon sasses to our little brother, treating him like a big dummy. However, Blade isn't wrong. I'm in a dry spell despite the dates from DatingDairy, and before that, the MateMe app, both of which my brother and his friend made me accounts on. Then they proceeded to communicate with women, pretending to be me to get me back out there.

"You need a one-night stand," Canyon reports, which surprises me coming from him. His past is riddled with them, leading him to all kinds of trouble. "You get in, get out, and move on. No commitments. No proposals. Just free and clear sex." He swipes his hands together and then shakes them off to the side, emphasizing the throwaway term.

"One and done, like that old cow theory," Blade suggests.

"Blade, have you been reading again?" I mock. "You know that's dangerous."

Ignoring me, he continues. "A bull only mates once with a cow. Twice, if *she's* lucky." He winks at me.

I huff. My days of one-night stands have long passed. That's what my twenties were all about until I met Jennifer. She was my everything, or so I thought at twenty-two when we hastily married. We divorced almost as quickly.

"I'm too old for one-night stands," I retort, lifting my lager and taking a hardy drink of the heavy beer. The Gin Mill houses all the Vermont specialty beers including Goldenpour and Shipley's ciders. Alec Rossi owns this cool place located by the river in Colebury. The old gin mill factories have been slowly converted into a dining and entertainment center of sorts, complete with this establishment; the Busy Bean Café, a coffeehouse; and a new brewpub, called Speakeasy.

"Never too old to get back in the saddle," Clayton prophetically states.

"I'm a cow man," I remind him, poking fun at my own name.

Bull—Harland Bull Eaton the third actually.

"Then it's time to let someone ride the bull again," Blade suggests, snorting before taking a sip of his beer. His head turns as the bar door opens, and we all glance over to see Rita Kaplan entering with a woman I've never seen before. Rita's roughly my age. I don't often see her in a bar, knowing her background as a recovered alcoholic. I'm assuming she's here for moral support of her friend.

And that friend is a looker with fiery red hair, falling in thick waves just below her chin. She slips off her jacket, revealing a sweater that slides off her shoulder, exposing creamy skin. When she looks up, she catches me staring, and deep dark eyes narrow in on me. A slow smile curls her purple-tinted lips, and then she looks away.

"Damn," Canyon mutters.

"I see her," Clayton replies.

"Wowza," Blade adds.

"Fuck off, all of you," I quickly say. "Settle your dicks." We're like our own lonely-hearts club at fucking forty-something, and it sucks. However, these guys are hornier than rabbits most days.

Canyon shakes his head again. "Bull, man, seriously. Here's your shot. One night. Just buy her a drink. That's the only commitment. One drink. No rings." He speaks like I'm carrying around diamonds in my pocket. Here's one for you, and one for you, and another one for you. I've actually never proposed with a diamond ring.

"Keep it slow. No big words like love, marriage, and a baby in a baby carriage," Blade adds as if I need coaching from the other eternal bachelor.

"What the fuck?" I mutter. The guys chuckle at my expense, and I get it. I do. I've been standing at the end of an aisle too many times. "I'm not doing this."

"Bull, dude. She keeps looking over here. Just say hi. That's not a commitment either. It's a way to start a conversation," Clayton encourages.

"Hardy-har, boys." These guys are such assholes. I know how this night is going to go. The more they drink, the more they razz, putting them almost on par with Redd and Dillard.

Look at Bull, dairy king handing out another ring.

Our waitress brings another round that I don't remember ordering. It doesn't stop me from chugging down the additional beer, though, before Clayton throws out a challenge.

"Milk time for a week." He tips his head toward the redheaded beauty I keep taking glances at. "Just a drink."

"For a week?" The boys know I don't actually mind milking. It's a repetitive process, and the soft lulls of the cows let my thoughts run their course before the rest of the day needs my attention. I wouldn't even know how to sleep in as I'm so used to getting up at four in the morning. Still, I double his challenge. "Two weeks."

"Done," Clayton says, reaching over the table and shaking my hand.

"Maybe she's your four-leaf clover. A lucky charm," Blade adds, rubbing his hands together, and right there, I know he's jinxed me.

"Hey, Rita."

My eyes leap to her tablemate and then back to her. Rita has dark hair with faint lines of white, giving away her age a bit.

"Hiya yourself, handsome. How are you tonight, Bull?"

Reaching for the back of my neck, I nervously scratch.

"Just thought I'd come over and say hi." I glance back at her friend, unnerved by the dark depths of her eyes.

"Uh-huh." Rita takes a sip of the cola in her glass. "Bull Eaton, this is my friend, Scarlett Russell. Scarlett, Bull."

Our eyes meet, and I swear my heart does a two-step dance. Struggling to keep myself in check, I slip my hands into my back pockets and rock on my boot heels. I'm a fucking teenage mess looking at her with those large coffee-colored eyes.

"My friends dared me to buy you a drink." The words rush out, bursting forth like hot air in a balloon. Scarlett laughs, looking like she's already had a few.

With a large smile curling those purple-painted lips, she says, "Well, I'll see your hello and one-up you. How about taking me home, Bull?"

"Pardon me?" I stammer, unbelieving my ears.

"I said, I'll see your hello and raise you to . . . take me to bed, partner."

I blink. I look at Rita. I glance back at her friend. It couldn't be that easy.

"How about that drink?" I nod toward her glass.

"Had plenty already," she states, staring up at me with saucer-sized eyes. *Damn, she's so pretty.*

"You drunk?" I have to ask. She shakes her head, and Rita leans over, saying something to her that I miss while taking in the light dusting of freckles on her nose and cheeks. She glances at Rita and then slips off the stool.

"Lead on." She holds out a hand before me.

Taking her hand, I don't look up at the guys as I pass them, but I'm certain their mouths are hanging open. Somewhere in the bar, I hope Redd and Dillard are watching. Holding up my hand, I give a raised V salute over my shoulder to whomever might be watching me.

Two weeks, buddy, I intend for Clayton. Or victory, however, they want to read it.

I'm not that crass, though, and once outside, I gently grab her upper arm and swing her toward the exterior of the bar.

"We don't have to do anything you don't want to do, darlin'," I say to her, leaning in and sliding my hand above her head. As she's several inches shorter than me despite high heeled boots, she looks up at me, biting the corner of her lip, and I swear I want to look into that swirling chocolate gleam as I enter her repeatedly, but I take a deep breath.

"Darlin'?" she mocks, grinning a little broader. "Seriously?"

"Don't like that one? How about baby girl?"

"Oh no, not that one." She laughs, and the tease in her tone tickles down my spine like a featherlight caress. My balls tighten, and I slide my hand down the exterior wall, bringing my body closer to her. Leaning in for her neck, I've never worked this fast before. I'm worrying I'm about to blow it as my nose glides up the side of her floral-scented skin, and I inhale.

"How about sweetheart?" I whisper, elongating the endearment as my lips brush the shell of her ear. Her breath catches, and her breasts heave, softly dragging against my shirt.

"That'll work," she whispers, and I slide my cheek against hers.

"Sweetheart it is, then," I say, my exhale hitting her lips like a kiss. Only I'm ready for the real thing, so my mouth takes hers.

She's quick to respond, giving back to me what I'm giving her. Soft sucks and tender tugs, then tongues seek, and I'm pressing firmer against her. She tips her head as I'm quite a bit taller than her. Hands slip up my chest and around my neck, latching onto me, and she uses her elbows at my shoulders to leverage herself higher. The next thing I know, her legs are around my waist, and I have her pinned to the exterior wall.

"How about that bed?" she says against my mouth.

"Anything you want, sweetheart."

Her lips smile against mine, and we return to kissing for another minute.

Yeah, I'll be giving this woman anything—for one night and one night only.

3

TWO MORNINGS AFTER

SCARLETT

"Well?" Rita asks, elongating the word and waiting on details. It's been two days since my one-night stand, and I don't know what to say.

"What do you want me to tell you?" I impishly ask, lifting my large coffee mug of dark roast. My eyes lower to the maple syrup walnut muffin on the marble coffee table before me. Rita and I sit on a plush peach couch in the Busy Bean Café, a local coffee house on the same property as The Gin Mill.

"Girl, I am living vicariously through you. Give me all the details," Rita says with a good-natured laugh. I'd love to tell her everything, but for some reason, I won't. I can't tell her how Bull took me against the door, over a desk, and on the bed, twice. How his thick fingers, wicked mouth, and amazing penis brought me to climax five times in twelve hours. How looking at that maple muffin on the table reminds me of the maple syrup sample in my rental at the Green Rocks and how Bull used it on me, making me a human muffin of sorts. Or how I woke alone in the morning torn between satisfied and disheartened.

"It was . . . fun."

"Fun?" Rita sputters, spraying a bit of her black coffee from her lips. "Going to knitting club is fun. Listening to kids laugh is fun. Watching a hockey game is fun. Bull Eaton is not fun. That hunk of a man is seriously hot *and hung*. I mean, I imagine he's hung. I have no idea if he is, but he has to be. His name is Bull." Rita's voice rises in exasperation at my lack of facts, causing me to laugh.

Rita is my oldest friend. We met in college and formed an instant connection with one another. I hate that life got in the way for both of us after graduation, meaning we haven't seen as much of each other in the past two decades. I've missed her. In a weird fluke of the cosmos, she called me on the day my life crumbled, and I'm so grateful I answered the phone. It's like some higher power knew I needed a friend, and there Rita was, encouraging me to come to Vermont to visit her.

"Would you keep your voice down?" I chuckle again, looking over my shoulder. The Busy Bean Café is a quaint establishment. Quirky and eclectic, it's the definition of fun. The place has large, leaded glass windows overlooking the Winooski River, wide pinewood floors, and walls in a warm brick color. Heavy beams painted in black chalkboard paint are decorated with cartoon figures of coffee drinks and sayings like "May the odds be ever in your flavor." Cute pun. Furniture like this plush peach couch is just a part of the novel collection of tables, chairs, and easy furniture arranged for maximum socializing. The coffee bar itself is topped with a thick zinc counter and holds a glass display case with various pastries. It's wacky, warm, and wonderful in here.

"Look, if I can't live through you, what is the purpose of my life?" Rita teases. While that might have been true when I had the lush apartment, the sexy husband, and the energizing job, it's no longer the case. No one wants to live through me, not even me.

"You don't think badly of me?" I hesitate. "I mean, it's only been a week since I left Boston." While I probably should feel a little more guilt that I so easily slept with a virtual stranger one week after leaving my husband, I don't. He slept with someone else first, but it's not as easy as tit for tat. Shelton and I have been distant for longer than I was willing to recognize. The reality of our waning closeness has weighed heavily on my mind this past week.

"Girl, I would never think badly of you. We all make decisions for a variety of reasons. Falling into bed with a hunky man doesn't seem like the worst to me. You deserve a reckless night once in a while."

"But I'm still married," I remind her.

"Which your husband seemed to have forgotten long before the other night." Rita's correct, and my guilt subsides a little more. There's no reconciliation in sight for Shelton and me. I don't want to go back to who we were or who I was.

"What I really want to know is when will you see Bull again?" Rita asks.

"I won't." I shrug. Bull was more than fun but waking up without his number was a good reminder I'm not really a one-night stand kind of girl. On the other hand, I'm not looking for a relationship that involves any kind of commitment.

"Why not?"

"He didn't leave me his number."

Rita stares at me, blinking behind red-framed eyeglasses. *They're fun.* "He didn't leave his number?" Rita's expression matches her incredulous voice.

I shake my head. "Maybe it's normal for someone like Bull to have one-night stands. Love 'em and leave 'em style." Even as I say the words, I don't think they're true. Bull wasn't so cavalier unless he's a damn good actor and lover, which he was *damn good* on the lover level. He was generous. *God, was he generous.* He made sure I came first and often, and then when I was finished, he made certain I was satisfied before moving forward. Unlike Shelton, who typically came first and offered me assistance second, Bull was attentive and considerate. I'd hate to think his generosity was a performance on his part.

"Honey, that does not sound like Bull Eaton. Not one iota."

I stare at my friend, waiting for further explanation.

"Rumor has it he's asked five different women to marry him. He has commitment written all over him. A man who makes engagements does not forget to leave his phone number."

Apparently, Bull did not want commitment from me. But I'm not in a position to start a relationship anyway.

"Five engagements? That sounds a little desperate, and since when do you believe rumors?" Rita's an attorney. She thrives on facts, not hearsay.

"Since it's all I have to live off as *you* won't share details." We both laugh at her emphatic answer. "I'm not saying the rumors are true. It's just . . . Bull doesn't seem like a one-night stand kind of guy, even if I did push you in that direction." Rita's voice softens, expressing her concern and compassion for my situation.

"You didn't push me. And thanks again for coming out with me to The Gin Mill. Was that difficult for you?" My friend is a recovered alcoholic, and going to a bar might have been the last place on her list of good times.

"Not my first choice of hangouts but also not the most difficult place to hang. I know my limits, and I'd have let you know if I reached them. Did my own stud finder scope out while I was there."

"Stud finder?"

"You took the bull. I need a stud." A moment passes before I catch her meaning, and I bend at the waist, laughing a good hard laugh. *I have really missed this woman.*

"I promise we will get you one the next time." Although, I'm not certain there will be a next time. I don't know how to do the day after, or in this case, two days later, when I don't know how to find Bull.

"I could get you Bull's number. Quick little social media check or database search." Rita wiggles her brows.

"I don't want to hunt him down like some stalker, and I'm going to ignore the fact you mentioned database searching. You shouldn't abuse your attorney privileges." I wink at her. I've done my own sleuthing like that in the past, seeking the next great gossip before it broke wide, but those days are over now. "I'm not in a position for long term. I have bigger issues, like finalizing my divorce with Shelton, finding a new job, and deciding what's next for me."

Rita nods, accepting the hard truth of my messed-up life. "What do you think should be next?"

As it will take three to four months to finalize my divorce in the state of Massachusetts where Shelton and I resided, I just have to wait out that time. I can't think about a new job just yet, uncertain the entertainment industry is right for me anymore, which leaves me with my final decision.

I look around the coffee house and take a deep breath. It's been roughly ten days since I left Boston.

"I think I'd like to stay in Vermont a little longer. I've checked with the rental office at Green Rocks, and I can keep my place until May first." It's mid-March, and the continued rental gets me through April.

My friend's brows lift. "That's wonderful." Her genuine smile reassures me of my plan. "Can you afford it?" Then she laughs. "Of course, you can afford it, what am I saying?"

Not only was my husband the lead heart surgeon at Boston General, but I have financial stability in my own right from my career, and it might be time to splurge a little on me for once.

"I'd still like a job. Just something to keep me busy, and in the middle of people. I don't think I'll be good company with myself." It's not that I can't be alone; it's that I don't want to be alone. I'll spend too much time self-evaluating, wondering where I went wrong in my marriage and career. Admittedly, I have negative self-esteem issues from my parents who laid the groundwork, so I don't need the self-demoralization.

As I look around the room, I notice a sign in the front window. *Help Wanted.* Like the phone call I received from Rita on the day I lost both my husband and my job, I feel like this is another message from the universe.

"I could work here," I say, glancing back at Rita.

"What do you know about making coffee?"

"Nothing, but how hard can it be?"

More than a month later, I still don't quite have the hang of it, but the owners Zara Rossi and Audrey Shipley are more than patient with me. The café is busy, and another warm body actually helps out. I don't mind the menial work of wiping off tables and straightening chairs, restocking the pastry case or even washing out coffee pots. It gives me a chance to talk to people, and I love a good gossip story.

The other thing about me is I'm timely. I have nothing else going on in life, so why not take any shift offered, even the ungodly early ones. My divorce is proceeding as we aren't contesting anything. I don't want the apartment especially after my delinquent doctor husband moved his little pregnant med student into our home, and Shelton isn't disputing that he pay me my share of the property. It feels like dirty money to me, but I just want to be done with him. *Happy ex-wife equals happy life*. I should write that on the chalkboard beams.

I am happy, mostly. I spend time with Rita. I explore Vermont, and steer clear of where I think Bull Eaton might be. No more The Gin Mill. No Dunham where I've learned his family owns a dairy farm. Dunham is a small community, and I vaguely recall the name from a story I reported on a while back. Something about cows, as a matter of fact, but I can't remember the headline. As if my thoughts conjure the only dairyman I know, Bull enters the café.

With a woman.

Blinking to clear my vision, making certain it's really him, I drop behind the peach couch, falling to my hands and knees. Crawling to the edge of the furniture, I watch Bull place his hand on the small of the woman's back—a possessive move if I've ever seen one. He strokes up her spine, and I feel a little sick watching him touch her so intimately. Actually, I've been feeling a little sick a lot lately, and I chalk up the current nausea to the upheaval in my life.

The woman orders and then turns to Bull, offering him a sweet gaze as though she's totally smitten with him. She also looks about fifteen years younger than him. The strange part is, he doesn't seem to notice her looking up at him with hearts in her eyes. He just keeps his eyes forward and places his order.

Please let it be a to-go order. I send up my silent prayer to the cosmos but have no such luck in it being honored when the two pick up plates with muffins on them and cross the café to the couch I'm hiding behind.

Frick. *Frick.* Frick.

I need to get out from behind this couch, but I'm trapped. I'm working with Audrey and Roderick today. Audrey has the patience of a saint with me and that Astra coffee machine that looks like something from outer space. It makes three cups of coffee at once, but I've only mastered black and pointing at the cream and sugar counter.

"Well, this is exciting. I've never been on a breakfast date."

I've never been on a breakfast date. My lips silently move to mimic her. Her voice is too high, and she sounds like Vermont Barbie. Only, I know that's not fair of me. I'm jealous, and I admit it one hundred percent. I haven't been with another man since Bull and don't have immediate intentions to do so, but most of all, I've missed him—the strength of his body, the tenderness of his touch, and the incredible orgasms. On top of that, Bull was sweet. We laughed about silly stuff, never mentioning anything about our pasts or our futures.

Only tonight, he said. *Us and this bed are all we need in our heads.*

Only one night, and my chest aches when I think of him. It's silly to consider, but the attraction to him was so strong. The way we moved. The way we connected. It was so different from Shelton, but then I chalk up the sensation to being with someone other than my husband after so many years.

I tip my head to the back of the couch and then lean forward, hoping they didn't feel the jostle.

"So how do you know Dillard Barnes?" Bull asks as if picking up an unfinished conversation.

"We're old friends," she casually states, and I'm shaking my head at the sound of things. *Old friend, my ass.* His friend didn't keep her, or she didn't keep him, and now Bull will be second-string. My lips purse, admonishing myself because I used Bull as a rebound, too. Although it didn't feel like a rebound. He felt like the start of something new. He felt like my fresh start. My shoulders sag, though, as I recall waking alone that morning.

"What should we do today?" Her voice is like nails on the chalkboard-painted beams around us. *Why do older men always go for younger women?* I don't want to hear about their plans or what Bull will do to her later, especially if it involves maple syrup or a hotel desk. My eyes close at the memory.

"Well, we're just doing this right here," he states, and I almost laugh. Bull isn't simple, but he's a simple man. He's living in the moment, and I'm hoping this means he hasn't thought past this coffee date.

"A dark roast and a caramel macchiato with exactly five drizzles of caramel, fifteen pumps of vanilla syrup, whipped cream, and an extra shot."

What the . . .?

Thank God, I did not take that order. I don't even know what that is. There's a pause of silence, and I'm wondering what's happening when Bull says, "You have a little something . . ."

I just want to die a slow death as I imagine him swiping at the corner of her lip or wiping off her nose, and that sweet, tender touch will be all the spark Vermont Barbie needs to want to pounce on this man behind me. Bull has these deep blue eyes and that silver-speckled scruff, plus his hair is artfully streaked with gray. He's all-around sexy, and he doesn't even know it. Then his touch. The soft strokes down my body and the delicate dips of his fingers, I just can't—

"Have either of you seen Scarlett?" Audrey asks.

Frick.

"Scarlett?" Bull chokes from his seat on the couch.

"Yeah, Scarlett. She's our newest barista, and I swear she was out here."

"I didn't see anyone," Vermont Barbie states. "But then again, I've only been looking at Bull."

Okay, that's enough.

"Found it," I say, popping up from behind the couch and holding my fingers pinched together like I've just found gold *in them there wood floorboards.*

"Scarlett?" Audrey blinks at me with those expressive eyes of hers. She's a petite blonde with a lot of power behind her personality. I slowly stand but find myself dizzy as I do and grip the back of the couch for support.

"Whoa," I blurt, unable to stop myself as the room spins and my legs tremble. My skin runs cold, but I break out in a full-body sweat.

"Scarlett, are you okay?" Audrey asks, rushing to the edge of the couch while Bull quickly stands to face me.

"I . . . yeah, I just think I stood too fast." However, that isn't the full explanation because that rush to my head has now settled back down to my belly.

"You sure you're okay? You look a little gray," Audrey asks.

"I . . . excuse me." Rushing around the couch, I fight the pull to look at Bull as I disappear behind the counter, bypassing our waiting customers with one finger in the air, and then press out the door to the grassy area behind the building for some much-needed fresh air. Once outside, I promptly bend forward and heave.

"Oh my God, are you okay?" Audrey says behind me, and I close my eyes, embarrassed by my position in front of my boss. Audrey's younger than me, but a good businesswoman and kind-hearted. She took me on without any prior experience in the coffee industry.

"Yeah. Just something I ate, I think." I honestly don't know. It's been a couple of weeks like this; nausea, fatigue, and then if I do get sick, which doesn't always happen, I feel a million times better once I vomit. "I just have a little stomach bug, but I don't have a fever. I'm so sorry about this." I point at the grass, which holds the evidence of how my stomach felt. "And that." I nod toward the café.

Audrey's brows crease as she examines my face. "What else is wrong? As far as how you are feeling?"

I consider it a second and then answer. "My boobs hurt. My back kills. And I had a lobster roll for breakfast the other day. I think there was something wrong with the mayonnaise." Then I reconsider what I've said. The other morning, that sandwich had been the best damn lobster roll in the world and the last thing I'd ever eat when it comes to a breakfast item.

Audrey's lips slowly curl, and her eyes spark like she knows something. "Scarlett, could you be pregnant?"

"What? No. *Heavens no*. Absolutely not. I . . ." I stare back at her, horrified at the notion. I'm forty-two. I'm recently separated. I cannot be pregnant at this stage of my life.

"No. I am definitely not pregnant."

4

SIX WEEKS AND COUNTING

BULL

The next day, I return to the Busy Bean Café in hopes to find Scarlett.

"Sorry, Bull. She asked for the day off," Zara Rossi tells me. Zara is the second owner of the Busy Bean Café and a dark-haired beauty with a willowy body. She's a tough one—married to a professional hockey player and running this coffee shop.

Zara checks something and then assures me, "She'll be in tomorrow."

Taking my dark roast coffee out to my truck, I sit a second, letting the steamy liquid cool as I try to collect my thoughts —again.

Scarlett popping up from behind the couch in the café yesterday was more than a shock. I nearly had a heart attack, and it wasn't just the surprise of seeing her. My heart did a two-step jig of excitement.

She was still here.

During our one night, Scarlett told me how she was visiting Rita and wouldn't be staying in town long. I took the information as further evidence that a one-night stand with her was best. No point in getting attached when you know in advance someone is leaving, and attachment was the last thing I needed. I'd already been left behind too often *without* a hint the person was going. The night with Scarlett was a sign the boys were right, and one night would reset me.

It's a reason I finally gave in and contacted Louisa Miller. I won't actually say I called her. More like stumbled into a conversation with her at the tractor supply store that left me agreeing to go out with her. After second-guessing that decision, I got Louisa's phone number from Clayton, knowing somehow he'd have it, and worked my way out of dinner plans to a cup of coffee instead.

Because I haven't stopped thinking about Scarlett. That vibrant red hair. Those dark brown eyes. That sexy mouth of hers. Sinful is more like it, and she used that mouth on me twice. She also made these little noises that turn me hard just thinking about her, and I've been overthinking.

I should have left her my number or gotten hers.

I wanted to linger in bed that morning, take her out to breakfast, and plan a day with her, but that defeated the purpose of a one-night stand, and that is all we agreed to. As soon as I felt that tug to stay, I knew I needed to leave. Even though I got out of two weeks of morning milking, which I did not take Clayton up on, I didn't like the empty sensation I had after that night.

My insides ached a little at walking away. Scarlett felt different than the women in my past. I couldn't explain it, but it felt like she belonged in my arms and in my bed. She belonged with me, but then again, wasn't that feeling always the first sign of my downfall.

Then there she was, springing up from behind the couch when I was sharing coffee with Louisa.

"Scarlett Russell works here?" I had asked Roderick, the baker, who stood behind the counter after Audrey followed Scarlett out the back door.

"Yes. She's been here about six weeks, I guess. She's the worst barista

ever but the best kind of person." My head lowered, and my cheeks flushed. How did I not know this? How did I not know Scarlett stayed?

Then again, it's rare I head into Colebury during the daylight hours and even rarer that I give in to the luxury of coffee from a café. We've got a pot that works just fine for brewing the liquid gold at the farm.

"Is everything okay, Bull?" Louisa had said from behind me yesterday, reminding me of where I was and why I was there.

My head popped up, and I stared at the closed door leading out the back of the building.

Crap. *Crappity,* crap, crap.

"Yeah, I'm good," I lied, scratching at the back of my neck. Roderick tilted his head, looking up at me, and I honestly didn't know how to talk my way out of what was happening. Before Louisa interrupted me, I was about to ask Roderick if he'd take my number for Scarlett or maybe I could get hers from him, or just anything.

"We should be going," I'd muttered instead, ignoring my cup of coffee on the low table and the muffin I no longer had the stomach to digest. Louisa wasn't happy, and I'd like to have said I'd make it up to her, but I knew I wouldn't. I'd be chasing down a woman who I let slip away from me instead.

Returning the following day, a startled Scarlett watches me stalk to the counter. Since two days prior, her color has returned. I'd never seen a person turn that shade of molten gray, not even my youngest brother, Blade, when he drank too much on his twenty-first birthday.

"Scarlett." My voice comes out a little breathless, considering I'm trying to play it cool and not rush to the questions hammering inside my head.

"Bull. What can I get you?" Her voice is tight, pinched even, which is not how I remember her. She nods at the menu.

You? "Dark roast, black only."

"Thank God," she mutters, turning around and working a machine that looks like one of our milkers. An awkward silence fills the air around us as the only sound is the stream of coffee pouring into a mug. Scarlett turns back to me, hands shaking and coffee wobbling against the insides of the ceramic. Without thinking, I reach for it, steadying her fingers with mine over hers.

"I got it," I whisper. Scarlett releases the mug to me, rings up the order, and I pay, but I don't take my eyes off her.

Once my transaction is complete, Scarlett turns around to poke her head into the kitchen behind the counter. "Bathroom break," she announces to someone. "Just a few minutes."

"Take ten," Zara's voice wafts out to the main café, and I watch as Scarlett quickly walks to the hallway where the restrooms are located.

Oh no.

Rushing after her, I catch the door to the ladies' room, and Scarlett spins to face me.

"You really need to go, sweetheart?" I nod toward the toilet.

Her shoulders fall, and her face turns away from me. "Bull, I—"

Stepping forward, confident she's only avoiding me, I lock the door behind me and lean against it, watching her.

"You stayed," I mutter, keeping my eyes on her. She'd told me she wasn't staying in town. *Did she lie to me?* Then again, we agreed on only one night. Still, I haven't been able to get her out of my head, and here she is.

"I can explain. Sort of." I wait her out. "I didn't think I was staying, but then I changed my mind. My life was falling apart . . . is falling apart . . . and this place just feels like a good fit for a while. Until I figure things out for my future."

"And your future is being a barista in Colebury?"

"For now."

"For how long?" I ask, unease coming over me.

"I don't know, Bull, honestly. I'm confused about . . . a lot of things." Her head pops up, and she swipes back at her hair, holding her fingers in those lush red strands on either side of her neck. She cut her hair a little shorter, and it springs in loose curls around her head. "You were gone the next morning."

"I had milking to do."

"Excuse me?" Her head tilts.

"I need to be up at four each morning to milk the cows."

Scarlett turns her face away from me. "You left me alone in bed to milk some cows." Her arms cross, disbelieving such a thing before she glances back at me. "That is the worst excuse I've ever heard. It's like me saying I have to wash my hair to get out of a date."

I snort. "Do you say that?"

"Say what?"

"That you need to wash your hair to get out of a date."

"No." She snorts, scrunching up that elegant nose, which accentuates her freckles at bit. "I don't date."

"Why not?"

"What do you mean 'why not'?"

"Why aren't you dating someone?" She's fucking beautiful, and men should be lined up to date her. Hell, I'm grateful I got one night with her, and the reason I'm standing in the women's bathroom is because I wanted a second night.

Scarlett takes a deep inhale and then slowly releases the air. "I'm newly divorced . . . or nearly divorced." Her arms flail out from her sides before falling to her hips.

"Which one is it?" I ask, hating how my insides twist with the idea of being with a married woman.

"Nearly. I have roughly six more weeks before it's finalized. There's no contest, though. I don't want anything, and he got what he wanted."

"What's that? What'd he want?" What kind of fool wants something other than her?

"A med student who he got pregnant while still married to me."

"Shit." My head tips back, knocking softly against the door. *Fucking idiot.*

"What about you?" she snaps. My head pops forward, and I blink at her. "You were here on a breakfast date the other morning, and I've heard about you and all your proposals."

"Oh yeah, and how many am I up to now?" I snark, hating the rumor mill around my history, and feeling as if she went right for the jugular with her snarky tone.

"Five."

I snort. "It's a small town. Stick around a little longer, and I'll probably be up to seven before you leave."

She glares at me, something unreadable in her eyes. *Wait?* Is she jealous?

"Do you do what you did with me often?" It's wordy, but my tongue ties with her looking at me the way she is. Our eyes lock together as her dark ones swirl. She's a red blanket, and I'm ready to charge, living up to my namesake.

"Bull, I know you don't know me, but I swear on a stack of coffee menus I have never had a one-night stand in my life."

I press off the door and stand taller.

"And I've never felt the way I felt when I was with you," she adds, her chest heaving as if she's ready to charge me.

Something in me snaps with those words, and I step toward her. Or maybe she steps toward me because we collide in a crash of lips. My hands slip into her hair, and hers clutch at my broad back. We kiss and kiss, and she makes that little noise I can't describe, but I'm instantly hard.

"Bull," she mutters in a soft whimper of want.

"What do you need, sweetheart?" I ask between kisses under her ear and along her jaw. She'd told me that night she just needed to feel wanted, and I was more than willing to want her.

"This is crazy." She groans against my cheek as we can't get enough of each other.

"Tell me. I'll give you anything." My lips crush hers before she can immediately answer. Our mouths move like they never want to be separated again, and I'd be happy kissing her the rest of my days. The thought forces me to abruptly break from her, but then she speaks.

"I need you inside me."

Holy shit.

Next thing I know, I'm unbuckling my belt, and she's hitching up her skirt. Her panties slip to her ankles, and I shove down my pants a bit. I pick her up by the back of her thighs, spinning her for the door, and her legs wrap around me. Her hand comes between us, positioning me where I need to be, and I thrust upward as her back hits the door.

"Jesus," I mutter, pressing my lips to hers as my hips dance. She's freaking wet and warm and clenching at me. Scarlett breaks the kiss and scrapes her fingernails through my hair.

"God, I've missed you," she admits, and I hammer into her harder, wanting to remind her of what she missed.

"You should have looked for me." I grunt, surging upward, and she softly gasps, covering my mouth with hers again. Her hands cup the back of my head, and she kisses me like I'm the air she needs to breathe.

"Bull," she gasps, pulling back once more. "It's gonna be so quick. It's happening fast. I'm . . . *ermygawd.*" Her mouth comes to my neck, stifling the scream as I rock faster than I ever have.

"That's it, sweetheart," I mutter to her ear, clutching at her ass until my own telltale signs occur. My lower back tingles. My balls stiffen. I thrust one final time before stilling and emptying into her. Jolting within her, I give into the glory of all things good and *holy shit.*

"Scarlett, I wasn't wearing a condom." I lean back only enough to look at her face. Her beautiful, flushed face with a crooked, goofy smile of contentment.

"It's okay." Her voice is groggy and rough as though she could melt into the door behind her. Then her eyes widen, and her hands tighten on my shoulders. "Oh my God. Bull, put me down."

She isn't upset, just insistent. I pull out of her, feeling her absence too quickly and ache at the haste to leave her body. She slides down the door, stumbles to the toilet, and leans forward.

What the hell?

Closing my eyes as if I can ignore the sound of her heaving, I reach for my pants. We just had incredible, spontaneous wall sex, and she's getting sick from it.

"Scarlett, sweetheart," I murmur, stepping closer to her as I right my zipper and work my belt, but her hand comes up, stopping me in my tracks. She doesn't look up from her position, bent forward and aiming for the bowl.

"Are you okay?" I question, my voice rising in a cross between concern and confusion.

"Please, Bull. Just leave me alone."

What the fuck?

"Scarlett." I step toward her. Her face ashen. Her lips pale.

"Please. Go."

Fuck. A woman doesn't have to tell me twice.

5

OVERALL A BABY

SCARLETT

The day I saw Bull and his date, and Audrey mentioned the possibility of pregnancy, I didn't want to believe it could be true. Shelton and I didn't want children. Correction: Shelton didn't want children. It was never the right time, he said, and I accepted that as truth. We were both busy in our own careers. As time went on, it just became a thing about us. We were the couple without children. We weren't going to be parents, so imagine my surprise when Shelton was having a baby with his twentysomething med student.

I remember the day like it was yesterday instead of almost eight weeks ago. I'd just been fired and gone to see Shelton at the hospital. I couldn't believe my day could get worse.

Dr. Shelton Blake was the chief heart surgeon at Boston General. He had all the makings of soap opera swoon with a cleft chin, chiseled cheekbones, and glossy dark hair perfectly styled on his very smart head. He was still incredibly attractive at forty-five, and the small flecks of silver that speckled his occasional five-o'clock shadow only enhanced his looks. I was a lucky woman, especially as Shelton had always supported my career.

I recall bypassing the nurses' station, breaking protocol in hopes of finding Shelton in a staff room before his surgery. Another day at the office for him, saving lives. Heart transplants. Repaired aortas. Stents and such.

I was aware of the surgical changing room and caught the door as someone exited, allowing me to enter without a security key card. Shelton had an office on another floor, but I knew he'd be here when I didn't find him there. We haven't seen much of each other lately, with him saving the most vital organ in every human and me scandalizing the world with the broken hearts of others. The dichotomy of us was not lost on me.

I just needed a hug. It'd been a long time since Shelton and I embraced for the sake of holding one another, and that day, I needed to be held. I needed to be assured everything would be okay. The night before, we'd made love for the first time in weeks. *I was such a fool.*

In my mind's eye, I can see the raven-haired beauty, young and freshly new to her rigorous program, once I entered the forbidden room. There was a finite moment where I questioned how close Shelton stood to her, knowing something was off about the situation but only aware of it afterward with hindsight and perspective and a tremendous amount of heartache.

He'd said my name, confused by my presence. The urge to rush for him, wrap my arms around him and fall into his firm chest stilled like a gate slammed between us.

"This is Scarlett," the younger woman had said under her breath, and I glanced from her to my husband, my stomach pitching. I had a sixth sense about this kind of stuff, the stuff that makes my nose twitch for more information, smelling for dirt.

Confused by my presence, Shelton scrubbed at his forehead like he does when he has something on his mind. I asked him what was wrong when I'd come to him seeking comfort for myself. I deferred to him first, as I found upon reflection I did too often. He'd told me it wasn't the time to talk, but I needed to know what was on his mind. I could see it weighing on him, pressing at his shoulders. My desire to console him took over despite my day, and I'd hate myself later for putting him before me during this crucial moment in my life.

"This is Brittney. She's a med student." Cute and perky, Brittney. Freshly scrubbed and ready to take on the world, Brittney. Becoming a future doctor, Brittney. "She's pregnant, and I'm going to marry her."

The words were cracks in the sidewalk, and I stumbled over each of them, knowing I was missing something.

"You made love to me last night," I blurted, staring at him. Brittney crossed her arms, jutting out her hip as her mouth popped open while she stared at my husband. *My* husband, who slept with her.

Med student. Pregnant. Marry her.

As I'd too often done with a story we were reporting on, I had to fill in the missing pieces, sometimes with my own presumptions. The filler I needed for this information didn't seem too difficult to surmise.

My husband had had an affair.

He'd dipped his scalpel in someone else's heart and torn out mine.

As I stand inside the tractor supply store, holding up a mini Carhartt pair of overalls and press the tiny clothing over my belly, I realize the universe works in strange ways.

I was pregnant.

Alone, at forty-two, I was having a baby.

Even though a pink plus sign on a stick told me what I suddenly suspected at Audrey's suggestion, the doctor in Montpelier confirmed it an hour ago, and I'd been feeling out of sorts ever since.

Elated one minute. Shocked the next.

After that awkward moment with Audrey, I calculated the

timing, discovered I'd missed my period back in March, and expressed my concern to Rita later that afternoon.

"Maybe you're just stressed out, or maybe you're going through the change," she had said like a horror film announcer. I felt too young for that kind of physical shift, but I'd heard women in their early forties could start the downward spiral to menopause. I'd originally chalked up being sick each morning to a stomach bug, like I told Audrey, or stress, as Rita mentioned. I'd worked through illnesses before and figured as long as I didn't have a fever, I could fight the fatigue, the aches, and the occasional upset stomach. That lobster roll for breakfast should have been a big tipoff.

"Scarlett?" My eyes close at the rough, questioning male voice, and my hand stills on the overalls over my midsection.

"Bull." His name is a breathless wave of regret—deep-seated, sorrowful regret. It isn't his fault I'm in the position I'm in. I'm not upset I'm pregnant. This is all me. Screwup Scarlett, as my parents would say. The only thing I did right in their eyes was marrying the dapper doctor, and even that was eventually a mess.

Opening my eyes, I find Bull's deep blue gaze on the outfit against my belly, which I quickly return to the rack.

"Baby clothes shopping?" His voice teases me because, of course, why would I possibly need baby clothes unless I was having a fricking baby.

Oh sweet, Bull. I need to tell him. This is the most awkward position I've ever been in, but he needs to know. His hand casually comes to the rack, and his forehead furrows while he forces a smile at me. I should explain what happened the other day in the bathroom, how the motion of what we'd done brought on a wave of nausea. Energetic, enthusiastic Bull lived up to his name, and that nausea was because I was pregnant.

"It's a gift for . . . someone." Someone arriving in, say, nine months. Actually, the timing is more like seven or so, as a rough estimation puts me at six weeks along with a pregnancy calendar calculation of a December due date.

Bull continues to stare at me, forcing that smile that doesn't reach his eyes.

"Bull, about the other day—"

"Yeah," he says, looking away from me and reaching behind his neck. "I just wanted to see if you were okay." His head turns back to me, and his eyes scan my body. This isn't the heated stares he gave me that night or even the desperate gaze of our bathroom tryst. This is a look full of concern, and guilt socks me in the stomach. Or maybe that's the hunger rumbling. The doctor says eating at regular intervals will help settle the morning sickness.

"I'm better," I tell him, grateful for his concern and comforted by his asking.

"Stomach bug or something?" he asks, still looking at me with all kinds of questions on his rugged face. Questions I can't answer yet. I just need a minute, or a day, to wrap my head around what I've learned about myself and my future. The future I didn't have a plan for has just gotten a whole lot more complicated.

I was going to be a mother at forty-two.

"Yeah, something like that."

"Hey, Bull, I found that part," a man with a store uniform vest on addresses Bull from behind him. Bull glances over his shoulder and nods to acknowledge the man.

"Tractor part," Bull says back to me and double pats the clothing rack where he placed his hand.

"Gotta fix the tractor," I awkwardly say, "in order to milk the cows."

"Tractors are for fields," Bull says, still watching me, and I swipe loose curls over an ear.

"Right, well, go do farmer stuff," I add, sounding even more like an idiot.

"Right," Bull says. Taking a step back, he spins away from me and then circles back to face me after a few paces. "You know, if you need anything, like say food, we could get food together. To eat, that is. We could go to dinner. Or hang out." He holds out a hand to emphasize his point, and his clumsy approach is endearing. My heart skips a beat. He's awkward in the sweetest manner, but once he hits the bedroom, that awkwardness disappears, and a self-assured man takes over. My privates do a little dance of remembrance mixed with a sigh of regret that they'll never experience him again. Under different circumstances, I'd totally take a chance on this man, but it doesn't seem like a good idea in my current condition. However, I'm full of bad decisions lately.

"Maybe," I say. Biting my own lip, I fight the grin on my face. "Come see me at the Bean sometime."

It isn't what he wants as an answer, and I instantly read it in his expression. I'm hurting him, and I hate myself.

"Yeah, well, see you at the Bean sometime."

I nod before Bull turns and walks away again, leaving me next to the baby clothes rack. My heart drops to my feet as a sense of aloneness washes over me, and the hollowness in my belly is not from a lack of food.

A few days later, I meet Rita at the Busy Bean Café even though I'm not on the schedule to work. She likes to claim the peach plush couch as her place to think, and we need to brainstorm. I only have a couple of days left on my rental and no future place rented. Rita suggested I move in with her, and it isn't a bad idea—roommates again—but it also doesn't seem ideal. Rita and I are both set in our ways a bit, and I can't lasso her with my condition or my future child. I need to find a place of my own.

However, we are sidetracked and scrolling the internet on her laptop for other things.

"I can't believe I'm looking at these," I say, staring at the white crib and baby bedding printed with sweet tiny ducks. "Who'd have thought? Me. Pregnant at my age."

"You're what?" The shout is enough to snap the chalkboard beams overhead, and Rita and I both jump at the strong male voice coming from before me. I look up and lock eyes with Bull.

37

"Hello, handsome," Rita mutters beside me.

"I . . ." I don't know what to say, as the heated seductive stares he's given me in the past have morphed into a tempestuous storm.

"Start talking," he demands. If his tone wasn't so growly, it'd be sexy, but he has every right to be upset.

"I just . . ." My eyes shift to Zara working the counter today. I've already told both my bosses about my condition, hoping for their sympathy for my situation and some continued compassion for my working here. I don't want to give up the job, and they've both been tremendously understanding.

Zara walks around the counter and crosses to us. "There's a nice bench out on the lawn facing the river. Why don't you two go there to talk?"

Rita pats my leg as I glance back at Bull. Zara is right. Bull and I need to step outside as several patrons are staring at us, curious about the wreck of a woman who can hardly make coffee and the steaming bull upset with her.

I can't run off to the restroom like I did the other day. With shaky legs and a weak stomach, I stand. As I pass Zara, she reaches for my wrist and squeezes.

"When I told Dave about my situation"—Zara had a baby but didn't know how to find Dave—"we were sitting on that bench, and things worked out for us. Maybe it will bring you good luck, too."

As I trudge outside, I am not feeling fortunate. The Busy Bean is located on the Winooski River. When we reach the bench facing the water, we sit in silence for a few minutes, watching the ripples race before us. It's the very end of April, and a beautiful spring day with a mild temperature. And I hate that I'm considering the weather because I don't know where to start.

"Scarlett, just tell me everything," Bull says as if reading my thoughts. Taking a deep breath, I dive into the highlights, explaining my job loss and my husband's infidelity. As I'm on a roll, I add in my parents' disappointment.

"They act like it's my fault that my husband slipped his raisin into someone else's cookie."

Bull bitterly chuckles. "I don't even know what that means."

"It means I'm a failure in their eyes, Bull, even though he's the one who stepped out on me. I didn't do all that a woman should do. Work, wife, motherhood—"

"Yeah, sweetheart, let's jump ahead to that last point." I have to admit every time he calls me sweetheart, I melt a little bit, and a part of my soul dies because of what I need to explain.

"The issue is, I'm pregnant now."

He sits up a little straighter next to me, and his chest heaves. Hope fills his eyes. "Is it mine?"

My voice falters as what I have to say next might crush him. I close my eyes, shutting out the river. "I don't know who the father is yet."

"What do you mean, you don't know yet?" Bull's voice is steady but stern.

"According to the doctor's estimation a few days ago, I'm six to seven weeks along. Considering how close we did what we did to my leaving my husband, it could be his." I swallow the lump in my throat at the possibility I could be pregnant from Shelton, and I don't want it to be his baby.

"You fucked your husband." The incredulous sharpness of his tone isn't unwarranted, but it still unsettles me.

"Yes, I fucked my husband." Shame fills me at the admission, which is disconcerting on a multitude of levels. A wife should have sex with her husband, and in turn, a husband should have sex with only his wife, not a twenty-three-year-old med student. That same husband should love his wife, not decide he wants to do right by the pregnant girl and marry her when he's still married to someone else. *What about doing right by me, his wife?*

Bull stands upright, walking in a small circle before turning back to me and waiting on more details. I can't look at him and glance back at the river as tears fill my eyes.

"Shelton and I had been . . . estranged a bit, but I didn't recognize how distant we'd become. The night before I left, we'd had sex for the first time in weeks. I thought it was the start of us reconnecting as though we'd just had a little blip in syncing our lives. I had no idea he'd been using his *stethoscope* with a med student. None."

Bull nods.

"I'd lost my job the next day, and when I went to him, hoping he'd console me, I found him with his student. He blurted out the truth. She was pregnant with this child, and he was going to marry her. I was such a fool, Bull. When Rita called me later that day, I was packing with no idea where I was going. Then I ended up here, and one week later . . ."

"I see," he mutters, softly, shakily. "I see." My hands curl around the seat of the bench. Taking two steps forward, Bull stops. His mouth opens and then shuts.

"And you haven't been with anyone else? I was your only one-night stand." There's no accusation, only a need for clarification.

"I've never done anything like I did with you before or after. I swear it on everything I am." Which isn't a good person.

"What were we in the bathroom a few days ago then?"

Pregnancy hormones. He just looked so good, and the tension between us set me off, especially when he stepped toward me. Or maybe I stepped to him. It didn't matter. We were like magnets drawn to one another by sexual attraction. His kiss brings me peace.

When I don't answer, he steps forward, pauses and, stands taller. "I guess it doesn't matter, though, if it isn't mine."

"But it might be," I offer weakly, knowing it's no consolation. Maybe a baby is the last thing he wants. I'm caught between a rock and a hard place if ever that cliché was true. "After our incredible night together—"

"You thought it was incredible?" The surprise in his tone shifts my position on the bench, and I stare at him. Large, soft midnight eyes meet mine, and the hesitancy I see in them almost breaks me in half.

"Of course, it was incredible. You're amazing, and that thing you do with your tongue . . ." I drift off. Now is not the time to recall his tongue or fingers or even his thick *thingy*. I clear my throat. "It was incredible because you're you."

I gesture my hand up and down, emphasizing his body—the muscles, the mass, the strength, the stamina. A slow smile breaks out on his face, crooked at first, but it does things to my body. Bull should come with a warning: may cause heart palpitations, pulsing between the thighs, and a brain malfunction.

That's one thing I've noticed already changing about my body —the libido shift. Sex is on my mind more than ever, and the way he's looking at me, I'm ready to pounce on him like I did in the bathroom the other day. I've been reading up on heightened sexual desire in baby books, and what the experts say is normal is a relief. I want it, and I want him, and that is all kinds of *not a good idea, Scarlett*.

"Yeah, I think you're you, too," Bull says, turning up the wattage on that lopsided grin, and I chuckle, feeling the tension ease just a little bit between us.

"So, it could be his?" Bull nods slowly. A hand lifts and swipes through his ink and silver hair, mussing up the short strands and making him finger-licking delicious.

"Or it could be yours."

"How long before you and I . . ." He drifts off, pointing between us.

"One week." It was one week between sleeping with my husband and sleeping with Bull.

His eyes close briefly. He's a foot before me, but he might as well be on the other side of the river. Slowly opening his lids, he asks, "Do you want it to be his?"

"No," I whisper as I seek his gaze. "No, I do not want him to be the father. Does that make me a bad person? I mean, I already know I'm a bad person. Never in a million years did I set out for this to happen. And I'd understand if you want no part of it if it is your child. I didn't mean to hurt you. I never ever thought this could happen to me. I'm on the pill. You used condoms, but I'm pregnant."

And I don't know who the father is.

Tears fall in earnest this time, and I lean forward, placing my elbows on my knees as I cover my face. This is another new development—emotion. I'm normally solid and steady. Nothing ruffles me, but lately, I feel like I'm coming apart at the seams. I cry over tissue commercials and insurance advertisements when I generally don't get worked up over sad stories or the misfortunes of others.

Bull plops down on the bench beside me. "You're not a bad person, sweetheart," he offers, rubbing a hand up my spine. His fingers find their way under my hair, and he massages the base of my head. *Frick, that feels good.* After a few seconds, I can't help the sound of contentment escaping as my tears settle.

"Like that?" Bull asks, his voice dropping and reminding me of our night when he often asked the same question in the same tone.

I wipe at my cheeks. "Do you hate me?"

"No," Bull admits, dropping his hand and looking off at the river. "But I need time to process this."

I snort. "I totally understand. It's taken me more than a hot minute."

Bull glances back at me. "Is that why you were holding those baby overalls the other day?"

I nod.

"You said it was a gift."

"They would have been . . . for the baby." Something in Bull's eyes drifts from stormy midnight to deep lake blue. "I didn't buy them, though."

Bull doesn't respond. Instead, he takes my hand and holds it, allowing us to just stare out at the river with our own thoughts for a few minutes. All I've told him is a lot to take in, and I will understand if he tells me to go to hell. Somehow, I don't think he will, though. The heat of his palm against mine hints that he isn't a man who walks away that easily.

"I'd make a good dad," he says under his breath. Startled by the hopeful sound in his voice, I pop my head up and look at him. With one glance, I know he's right. Sitting here, holding my hand, he exudes the qualities of a decent man. A man who would love and take care of his children and perhaps love a wife one day.

"I'm sure you would."

Bull pulls my hand up to his lips and kisses my knuckles. His eyes momentarily close, but his entire face expresses how much he wants to be a father. Would he want to share that experience with me?

"I never thought I'd be a mom," I admit. Bull turns my hand palm up and strokes his against mine. "The irony in all this is Shelton didn't want children, and now he might have two women pregnant."

I shudder at the thought. However, I also have this weird sense it isn't Shelton's child. Like I'd just know if it was. Maybe it'd be a sense of the devil inside me, but I don't truly feel that way. No matter whose child this is, it's not something evil, though I'm scared out of my mind.

Am I too old to have a child?

"If it's all the same to you, I don't think I want to consider your husband right now." The words are said with teasing sarcasm, but it's a hint to his alpha-ness. He'd be fiercely protective of his woman. Instantly, I recall our night together. He was all about me. What I wanted. How I felt. How I made him feel.

"Right, of course. And he's soon to be an ex. There's no going back," I remind Bull. I will not be getting back together with Shelton, although I suppose he deserves to know about my condition. The thought makes me sad, and I glance up at Bull one more time. Would it be wrong to want him to be the father?

"You're going to be great." His voice is low while he concentrates on our hands.

I huff. "How can you even say that? You don't know anything

about me, and I'm obviously a hot mess lately." I'm not being defensive, just stating the facts.

Bull shrugs, squeezing my hand. "While this might seem like a crazy situation, I just have a feeling about you, Scarlett Russell. It's like with my cows. I just know which ones are good and which ones are done."

My mouth falls open. "You did not just compare me to your cows."

He chuckles. "'Fraid I did."

"Do not do that again," I demand.

"Are you saying I'll have the opportunity to see you again?" His eyes focus on where his hand is still skimming over mine.

"Not if you're going to compare me to your cows," I tease, and Bull smiles, spreading my fingers with his, then linking them together. His hand is a comfort I didn't know I needed, and I wish he could just keep holding mine. Collectively lifting our clasped hands, he presses another kiss to my knuckles.

"Then I'd like to see you again. Tomorrow?"

"I don't know if that's a good idea. Things are so messy right now." Middle of a divorce. No career path. Uncertainty of the father of my child. Need a place to live. I don't think I need to spell it all out for him again.

"Then let's get messy together," he states, and I blink at him. "Tomorrow."

That's all he says before kissing my fingers one more time and standing. Releasing me, he walks away, and I watch his retreat, longing filling my chest. Complicated does not begin to describe our status.

6

A RIVER DOES NOT RUN BETWEEN US

SCARLETT

True to his word, Bull appears at the café the next afternoon near the end of my shift. I don't know how he knew when my shift ended, but I'm blaming Audrey and the sly smile she gives me when she sees him enter the coffee shop.

"Bull," she elongates his name. "What can I get you this afternoon?"

"Scarlett," he says like I'm an option on the menu, and my insides do a little flip flop. The crooked smile he's giving me is like a beacon in the night and lights me up just as much. I want this man when I have no business being with him until I know who this baby's father is. I haven't called Shelton, and it feels like that says something about us. I don't want this child to be his, even if he is the biological parent. He's made decisions without my input—aka, sleeping with someone else and impregnating her —so I don't see how being pregnant myself, even if it is his child, is his business.

Rita tells me he has a legal right to know, though, and I know I have a moral obligation to tell him. But not yet. I'd like to know something certain before I share anything with Shelton. Plus, I'd like to give Bull a chance, which is just crazy as we've only had one night together and fifteen minutes of paradise in a public restroom. Still, something draws me to Bull. Maybe it's the baby. Maybe it's my sense that he's a good man.

After collecting my things, I clock out and circle the counter. Bull holds the door open for me, and I step outside the café. It's another glorious spring day. The sun stays up a little longer each afternoon as a sign of good things coming soon.

"I was wondering if I could take you somewhere." His eyes shift as we stand between a truck and my sporty BMW, a gift from Shelton when I turned forty.

"Sure."

Bull reaches for the door handle of the truck and opens it. He holds out a hand to help me up the running board and closes the door once I'm settled. He's a perfect gentleman, and I'm a little stunned for some reason. Not that he wasn't a gentleman the night we hooked up, but this is just different. Shelton didn't do doors—cars, stores, or restaurants. He was a get your own door kind of guy, and I admit I might have been that kind of woman. *I can open my own door, thank you very much.* But it's still sweet and considerate.

We ride along quiet streets and curvy roads until coming to a gravel drive marked by a sign.

Eaton Dairy Farm.

Once again, the last name sounds familiar, but it's basic enough it doesn't trigger anything in my memory. The truck bumbles and bounces down a stretch of rocky road, passing a two-story farmhouse, a long, large white barn with silos behind it, and a traditional red barn next to them. Following a split-rail fence, we continue down the gravel drive to a smaller, more traditional looking farmhouse, and Bull pulls up before it.

"Home sweet home," he announces. I stare at the building that looks storybook yet slightly more modern than the larger house down the lane. With a white tin roof and fresh siding, it's pristine looking with character, but it needs a splash of color on the low front porch.

I follow Bull as he leads me inside and find the space within an open concept. The kitchen is to the left, while the living area is to the right. In the middle, a chimney with a wood-burning stove faces a dining room table that seats eight, dividing the overall space in half. The woodstove chimney acts as a natural barrier to the kitchen. Double doors behind the dining table lead outside. A fieldstone fireplace is the focal point of the living area.

"It's beautiful," I whisper of the quaint space with New England charm while modernized just a touch. It's also the complete opposite of the sleek apartment where I once lived in Boston with its steel and glass décor. Bull's color scheme is muted browns and earth tones, softly masculine, farm-ish, and homey.

"My grandparents lived here. My dad built the front house when he married my mother. After my grandmother died a few years back, I inherited this house and fixed it up."

Bull proudly gazes around the rooms.

"That's impressive."

"I'm good with my hands." His innuendo is accentuated as he smirks. *Don't I know it, partner.*

"I have something for you." Bull steps up to the table and lifts a package poorly wrapped in brown paper. "The wrapping paper gave me trouble." As he holds out the gift, he scratches under his chin at the scruff creeping down his neck.

"You didn't have to get me anything," I say. "But I love presents." Shelton and I stopped exchanging gifts, minus my BMW, opting for vacations instead of items for birthdays and holidays. However, I can't remember the last vacation we took.

I rip at the not so artfully wrapped paper and dive into the box. Staring at the item inside, I feel my eyes prickle and blink away the threatening tears. This crying business needs to stop.

"For the baby," he says, his voice lowered but still rough while hesitant.

"For the baby," I repeat, staring at the little brown overalls from the tractor supply store. "Thank you, Bull. This means a lot to me." Stepping up to him, I kiss his cheek and then step back, taking a second glance at the thoughtful gift.

"Scarlett, I'd like to make a proposal."

Oh no, I've heard about these things from him.

"I'd like to suggest you live with me." My mouth falls open, and Bull steps forward, jumping into the rest of his speech. "I figure I have a fifty-fifty chance of being the father, right? And you already said you aren't going back to your husband. Hell, you even said you're hoping it's not his, so let's say for now, it isn't. Move in with me and let me take care of you."

"Bull, don't you think it's a bit much?"

"I'm not suggesting marriage. Absolutely not asking you to marry me." He makes a face, cringing at the thought. "Just me watching out for you and the little one. I want to share this experience with you, in case it is my kid. You can still work. We'll just be partners, roommates, and take it day by day." His face brightens a little before he adds, "Maybe, consider benefits occasionally."

"Benefits?" I choke.

"Then again, you did get sick the last time we had sex." His hopeful expression falls.

"Bull." I laugh. "I wasn't sick because of you. It was because of the baby. I hadn't eaten that morning and all that jostling around we did just shook me up."

"No jostling then. Got it." He grins, the hitch to one side of his mouth grows bigger. "Look, I figure you can't keep staying at the Green Rocks resort. You need a place to live if you're staying in Vermont." He pauses, looking at me to confirm my calendar.

"I'm staying. At least for the next several months, and you're right. My rental time is up tomorrow, actually, and I still haven't found a place to live."

Bull exhales. "Okay, for the next few months, then." Bull looks toward the ceiling as if he's calculating something. "You'll be pregnant three-hundred days, give or take a day, which is only a few days longer than the gestation of a cow, so—"

My mouth falls open. "Did you just compare me to a cow again?"

"Just wanted a second chance to do that." He winks at me, and I slap his chest with the box in my hands.

"I don't want to miss any more days, though, Scarlett." Hugging the box in my hands to my chest, I look around the comfortable room and sigh. It really is beautiful, but Bull is too much. I hold the present away from myself, staring down at the overalls. He says he wants to share this experience with me, and as I have no idea what I'm doing, it would be nice to have a companion on this journey. A partner, he said.

"About that sex. What were you thinking? Every Tuesday and Thursday?" I'm teasing. For as much as sex is on my mind, I don't think we should have it again until I get a few other things straight in my head. And my heart.

"Is that a yes?" Bull's brow lifts, furrowing his forehead.

Is this crazy? This is definitely crazy, but I nod, biting the edge of my lip as Bull's surprised expression turns to a genuine smile. And that smile makes me feel like I'm making the right decision for the first time in weeks. Being here feels right.

"Any day ending in day is good enough for me," he says, circling back to our *benefits* discussion. As we stand close to one another, he lifts me off my feet. My arms are crushed to my chest as Bull spins us in a circle. Suddenly, he stops and sets me down, holding me at arm's length with his hands on my shoulders.

"Sorry, no jostling. I'll figure that one out." His eyes focus on mine. His face loses some enthusiasm as his expression turns more serious. "There's no pressure for anything, though. I only promise this will be good for us both."

I want to believe him. I really do.

NIGHT TWO

BULL

Holy hell, she agreed to move in with me.

Not wanting to waste another moment apart, I suggest we drive her back to the Busy Bean, and I follow her to Green Rocks to collect her things. I'd have liked to take her to my room and bury myself inside her to celebrate our new beginning, but I fought the urge. I need to keep my wits about me. This is nothing more than living together.

Parenting partners or something like that.

Because holy shit, I might be a father.

If I'm half as excited about actually being one as I am about the *possibility* of being one, someone's going to need to rope me down from the moon.

In my relationship history, I never got past the idea of marriage. I hadn't considered fatherhood, and with each waning, complicated situation, spreading the family name onto the next generation did not seem like a probability, at least not from me.

This is everything I could have ever hoped for, but I will not allow myself to get carried away. I will not look further than today, and maybe tomorrow, when I need to face my family and tell them what I've done.

I've asked a woman to live with me.

A woman who might be the mother of my child.

Like I told Scarlett, there won't be a marriage proposal. *No siree, she does not need to worry about that from me.* I'll be perfectly happy to stand by Scarlett as a friend—with some benefits if she'll let me. Or not. We can just be partners, like I said.

Slowly, my thoughts catch up to me as we wind the mountain roads, once we've collected Scarlett's things. There's still the possibility of her ex being the baby's dad. A week between Scarlett and me, and him and her isn't much to work with. I should be more upset about this, but I'm not. The excitement of having a baby overshadows everything else in my head. Like she said, he was her husband. He's a fucking idiot for wanting someone other than the beautiful redhead following me back to the house in her car. He's double the fool for getting someone else pregnant when he could have kids with his wife. *What a fucking schmuck.*

But his schmucky-ness might be my luck.

Still, I warn myself not to get wrapped up in Scarlett. *Do not get ahead of yourself.* Helping her out with living arrangements is not a promise of forever. If I happen to be the father, we can tackle what that means next. I don't need to marry her.

When we finally return to my house, we each park next to one another, and I quickly jump out of my truck, heading for the bed to gather Scarlett's things. Her car is a flashy, sporty thing, and I don't know how she got her three suitcases inside it in the first place. The three cases weren't light, and I surmise she owns more than these belongings. She strikes me as the type to have a closet the size of a small bedroom full of clothes and shoes. The fancy car hints at such a thing as do the designer bags in the back of my truck.

Why would she want to stay with a man like me anyway?

"I got it," I say, more aggressive than necessary when Scarlett meets me at my tailgate. I tug each suitcase forward, recognizing

51

the tension in my words comes from a sudden fear. She could leave. She could decide she doesn't like me or learn he's the father and return to him. She could walk away like all the rest of the women in my life have.

I'm not some self-deprecating sap. I know my assets. I'm dedicated to a fault and loyal despite everything. I'm openhearted, and that shit gets me in trouble too often.

I will not be falling in love with Scarlett.

It'd be easy to do and stupid of me. I've learned my lesson. Then again, I've had some time to reflect on my past mistakes and learn how each one of them wasn't love. At least, not the long-lasting kind of love I wanted to have like my grandparents and parents did. I'm a love fast, learn later, kind of guy, and it has bit me in the ass too many times. It won't happen again.

Scarlett heads to her car for a laptop bag and her purse. Then I point the way forward and follow her as she walks up the short path to the porch. The lights are on in my house, welcoming us home.

Could Scarlett see this place as a permanent home for her?

I can't consider the thought. I didn't live here with my wife, then I practically moved in with the next girl. And by my third turn, I'd learned some things about practicality, location, and romance.

Never bring home a woman who isn't going to be a permanent fixture in your family.

I'm already breaking my own rules.

"There are three rooms upstairs," I say, leading us in the direction of the staircase. "I use one as an office. Then there's my room and a guest room." I walk directly to the guest room and set the suitcases on the floor.

If Scarlett would prefer to be in my room, in my bed, she doesn't mention it, so I leave her things where we are. *Roommates, it is.* I sit on the edge of the bed as Scarlett sets down her laptop case and scans the room. It's light-colored and stark like the other rooms in my home. The furnishings are simple with a double bed and a wrought-iron headboard plus a maple wood dresser with a matching mirror over it.

"I'm surprised," she admits, checking out the clean but sparse space.

"Too bachelor-ish?" I tease.

"Homey," she says, surprising me.

"I want you to think of this as your home."

"I really want to thank you again for this. It's more than generous . . ." Her voice drifts, and I pat the space next to me, suggesting she sit.

"Wow," she mutters. Still standing, she faces me, but she's looking over my shoulder at the view out the window above the headboard. It's a vision of slight hills and rolling fields. Twisting to look in that direction, I agree with her assessment as the early evening sunset casts a golden glow over everything.

"It's probably not going to be enough for you," I admit. She is from Boston. She lived in the busy city. Her suitcases alone suggest she was well off, and farm living isn't for everyone.

"It's perfect," Scarlett says. She collapses next to me, our thighs brushing as we sit on the edge of the bed. Those dark eyes of hers look like freshly tilled soil, reminding me of earth and land, and how those objects make me feel. Home. Happy. Heart. "I'm so sorry again—"

My fingers slip into her hair, stopping her apology. Leaning toward her, I hesitate just above her lips, fighting the urge to kiss her. I want to lay her back on this bed, bury myself within her, and fill her again with my seed. The thought makes me smile. She could already be full from me.

God, please let it be mine.

Scarlett takes a short breath, and the air whispers over my lips like a soft caress. My mouth waters as my thumb strokes the side of her neck. Her skin is warm but delicate, and she smells floral, like a combination of meadow flowers.

"I think we should . . . keep our distance until we know something for sure," she says although her hooded eyes say the opposite. "We shouldn't be together . . . until we know more about . . ."

The baby.

She doesn't want to be involved with me if it's not mine, and I should agree. I do agree. I shouldn't want to be mixed up with a woman pregnant by another man. Only, everything in me says this baby is mine. It has to be. Sitting here, stroking her skin, she feels like she belongs here. She belongs with me.

Still, I tip up my chin and try to tamper my eager dick. Slipping my hand free from her neck, I suggest I make dinner.

"You are going to spoil me," she says thirty minutes later as we share a meal of baked chicken, mashed potatoes, and a salad of spring veggies.

"I normally eat at the main house but figured tonight it'd be best to eat here."

"Who lives up there?"

"My dad. This is his farm. Five generations of Eatons. Then there are my younger brothers Canyon and Blade, who you might remember from the bar."

"I wasn't exactly looking at other men," she admits, and my chest swells at the confession. My grin matches hers.

"Canyon is three years younger than me, so thirty-nine. He has a child who is thirteen and lives with him. Then there's my baby brother Blade, who is thirty-six."

"And which one is which again?"

She's referring to their creative talents. "Canyon writes songs and plays guitar. Blade fights but loves poetry."

Scarlett smiles. "And what's your specialty?"

"I milk the cows."

She snorts. "I don't think that's it, and that's definitely not what I meant." She looks around the rooms open for viewing from the dining table where we sit. "I'd say working with your hands is your specialty." She winks at me, and I fight the goofy grin creeping higher on my lips. I'd like to show her my special talent, but I don't want to push. Tonight is about acclimating, getting to know one another in more than the biblical sense. Despite my disappointment she chose to stay in the guest room and stopped our kiss, I'm still excited to learn all I can about her.

"So what about you? What's your specialty?"

She shrugs, looking off toward the double doors leading out to a small patio area. "I don't really have a talent."

"Of course, you do," I say. "Everyone does."

"According to my parents, I don't. I wasn't exactly the journalist they'd hoped I'd be after journalism school, nor was I the society wife they thought I'd grow accustomed to being with the good doctor. This is just one more thing I'll have fricked up with them." I ignore the mention of her husband as Scarlett rubs a hand over her belly where there isn't a trace of her condition. She lowers her head.

"I don't really see how being a mother is a frick up." I chuckle at the term.

"It's the way it might have happened." Her eyes drift. "Either I slept with my husband after he impregnated another woman, or I got pregnant from a one-night stand. I haven't told them about my condition yet."

One-night stand does sound like a dirty deed at this point, and I reach across the table for her hand. "Scarlett, let's count this as night two then."

She looks over at my outstretched palm and slowly lifts her hand for mine.

"Night two," she whispers.

"To many more," I say, lifting my water glass, and her smile cautiously returns.

"Many more."

When we finally arrive at bedtime, we circle one another as the only bathroom upstairs is outside my room. Scarlett is good at this, and it's evident she's recently been living with another man.

We work around each other brushing teeth and finalizing bedtime rituals, but something is unsettling about it. We're ships passing in the night, and I want to moor her to me. I want us to move in the same direction, toward my bedroom, toward my bed.

She pauses outside her new bedroom door, leaning against the jamb with half her body in the room and half in the hall. She's wearing long flannel pants but a tank top for a shirt. Her breasts are heavy in the skintight material, and her nipples peak under my gaze. My mouth waters for another taste of those succulent globes.

"Good night," she whispers, her voice husky and low, and the soundwaves travel directly to my dick, long and hard in my own pair of flannels, which I'll be removing as soon as I crawl into bed. I'll need to relieve myself, taking matters into my own hand tonight to take off the edge.

"Good night," I offer with a wave and then want to kick myself once she closes the door behind her.

Waving? What an idiot. I should have rushed her and kissed her senseless to remind her of our night together. That would be a good night salutation.

Because deep down, I don't want to be just roommates with her.

"Morning," my dad says to me as I finish cleaning up after the milking by spraying down the concrete flooring of the barn. We handled one hundred and thirteen this morning. Not bad for one morning, I consider, fighting my thoughts from wandering to a woman warm in a guest bed in my house.

"Got a guest?" Dad asks. My dad's an easy enough going man. He claims my mother softened him over the years. Currently, as a houseful of men, we're well past incriminations, but I've never brought a woman to my home.

"Yeah. She'll be staying with me a bit," I say, not looking up, afraid of his disapproval. I don't need his permission, though. He'd be the first to tell me it's my life, and I can make my own choices. I chose the farm before anything else. We had trouble a couple of years back, and I could have walked away from it all, but I didn't. I stuck it out same as I have for some twenty-five years.

"Going to explain more," Dad wonders.

"Nope."

"Keeping things in perspective?" He's referring to my past relationships. Most people assume I'm in a rush to marry, and they wouldn't be wrong. I want what my parents had, what I witnessed between my grandparents, which was a total commitment and dedication to one another. *Love.* Marriage equates to such a thing, but I've been known to be wrong.

I give my dad one glance before turning away from him.

"Okay then. Good talk," he mutters, slapping me hard on the back and turning for the office. I'm certain I'll be a topic of discussion at the breakfast table, but I'll be skipping that meal, heading back to my place to check on sleeping beauty. My internet research on pregnancy informs me a woman can sleep a lot during her first trimester. Scarlett's considered high risk as she's over forty. It's not the most optimal age to be pregnant, so I won't be doing anything to disturb the rest she needs.

Returning to my house as soon as I can, I find Scarlett standing in my kitchen staring at my coffee maker.

"Whatcha doing, sweetheart?"

She jumps at my voice, turning to face me in the tight tank and flannel pajama pants ensemble.

"I'm willing that coffee machine to work." Her hands land on her hips as she looks up at me, sleepy-eyed and rumpled

She's cute in the morning, and I once again regret missing out on waking next to her at Green Rocks. As my eyes have a mind of their own, they lower for the fullness of her breasts and the dark nipples protruding from the thin white material. Her nips peak, poking at the soft fabric, making me lick my lips.

"Bull," she whispers. My name is like a breathless call in the night. However, I fight the urge to plunder her mouth, tug down that neckline, and suckle those supple swells screaming for attention.

"Bull," she says sharper, crossing her arms, which does nothing to distract me from wanting those lush breasts. Snapping out of it, I glance up to see a knowing smirk on her lips. *Busted, buddy.*

"Coffee?" she questions, and I lean around her, brushing my body against hers. I hold up the plug.

"Helps if you plug it in."

She shakes her head, looking up at me. With us this close, I could kiss her. I could lean down and take her mouth, but she wants distance, and I can respect that—sort of. I plug the extension into the outlet and turn on the machine already primed to make coffee. I must have unplugged it to move it around the counter when I made dinner last night and forgot to return it to the outlet after washing dishes.

"How'd you sleep?" I ask, still crowding her in against the counter.

"Like a baby. That bed is too comfortable."

I wouldn't know as I've never slept on it, but I want to sleep on it with her.

Settle down.

Glancing up at the coffee machine as it hisses to life, I ask, "How do you work in a coffee shop if you don't even know how a pot works?"

"Oh, well, I'm not a very good barista." Her face pinkens, and I sense a story.

"Tell me more," I tease.

"I just wanted a job, something to fill my time."

"Did you work before coming to Vermont?" Her eyes meet mine, and she quickly looks away.

"I worked for an entertainment company."

"What's that?"

"It's like a television station." I'm not much for television, preferring movies on occasion and a hockey game on the regular. She waves her hand, dismissing the topic, and turns to face the coffee machine as though she can make it work faster. As she presses her hands against the counter, strumming her fingers, I reach over her for the cabinet. My chest meets her back. The front of my pants hits the seam of her flannels.

She stills, and I inhale the sleepy-scent of her neck.

"Coffee mugs," I whisper, blowing air at her moist skin, and she shivers. Opening the cabinet over her head, I pull down two mugs with one hand. Resting the other on the opposite side of her body, I cage her in. My nose trails up her neck. She doesn't move away from me like she did yesterday. *So much for distance.* After I set the mugs on the counter, my mouth hovers over her neck, and she tips her head, allowing me better access. Her body is begging me to taste her. Breathing her in, I lift my hand for her belly, landing over the spot where one day soon she'll swell. The idea of it causes me to inhale, and her breasts heave. Those nipples are so ripe, teasing me for attention.

"Knock, knock." The soft click of the front door tells me someone entered. *Dammit.* Everyone has a key to my place, and I might need to impose a no-entry policy for the length of Scarlett's stay. Instantly, I step back and turn toward the entry door, placing myself in front of Scarlett in her revealing tank top. However, there's no way to disguise the raging hard-on in my pants.

"Heard we have a visitor." My youngest brother's teasing voice lets me know he's here to scope out the situation. *Nosy bastard.*

"What do you want?" I snap.

"Is that any way to greet your favorite brother?"

"Good thing I have another one who can take the spot," I groan, needing a second to cool my thoughts of Scarlett, the kitchen counter, and what I'd like to do to her against it.

"Hiya Red," he says, tipping his head to look around me.

"Please don't call me that," she whispers behind me, and the sound of her voice tells me she doesn't like that nickname. It's more than disliking a play on her bright hair but something deeper.

"Blade, this is Scarlett Russell. Scarlett, my pain in the ass, little brother Blade."

She waves around my arm.

"Carly sent me down to tell you to bring your guest to breakfast." *Guest.* I am not liking that word, as I want to claim Scarlett as more, but I can't.

"Ever heard of a telephone?" I mutter.

"Where's the fun of walking in on something if I called?"

Sometimes I want to strangle my brother.

"Who's Carly?" Scarlett asks, leaning her chin against my bicep.

"Carly is our cook, housekeeper, and all-around woman about the house."

Scarlett doesn't respond, and I hear the coffee behind her percolating. "We'll figure out breakfast ourselves today."

"Dinner tonight?" Blade questions, knowing Carly likes to be informed if people are going to miss a meal.

"I'll consider it," I say, speaking for both Scarlett and myself.

"Dinner for two then. Wonderful," Blade adds, making the assumption I won't be at dinner. He sees himself out, and Scarlett presses the top of her head into my shoulder blade.

"Is that what you want in a woman? Cooking, cleaning, a person about the house?" There's a softness to her question, and I turn to face her again. Her head remains lowered, and I lift her chin so she can look at me with those rich, dark eyes. "I didn't really do those things in my past life. I ate out a lot. I had a cleaning service. I hardly did my own laundry as most things were dry-cleaned." She looks toward the chimney of the woodburning stove behind me. "I sound shallow, don't I?"

Unable to stop myself, I brush back her hair at her forehead, tracing her hairline to push the reddish strands behind her ear.

"Not shallow, just different." Focusing on my fingers, I scoop around her ear again.

"I have a feeling we're a bit of Green Acres here. Farm loving and city living coming together."

"Is that bad?" I ask.

"No, just different." She smiles up at me, and I want to kiss her so badly I ache. The beep of the coffee machine saves me from pushing my luck.

"How about eggs?" I ask, assuming she doesn't know how to make those.

"I'd love them," she says, sounding relieved at the offer. She turns to reach for the coffee pot, giving me a look at her perfect backside while she pours us each a cup. Teasing me, she hands a mug over to me. "At the very least, I can pour coffee."

EXPOSÉ

SCARLETT

For a few days, Bull and I dance around each other. He's up and out before I rise, and I'm off to the Busy Bean Café before he returns for breakfast. I assume he's eating up at the main house, as he calls it, during the meals I'm not present. He told his brother we'd have dinner with the family soon, but I have yet to meet them as Bull's been careful to keep me away from his father's house.

"They're special and nothing special, all rolled into one," he tells me, explaining the relationship between the three brothers and their father as just the two of us eat dinner again.

Bull tells me how he went to college, majored in agricultural studies, and returned to this area, knowing his practical experience on the farm taught him more than any classroom. Canyon ran off to start a country band and returned home one day with a teenage child, and Blade is in love with Carly but won't admit it.

"Unrequited love is the worst," I tease but immediately regret the words. I mean them in reference to myself and my messed-up marriage, but when I consider Bull and me, we are in a similar position. He isn't going to love me. He feels obligated to me. *If* this is his child, he wants to be here for the baby experience, not me directly. And *if* the baby isn't his child, I'll soon be looking for another place to live.

My family is right. I'm still a screwup even over forty.

Despite the confident woman I am in front of the camera or behind the scenes for research, no one can bring me down more than my mother. When I told her what happened with Shelton, she blamed it on me.

"You worked too much," she prefaced as if that threw the ever-working doctor into the arms and bed of someone else. Even admitting his new girl was pregnant was my fault. *"You should have gotten pregnant yourself, when you were younger. A child is how you keep a man."*

I could not swallow her antiquated attitude. However, it concerns me that Bull might think less of me as well. Will he think I've trapped him if the baby is his? We'll be linked for life.

"Yeah, the worst," Bull mutters, drawing me out of my head where I've forgotten what we are discussing.

"Excuse me?"

"Unrequited love. I might know a thing or two about it."

"I might have heard a thing or two about some proposals," I tease, perching my chin on my hand, wanting all the juicy details. It's weird how sometimes I miss all the gossip I used to report on, and I'm expecting Bull to share some teenage story of angst and broken hearts.

"My wife left me."

"Oh God. I'm so sorry." My hand lowers for his forearm, and my heart sinks to my belly. Bull loved someone else. *Of course, he loved someone.* He's him. But why wouldn't she love him in return?

"It's a complicated story," he begins. "But the long and short of it is, we were married too young, and she wanted babies."

Oh no.

"And we couldn't make them. With all the tests and schedules and practice, we couldn't conceive."

"I'm so sorry, Bull." What must he think of *our* situation? If this isn't his child I'm carrying, he'll feel emasculated.

"It wasn't me," he says, offering a weak smile as if reading my thoughts. "At least, that's what the doctors said." He shrugs, looking toward the end of the dining table. Did they sit here every night like we've been doing, talking about babies? Bull and I have random discussions about how I'm feeling, our thoughts on a birth plan, and baby names. He knows more than I would have expected about pregnancy.

"It was still my fault, though. We could have done artificial insemination or adoption, but Jen was on a mission. I reached a point where I didn't believe it would happen, so I gave up."

He speaks as if he's beat himself up a bit over the years, taking the blame for something that is just biology.

"Eventually, she had enough, as had I, and she left." With the faraway look in his eyes, I recognize the sting of a failed marriage.

"Did you live here together?" I wonder, looking around the room, suddenly feeling like an intruder in someone else's dream.

"No. Jennifer left fourteen years ago. We lived in the main house, and sometimes, I thought that was the thing preventing us from getting pregnant. Although my family knew we wanted a child, and how to make that happen, it wasn't always the most romantic setting, especially when Jen was checking herself for ovulation." Bull shakes his head. "Once she left, I needed some space. This house didn't become my project until each of my grandparents passed, which was about ten years after her departure." He glances up at the ceiling before scanning the large room with pride.

"I'm sorry for your loss." For all of them. His wife, his grandparents, babies he never had.

Bull shrugs, gazing back at his dinner plate. Tonight, he made pork chops with diced potatoes and green beans. He's really too good to me. "I don't know what happened between Jen and me. One minute, you think you're in love, and the next, it's all temperature-taking and baby-making business, minus the tenderness needed to be close to someone."

My thumb rubs back and forth at the hairs on his forearm. He's such a strong man. His arms define arm porn, but it's his heart that's the strength of him.

"It was never the right time to have children with Shelton," I explain of my own situation. "I didn't think I even wanted a baby until he was suddenly having one with someone else, and I was left questioning everything in my life." My other hand automatically moves to my belly although there's no outward evidence of my condition yet. Bull smiles a little deeper, but it still isn't setting off sparks in those deep eyes surrounded by thick lashes.

"I'm glad I'm pregnant now," I offer, my voice quiet while my thumb still rubs at his skin. Bull's hand covers mine and lifts my fingers. He turns my hand to press a kiss to my palm, closing his eyes a second before re-opening those beautiful lids.

"I'm glad you're pregnant, too." His words are full of so much sincerity, and I don't want to disappoint him. It's embarrassing enough to question who the father is, but it will be devastating to discover it isn't Bull. I haven't allowed myself to consider one man over the other. It's too hopeful for me. For now, I concentrate on how the baby is mine.

"You're starting to spoil Sprout and me."

"Sprout?" Bull inquires, and I tip back so he can see my hand patting my belly. He pushes back his chair and reaches over for mine as I'm sitting to his left. After pushing it out as well, he drops down to one knee and faces my tummy.

"Hello, Sprout." He places a hand over my hand on my stomach and then lowers his head, pressing kisses to my covered belly. I slip my fingers through his hair. He's so sweet like this, so tender. Every part of me vibrates—my inner thighs, my hammering heart, my shaky fingers. I want to tug his hair and pull him up to me, kiss him with the pregnancy passion churning inside, and tackle him down to the floor, but I don't. It wouldn't be fair to Bull to keep taking advantage of him, especially sexually. His heart is too big for just sex.

He wraps his arms around my back, scooting me to the edge of the seat to hold me like this—his head on my belly—and I send up a silent prayer.

Please let him be the father.

The next night, Bull and I walk to the main house for dinner. The sun is up a little longer. The air is heating. Everything is bursting into bloom, and soon, so will I.

"Let's not mention our predicament to my family," he states as we walk down the dusty gravel drive. "Not yet, at least."

"Totally agree. What will be our story? How did we meet? Why am I here?"

"Pretty sure Canyon already told them we had a one-night stand." Bull cringes as he speaks. "We can say we're friends. I'm helping you out while you're between places." Bull glances off in the distance, not liking his own explanation, but it's as close to the truth as we can get for now.

When we enter the main house directly into the kitchen, I'm accosted by the smell of something mouthwatering and spicy. "What is that?" I ask of the intoxicating scent.

"Grilled steak and Brussels sprouts are tonight's specialty," a feminine voice answers me, and I glance across the kitchen to find a gorgeous woman with raven black hair and deep blue eyes. "Hi. I'm Carly."

"You're stunning," I admit, not holding back. Her face pinkens at my direct compliment, but when someone is beautiful, it needs to be stated. She has movie-star good looks with high cheekbones and sultry lips. Brushing hair over one ear, she mutters her gratitude at the comment while another person enters the room wearing a ballcap. Nearly as tall as Carly, the body is of someone young, and I surmise this is Canyon's child.

"Aw, Carly. I hate Brussels sprouts," the teen whines. I squint a bit, trying to decipher if this child is a boy or a girl with his or her back to me. The solid shoulders and loose jeans suggest a boy, maybe, but the high voice hints at a girl.

"They're good for you," Carly argues, slapping at the bill of the cap, lowering it over the teen's face.

"Since when?" the teenager argues before glancing over a shoulder at me. "Hey, who is this? This the woman shacking up in your place, Uncle Bull." The kid hitches a thumb at me while addressing Bull, and I'm a little taken aback at the description.

"Joey, mind your manners," Bull warns. "Who said such a thing?"

Joey. Boy.

"Uncle Blade said you met another damsel in distress and brought her home with you. She from one of those dating apps you were on?"

Bull rolls his eyes, but I immediately react. "What dating app?" Bull reaches behind his neck, scratching nervously at it.

"Oopsy," the child states, hand flying upward to cover thin lips, but the shadowed facial expression shows no sign of remorse. "Uncle Bull is *the bull* of DatingDairy."

"Joey, make yourself useful and set the table," Carly interjects, placing hands on the teen almost taller than her and redirecting Joey to a room off the kitchen. "And no hats in the house." Carly tugs at the cap, and a tumble of ginger-colored hair flows from the headgear.

Oh. Girl.

"Joey?" I choke.

"Josephine Elizabeth. My brother Canyon's daughter. She's thirteen."

"Ah," I groan as if that explains everything.

"She's also being raised by a gaggle of men, and she's taking on characteristics of being one," Carly states. "I apologize on her behalf. I'm trying to do my best." Her eyes lead to where the girl disappeared into the dining room, and Bull shakes his head.

"You're not her mama," he states, making me question where the girl's mother is. Bull mentioned Canyon just showed up one day with the child next to him.

"I know," Carly whispers, and sorrow fills her voice. Looking up at Bull, I'm curious as I thought he said Blade was the one in love with Carly. Was Carly in love with Canyon?

Oh, this has all the makings of a good love triangle, but I have my own issues.

"Tell me more about this dating app." I intend to sound teasingly intrigued, but jealousy lingers beneath the surface. With Bull's head in my lap the other night, I wanted desperately for him to lift my skirt and nuzzle his face between my thighs, restoring us to who we've been together. But I'm the one who set the limits. I'm the one who said we should wait until we have an answer because I don't want to be unfair. However, I'm dying a slow death over my attraction to him. I want to touch him and have him touch me. I want our mouths to meet and explore like they did during our night together. Fighting off the urge to throw myself at him like I did in the Busy Bean's bathroom is a constant battle.

"It's just something I've done in the past," Bull mutters and steps over to Carly to avoid further explanation. "What can I help you with?"

Giving me a sympathetic glance, Carly nods at a large bowl with a salad as she answers Bull. "Take that to the dining room and then maybe fill glasses with milk."

"Oh, I don't drink milk," I state. Like a screeching car crash, everything in the kitchen halts. Carly stares at me. Bull rounds to face me.

"Excuse me?" he asks, brows raised high.

"I don't . . ." My voice trails. I'm on a dairy farm, but I don't ingest the product. I'd like to argue lactose intolerant, but that isn't the explanation. I just haven't drunk milk since I was a child. I don't like it, but I can't say that.

"Blasphemy." A deep tenor breaks the sudden silence, and I

turn to my side, watching a man with long hair tucked into a man bun stride into the kitchen from the outside door. He gives me a smile and then winks.

"Canyon," Bull greets his brother. Canyon Eaton should come with a warning of his own. Compared to his brother, he's just as broad and sturdy, yet Canyon has an edgy and artistic side. He has former musician written all over him despite dirty hands and something smudged on his shirt.

"Off with her head," he continues to tease, stepping up to me and playfully wrapping an arm around my neck. He presses an unexpected kiss to my temple before releasing me as quickly as he embraced me. Bull's eyes narrow on his brother.

"Keep your hands to yourself," he warns Canyon.

"Or what? According to you, Red here isn't yours," Canyon teases. "And I like me a redhead." Seeing the dull color on his daughter's hair, I'd say her mother was a redhead, as Canyon's hair is dark brown. However, I'm focused on the fact that Bull's mentioned I don't belong to him, making me sound available to everyone else. I am not liking that assessment.

"I'm taken by me," I state, defending myself and my honor.

"That's not what I meant," Bull growls again at his brother, nostrils flaring with steam like his namesake implies. Then again, Bull has explained that he's named after his father, Harland Bull Eaton, but goes by his middle name.

Canyon steps over to the sink and washes his hands while Bull turns away, disappearing into the dining room with the large salad bowl, and I'm left wondering what these brothers have discussed about me.

"He's not on that app anymore," Carly offers, opening the refrigerator and reaching inside.

"How do you know?" I question, stepping over to her and taking the milk jug from her hand.

"I'm on there, and he's not." She gives me a sheepish grin, and I softly smile. However, I'm still uncomfortable with Bull ever being on a dating app. What's with this about damsels in distress? Is that how he sees me?

"You shouldn't be on that site either, beautiful," Canyon says to Carly, and she blushes before waving out an arm for me to follow her to the dining room.

A table big enough to seat twelve is sporadically set, and I assume this has to do with people's preference in sitting arrangement. After pouring the milk into glasses and skipping my own, I carry my glass back to the kitchen for water. When I return to the dining room, a version of what Bull will look like one day when he's older sits at the head of the table. With solid gray hair and wrinkled facial skin, he's still ruggedly good-looking in his mid-sixties.

"Scarlett, right?" he addresses me, giving me a warm smile. "Canyon was correct. You are beautiful and look just like her."

For a moment, I'm thinking he means Bull's first wife, Jennifer, and I don't know how to respond.

"Looks just like who?" Joey asks of her grandfather.

"Grandma," he whispers, still watching me round the table.

"Sit here," Joey says, patting a chair next to her. "Uncle Bull sits there." She points at the other seat at the head of the table, making it appear the top two males of the family face one another. I'll be sitting to Bull's right. Carly enters with another large platter, Bull behind her, and Canyon follows.

"Where's Blade?" the middle brother questions, and we hear the stomping of feet down a staircase somewhere in the house. Canyon smirks and sarcastically remarks, "Right on time to help."

The errant brother rushes into the room and halts when he sees me at the table. "Holy shit."

"Language," Carly groans as Blade stares at me.

"Did she drop from heaven?" He doesn't direct the question to anyone, and Joey chuckles beside me. I don't respond to his compliment other than a deep blush. He's already seen me the other morning.

"Actually, she walked into The Gin Mill," Bull answers.

"And that's all it took," Canyon teases, winking at me over the table.

"Of all the gin joints," Blade throws his voice, mimicking Humphrey Bogart in *Casablanca*. I laugh at his impression while Carly takes a seat, and it appears Blade will sit next to her, opposite me. Canyon rounds the table to sit next to his daughter.

"Harland, grace," Carly addresses the table once everyone is seated.

"Joey, your turn," Harland states, narrowing his eyes at his granddaughter. "I heard what you said in the kitchen."

Joey's eyes shift to me. "Sorry," she mumbles of her accusation about me. Then she folds her hands in contrition.

"We are grateful for this bounty, which is always good." It's sweet, but Harland shakes his head in disapproval.

"Next time, rhyme," Blade teases his niece. The meal erupts into chaos as bowls are passed, and food served, and appreciation spoken for Carly's delicious dinner. The tender steak strips melt in my mouth, and I hum.

"Like Bess?" Joey says to me, and Bull pauses his fork midair. Carly drops hers.

"Josephine Elizabeth, what has gotten into you?" Carly hisses across the table.

"Who's Bess?" I ask, slowly chewing the remainder of the meat.

"She's in your mouth," Joey clarifies, and I stop chewing.

"Excuse me?" I say around the food.

"Course it could be Ilsa or Esther or—" Joey continues sing-songing the names.

"That's enough," Canyon warns of his daughter, and I glance over at Bull for an explanation.

"She likes to name the cows."

Oh, God. I swallow the remaining lump in my mouth, reaching for my water glass and chugging the remainder of the liquid.

"Gonna not eat meat, too?" Joey questioningly sasses me, and I realize she must have heard what I said about milk and not drinking it. To prove her point, she picks up her glass and guzzles the entire thing, making a satisfying *ah* after finishing the refreshing liquid. She slaps the glass to the table and takes a large bite of her steak.

"How's Bess taste to you?" I question, watching her chew without a conscience even though she tried to make me feel guilty for eating the cooked meat.

"She was done producing, so off to the slaughterhouse she went." Joey draws a line along her throat.

Again, I peer over at Bull, who has returned to eating, ignoring his niece. Deciding this is a test, I move to my salad, no longer hungry for the rest of my savory steak.

"You know, you look familiar," Joey continues.

"Stop torturing Bull's guest," Carly demands across the table.

"Oh, is that what we call you?" Joey asks, and the angry vibe coming off this teen raises the hackles on my neck, but I remember this age and this attitude. I had it myself.

"We're friends," I state, proud of the label.

"Ri-iiight. Friends," Joey annunciates, rolling her eyes.

"JoJo," Canyon warns of his daughter.

"So, are you someone? Because you look like someone famous. Are you hiding out here? Did you commit a crime?"

I wouldn't say famous, but I can be recognized in certain circles. Convinced this teenager won't know who I am, I proudly state my name. "I'm Scarlett Russell, and I don't have any known felonies on record."

Bull pauses again, glancing over at me with wide eyes.

"I'm teasing," I state, choking back the joke.

Joey reaches into her lap and picks up a phone. Tapping at it quickly like kids can, she holds out the screen for me to view.

While this happens, her grandfather warns her about electronics at the table. Without breaking his rhythm to eat, Canyon reaches across his daughter to take her phone. However, when he brings the device before himself, his brows pinch.

"This you?" He holds up the screen so I can see my name in

bold letters underneath an image of me. My makeup is done to perfection as I remember exactly where that photo was taken. The Emmy's.

"That's me." I nod.

Canyon presses on the screen while his father reminds him no phones at the table. He ignores Harland and narrows his eyes.

"It says here you worked for KTEL at one of their entertainment rags." Canyon hisses, and I instantly wonder if I ever reported on him. I haven't done a search of his name, although Bull told me he was famous in his own right for a bit.

On his way somewhere, Bull explained.

Thankfully, Harland reaches over to his second son and yanks the device out of his hands. He tucks the phone under his leg and continues eating without breaking stride to finish his dinner. I glance back at Bull, who's watching me.

"You never mentioned you were famous."

"I'm not. And I no longer work for KTEL, obviously," I say, noticing the table has grown quiet as I speak.

"What happened?" Joey asks, and Carly hisses her name again.

"I was fired because I was too old."

A chorus of *what, are you kidding me, no way,* and *how could that happen* rounds the table.

"Forty-two isn't twenty-two," I admit, shrugging to dismiss the truth as I push my salad around my plate. I'm no longer hungry for anything at this point.

"You're still pretty. Will you get another television job?" Joey asks, her voice lowering.

"Unfortunately, talent doesn't outweigh looks sometimes." It's a hard lesson to learn. "And I don't know if I'll go back to television. I haven't applied anywhere. Just taking a life break." I look up to meet Canyon's eyes over his daughter's head, and his chin tips as if he knows what I mean.

"You'll get another fancy job, and then you'll leave," Joey

mutters, and my eyes narrow at her. Did something like this happen to her? Did her mother leave for a job?

"For now, I'd like to stay." I peer over at Bull and then drop my eyes again.

"We're happy to have you here," Harland says from his end of the table, and when I glance up to look at him, sincerity shows in his face. "You stay as long as you need."

"Thank you," I answer. I'm lost in my head through the remainder of the meal. Should I be looking for another job in the entertainment industry? I'll have another mouth to feed, and I need to consider making more than the part-time wages of a coffee shop to support myself and a baby. I don't want to rely on Bull, father or not, and as he already said, this won't be a marriage. We're partners, parenting together, but I'm only a houseguest until we have particulars.

Maybe I should reach out to some old friends, see what's out there for someone older in the industry. It doesn't need to be entertainment news. I'm a damn good reporter. With this in mind, I decide it's time to take more steps toward a new future.

9

MORE THAN A JOB

SCARLETT

The remainder of dinner turns to more family-related issues—school for Joey and the farm for the men. Later, as Bull and I walk home on a quiet, cool evening, I slip my arm into the crook of his. I imagine this is the life he would have had with his wife or any other woman he was engaged to marry. Share a meal with his family. Take a stroll down the lane. The thought reminds me Bull hasn't told me about the other engagements rumored about him.

"Saw the wheels spinning in those pretty eyes of yours after Joey grilled you about your job. I'm sorry you lost it because of something ridiculous, and probably unlawful, like age discrimination. What happened?"

"One day, I walked into my boss's office, full of new scoops and angles, and the next thing I know, I'm being fired because of crow's feet and saggy breasts."

"Your breasts don't sag," Bull admonishes. "And if they did, I'd volunteer to hold them up."

I chuckle at his teasing suggestion but fall prey to the memory.

"I hate to do this to you, Red, but we're letting you go."

I stared at my boss, Lex Steinburg, disbelieving what he just said.

"Good one, Lex. Now, Adrianne Grosse had another mishap in a donut shop, using her tongue to imitate how she'd like to take her girlfriend, and it's making the rounds on social media that she's secretly been having an affair with Ellen Lux, which does not make Ellen's wife happy."

"Red, you're not listening to me."

He was right. I wasn't. "And then there's the continued scandal of Ben Alex doing his nanny while his sweet wife raises their three children. I mean, how do you cheat on her? She's quirky and cute, and devoted. What a dick."

"Red—"

"And finally, I think we have some inside scoop on the royals. Mikayla Martin has really done it now." I glance up at him from my tablet, pleased that I've made friends with the second cousin of the first person who once worked with the new duchess-no-longer a duchess when she had a job in a coffee shop for a few months at fifteen years old. "So, on that note—"

"Scarlett," Lex interrupts me again. "You're fired."

The words were like one of those slow-motion scenes in a commercial for spilled milk, where the mom reaches for the glass too late and the child gasps, and the background sound is an elongated no.

"Ye – or – fy – err – ed." Phonetically, the words traveled through the ear canal and stumbled across my brain, and I had no response. I just stared at the man I've worked with for twenty years.

"I'm sorry." He wasn't. Not the least bit of chagrin showed on his paunchy face. Over the years, the alcohol had caught up to him, and he was puffy in cheeks, chin, and jowls. He'd also lost hair giving him a landing strip down the center of his head, and no amount of combing this way or that covered the fact he was balding in the middle at forty plus.

"I was told they wanted someone younger, trendier. More perky. Those were literally his words, snapping his fingers to emphasize them." I snap one set of mine as I explain.

Lex's eyes dipped to my breasts. There's nothing wrong with my breasts, I remember thinking. They're perky . . . enough. And to prove *my point, I sat up straighter, adjusting my back to thrust said breasts forward in my tight-fitting sweater.* See perky. *But Lex looked away.*

"My boss said my airtime wasn't getting the same ratings as it once did. To which I suggested perhaps they needed new material. People were getting tired of the scandalized bits of the rich and famous. They wanted more heart behind their celebrities. Not just the nasty parts."

My business was other people's business, and I worked hard to prove myself for two decades in an unforgiving industry. But I was growing weary myself of the constant negativity. The failed marriages. The drug issues. The malignant behavior. I'd been making suggestions for a new twist for years and getting turned down with each special interest story. How many times can you hear about Brad Smoltz dissing Jennifer Allister before you just don't care? It's over. Move on. Tell me more about Sally Superstar and the twenty million kids she's adopted, homeschooled, and drags around the world doing philanthropy work while still winning Academy Awards. There's a role model, sort of. There's a reason Princess Diana was such a hit in her day. People want the soul of a star not all their shit.

"I was told outright I was too old for the position."

"Excuse me?" There was no way I could have heard Lex correctly. "I'm forty-two."

"Past your prime."

"You've got to be kidding me. What does that even mean?"

According to *Glimmer Magazine*, I've just entered my prime. Wasn't Lex aware that forty was the new twenty? I was seasoned. I was wise. I was entering a new phase of my life that would bring me renewed energy, increased libido, and a zero-fucks attitude. I wasn't old. I was goddamn tired.

"Lex, my boss, was happy to point out all my flaws. A little sag here." I mimic Lex's voice while I tug at the loose skin under my eyes.

"A crinkle too many here," I mock of him again as I point at my temple.

"And then, he insulted my breasts." Lex's eyes simply dipped to them.

Bull chuckles, shaking his head in disbelief.

"Then he tried to argue that he defended me. If I only had a few surgeries—"

"Surgeries," Bull interjects, aghast. "You're fucking perfect. Are they blind?"

I chuckle at his strong admonition of my former employer while my face heats at the compliment. No one has ever called me perfect.

"A boob job and Botox, and I'd get to continue working for them."

"That's ridiculous," Bull states. "You know that, right?" His voice shifts, dropping stern as he squeezes his arm where I'm looped through it.

"Yeah, well, it's a man's world in some manners. I wanted to ask Lex if he'd looked in the mirror lately and noticed his receding hairline." I bit back the insult at the time. Unfortunately, parts of the industry were still an ol' boys' club. Special handshakes. Pats on the back. And blind eyes especially when it came to men looking at one another's behavior.

"Unfortunately, it was the same day I found out about Shelton, my husband, and his affair."

"That's awful, sweetheart," Bull sighs beside me, and I narrow my eyes, keeping my focus straight ahead as we walk.

"Like everything else in the last few months, I guess I've taken it as a sign that change was inevitable." Unfortunately, there has been a lot of change all at once.

"Was that the type of reporter you wanted to be? A gossip journalist or whatever they call it." Bull's voice strains as he asks.

"I went to school to be a reporter because I wanted to share editorials and interviews like Barbara Walters. Somehow I ended up with KTEL instead."

"I'm not familiar with KTEL," Bull admits.

"Well, it's for the best." I wave a dismissive hand. "The show I worked on was an entertainment rag as Canyon so eloquently put it." My eyes squint in the dark, gazing off toward the distance before us. There's a peacefulness here, a stillness unlike city life. The only sound is the crunch of gravel under our feet.

"Will you look for another job? Be a different kind of reporter?" Bull asks.

"I have a job," I tease, although pouring coffee isn't really a career move for me. I'm also terrible at being a barista, so I don't see it as long term. However, I do like the place, and I adore Audrey, Zara, and Roddy. In general, I really like Vermont. "But in answer to your question, I just don't know. I'm stumbling over every step right now as there have been so many changes at once."

Bull nods. "Was it satisfying?"

"What do you mean?"

"Did you like your former job?"

Staring off in the distance again, I take a minute to consider my answer before I speak. "I was good at what I did. I'm a reporter. But did I always *feel good* about my job? The truth is, I didn't. It wasn't always pleasant information we shared, and some of it wasn't even true. It was more sensationalism, for ratings and rank." I snap my fingers again like Lex used to do.

"As I told your niece, I haven't been looking for anything. Maybe I should reach out to people I know, though, see if anything is available. I'm going to need more of an income eventually. The longer I'm out of the industry the less likely I'll be able to re-enter it. But I'm also in quite a predicament at the moment. Not certain an industry that fires women at forty-two wants to hire a pregnant forty-two-year-old."

Bull huffs to agree.

"I'm content where I am for now," I say, giving his arm a squeeze.

"For now." Bull nods but remains quiet. Tipping my head to his arm, we walk the rest of the way in silence, but my thoughts are loud. I don't know that I want to return to the entertainment industry. I feel a bit betrayed from the years of commitment, the dedication to the network, and the way I was so easily tossed aside. However, I can't rely on my savings for everything. Eventually, I'll need to work.

"You know, you can rely on me, Scarlett. I'm willing to pull my fair share with the baby when the time comes." He's talking finances, and I guess it's a sweet enough gesture, but I don't want Bull's money.

Once we're back at Bull's home, we fall into our nightly routine of circling one another for the bathroom. I hear the door open and decide to tell Bull one more thing before I head to bed, only I'm stopped in my tracks, forgetting what I intend to say as he stands just outside the bathroom door with only a towel, wrapped around his middle. Hanging low enough to expose a trail of hair leading lower, I swallow hard knowing well what's under that terrycloth material. My hands clutch at the door jamb, holding myself steady as my mouth dries. He has such an incredible body, lean and firm from labor on this land. A smattering of hair curls over his pecs and a tattoo circles one bicep.

"Did you need something?" Bull points over his shoulder with his thumb, suggesting the bathroom. What I need is to enter the shower *with him* and wash away my dirty thoughts while we clean each other's bodies. I blink as he steps closer to my room, his presence filling up the hallway and all the oxygen I need to breathe.

"I-I just wanted to tell you I think your family is great." As I'm an only child, my parents laid the pressure on thick when I was young and didn't relent as I grew older. I can't recall loud family meals or laughter around a dinner table. Even with Shelton, there were nights of only scraping forks against china and the soft swallow of wine. Perhaps that's what happened to us. Where I thought we had quiet companionship, we only had simple silence.

"Yeah, they loved you." I blush at the thought as they don't really know me, and they don't have all the information about Bull and my situation, but I want them to like me.

I'm still holding the sides of the door jamb, half my body inside my room, half of it out, but I don't miss Bull's eyes lowering to my breast, covered by my tight-fitting tank top. My boobs ache from both the changes in my body and the desire I see in his eyes. He wants to touch me, and I want his touch. My nails dig deeper into the wood framing the door.

"Oh, and I have another doctor's appointment coming up soon," I say. My voice catches on the words, raspy and rough as my own eyes focus on his chest, lowering for the dark trail leading into the towel. I've just made a mundane visit sound sexy in the tone of my voice, and I lick my lips before glancing back up at Bull's face. His hand has flattened on the wall. His body stills while I worship it. "Want to come with me?"

The corner of his mouth slowly lifts, and I realize what I've said has two meanings.

"I mean, attend the doctor's visit with me," I clarify, still gripping the door.

"I know what you meant, and I'd love to come with you . . . to the doctor appointment, that is." We stare at one another, breaths shallow. My heart races.

"Need anything else tonight?"

The list of my wants is rather short. I only want him, but I promised myself I'd roundup my libido. I don't want to give him false hope of us, although he's made it clear he doesn't want us. *You said Red wasn't yours.* He only wants his share in fatherhood, *if* he's the father.

With the sour potential he's not my baby's daddy, I slap a hand lightly on the door jamb.

"We could talk to the doctor about a paternity test," I state, nearly bursting the bubble of sexual tension between us.

"We could," he agrees half-heartedly answering me. With nothing else said, I tap the doorframe again.

"Well, good night then."

Bull nods, pushes off the wall, and spins to give me his retreating back. My forehead lowers for the trim, rolling back and forth against the wood. His back might be as incredible as his front with dips and cliffs of muscles. Suddenly, Bull turns on his bare feet, facing me once more and taking a few extra steps toward my door.

"Just putting it out there, that today's a day ending in day, and if you needed me for something, I'm here for you." His hand lightly pats his chest before coasting downward, forcing the coarse hairs to spring a little and then his abs flinch as he lowers his palm to the edge of that dangling towel.

"I'm good," I lie, raising a hand as a little wave of good night. Stepping sideways, I knock my knee on the wood casing, bite my cheek to hold back a curse, and reach for the doorknob. Once inside the room, I collapse against the closed door, cursing from more than the ache at my knee, but the one in my heart.

Rita comes to the Busy Bean near the end of my shift the next day. Wishing I could enjoy an afternoon coffee, I sit with her instead as she sips a cold brew. The doctor has already warned me I need to cut back on caffeine products and I've already had my one cup this morning. Another irony of working at a coffee shop is how I must resist the temptation, just like I must resist Bull.

A full-body shiver occurs with the images in my head of Bull crowding me near the coffeepot in his kitchen or walking down the hallway in only that towel of his.

Rita and I have been discussing whether I should be looking for a new job or not.

"I'd just like to do something with more purpose." My reference did not imply working at the coffee café was less than admirable. I simply meant any employment in general, I wanted to have purpose behind it in the future.

"It's okay not to know what you want," Rita tells me as we slouch on the comfy couch Rita claims as hers.

"I'm forty-two. Shouldn't I have life all pulled together by now?"

"Your life was pulled together. It was wound tighter than a knitter's knot. It's okay to loosen the loops a little. You're never too old, or too young, to start over," Rita encourages.

"But I don't want to start over." I sound like a petulant child, but the truth is, I actually do want a fresh start. My hand coasts over the tiny bulge of nine weeks, or is it only eight, of pregnancy. I have an appointment this week to listen to Sprout's heartbeat. It's still a bit surreal that some tiny creature is growing inside me, let alone unbelievable at my advanced age, as the doctor lovingly called it during my first visit. When the doctor also told me this pregnancy was considered a geriatric pregnancy, I almost fell off the table. I wasn't *that* old. It's not improbable or even uncommon for a woman over forty to be pregnant, but it also comes with loads of potential risks. My own research on the topic taught me that while the average age of a pregnant woman is twenty-six, there is an increasing proportion of women who are in their thirties. And while that number has actually dipped in the last decade, pregnancies among women over forty is actually on the rise. It's up only a few percentage points, but it's still noteworthy.

The issues rest in the risks—heart concerns, skull abnormalities, developmental delays—and those were just concerns for the baby. Personally, I could develop high blood pressure, gestational diabetes, or pre-eclampsia. Even worse, though, is the possibility I could miscarry. I could lose the baby and all the trouble I'd been to Bull would be for nothing.

He's been so good to me. Every night, we have dinner together like a real couple. No late-night dashes off to a local bar for a quick bite. No takeout ordered in for one while my other half works long hours. Bull and I sit at a table together, with a home-cooked meal before us, from either Carly or Bull himself. He's an amazing cook, and I've felt guilty that I don't offer more home engineering. I'm terrible at domestic deeds as I proved the other evening when I tried to make Bull chicken in a skillet and burned the outside while the inside was still raw.

He's also been more than generous with his home. We've continued to dance around close calls in the hallway and finding too much comfort on his couch. I'm sleepier than I've ever been, and Bull is like a giant heating pad. Too often, I've found myself slumped over against his shoulder, snoozing in the early evenings when he physically works twice as hard as I do.

"I totally understand the desire for purpose," Rita says, looking at me over her cup. She's been struggling herself lately, as she's been saying for years she plans to retire from her law practice in Montpelier. She hasn't found that thing either—that passion—to push her forward on a new path, though. "But have you considered that where life leads, you can shift your priorities and motherhood might be the next great adventure for you? Maybe motherhood is your next great purpose."

"I . . ." I actually hadn't thought of it that way. I'd always been so career driven without a thought for children that I hadn't considered being a mother could be a role in my life as well. Rita watches me as I wrestle with my thoughts, uncertain how to answer her. I'm stumped.

"Let's talk about Bull," Rita prompts, releasing me from trying to decipher motherhood and how I see myself fitting that future role. "How are things going with the hunky heifer king?" She wiggles her brows. As she knows all my secrets, I admit the truth to her.

"We're waiting to find out who the father is before we do anything . . . between us. I have a doctor's visit soon, and we're going to discuss a paternity test then."

Rita lowers her afternoon treat and stares at me across the couch. "You mean to tell me, you're living with that hunk of cowhide and not riding him?"

I snort. "Rita, I swear . . ." She says the damnedest things.

"Well?" Her voice rises.

"No, I am not sleeping with him." We cuddle on the couch

sometimes, but that's not what Rita means. Even that is more than we should be doing because each night I settle in next to Bull, I don't want to separate from him when it's time for bed. I never liked sleeping pressed up against Shelton. We actually didn't curl into each other like we once did when we were young, keeping to our own sides of the king-sized bed we used to share in our marriage. The experience would be different with Bull. I'd want to be touching him. I'd want to be near his heat, pressed against his skin. I'd want to hear his heartbeat.

"Is that paternity test safe?"

"Considering I'm at high risk because of my age, I'm not sure. I'm not even certain how it works exactly, although I looked it up." Somehow a sample is taken from both Bull and the baby. I'm not convinced it's entirely risk-free and I'd like to discuss options with the doctor. "Either way, Bull's attending my next doctor's visit with me."

"So, things are going well, even if you aren't heating the sheets with a hot man," Rita teases as her eyes narrow in on me. "You like him, don't you?"

"Of course, I like him. He's a great guy."

Rita snorts herself. "Great guy? That's like saying someone has a nice personality."

"What do you want me to say? When he looks at me, I feel like he wants to devour me. Or how I can't take my eyes off his body even when it's as simple as him walking across a room. Or how I miss the way we were together that one night, putting us into this possibility of being connected forever." I glance down at my lower belly again.

"It's crazy. It all seems like too much too soon." I huff. I'm not even officially divorced yet. If all goes as planned, Shelton and I only have another six weeks.

"Everything happens for a reason," Rita says, and my head pops up to look over at her. It's a phrase she lives by. I'd argue against it if I didn't suddenly believe that this unplanned pregnancy at such a late-in-life age meant something. Even if I don't know what the reason for such a life shift could be, I can't deny I'm happy with this directional detour.

"What do you know about Bull and all those proposals?" It's something he still hasn't explained to me.

"I think you should ask Bull. It's always best to go to the source rather than believe all the hearsay." Rita tips a brow at me, hinting at my past profession. I'm just curios as Roderick said something to me the other day as well. He was sweet in his warning, telling me not to believe all the gossip in the community, but he was equally concerned that I protect myself.

"He's been called the perpetual proposer and there's something behind the fact he's been engaged a few times." Roderick was not speaking ill of Bull or even trying to perpetuate the rumors but looking out for me. He knows my condition. He knows my position, and he knows Bull and I are living together, platonically.

"Let me know how that works out for you," he teased as he fell for his roommate and they've been together ever since.

"So, back to the original matter at hand. Are you really thinking of looking for a new job in entertainment news?"

"Don't you think I should?" I question, as I don't want to keep taking advantage of Bull. I need to plan as if this child isn't his, because if it isn't, he's going to want me to leave. He'll want as much separation from me as he can possibly get.

"I think purpose and passion are what you make of it. And there's nothing wrong with being a mother and pouring coffee for a little longer," Rita says, reaching out to pat my knee. "It certainly gives me purpose that you work here. I get to see you more often."

I've really missed my friend and decide a little more time at the Busy Bean Café is just fine with me as well. Besides, I have her to thank for bringing me to Vermont and introducing me to Bull.

HEARTBEATS

BULL

At night, Scarlett and I assume our normal position on my couch. A hockey play-off game is on, and Scarlett's been reading from a baby book. We typically start in opposite corners, but eventually her legs stretch, as if her toes are seeking me, and I tug her feet into my lap, massaging her ankles. Sometimes, we sit closer, more in the middle, and she'll inevitably flop toward me, as if her head is too heavy. I'll tuck her under my arm, leaning her against my chest, and breathing in the comfort of all things. It's been torture.

Tonight, I'm tired myself. We've had to make decisions on a few heifers not producing and I had to round them up for slaughter. It's never an easy decision, but it's a part of the farm process. When Scarlett's feet slide across the couch to my thigh, I don't shift them to my lap like I normally do but slip my whole self behind her. With her back nestled into my chest with each of us on our sides, and we face the television set.

"This okay, sweetheart?" I ask too late as I'm already in position to hold her and not interested in giving it up.

"This is good, Bull." My arm slips over her waist as we each stare at the hockey game, but I'm hardly hearing the announcer.

"Can I ask you something?" Her quiet voice has me nervous.

"Anything, darlin'."

"What's the deal with the rumors about you as the perpetual proposer?"

My forehead lowers for the top of her head, and I close my eyes. This is a conversation I've dreaded having. Marriage talk is always an issue for me. However, Scarlett and I are in a different predicament, and we aren't discussing *our* marriage, just my relationship history.

Taking a deep breath, I begin my explanation.

"First, there was Jennifer, who you already know was my wife. We were married young and divorced early. Then there was Sabrina." I take another deep breath as Scarlett's fingertips stroke over my forearm. "That's a bit more complicated, but let's just say she left me at the altar."

Sensing Scarlett's shift under my arm, I tighten my hold around her. She attempts to look at me over her shoulder, but I won't be able to face her until I get this story out.

"Not much more embarrassing than standing at the altar, waiting on your bride to walk down the aisle. Church filled with people who'd been calling you a match made in heaven. Then her father approaches me and leans forward, telling me Sabrina needs to speak with me."

The memory rushes back to me. Sabrina Carrera was different from anyone I'd ever met before. First, she was ten years younger than me in my thirties. In contrast to Jen's acorn brunette coloring, Sabrina had midnight black hair and looked sleek in business suits and fitted skirts. She had dreams and ambitions of being something bigger than our small community, but her energy never bothered me. In fact, she was refreshing after Jennifer, who was a little too complacent at times and often gave in to my whims instead of following her own desires. If I liked pepperoni on pizza, Jen liked pepperoni. If I wanted to wear jeans and be casual, Jen wore jeans to be casual. If I wanted to watch a ballgame, then Jen watched a ballgame. Jen only had one focus all her own—a child.

"Sabrina wanted bright lights and big city, so it never made sense for us to be together. She should have gone to New York, but instead, she worked in a bank in Montpelier. I could never quite explain it, but Sabrina was just vibrant. She was also superficial."

She loved gifts, and the fool that I was, I showered her with them. I gave her whatever she wanted, and in return, I had a young, beautiful woman on my arm, reviving my sexuality.

"After the breakup with Jen, I just needed different, and Sabrina was it. It felt good to be wanted for more than my sperm donation."

Scarlett stills her fingertips on my forearm, and I mumble an apology. It isn't like that with Scarlett. Jen and I had become so perfunctory in our relationship, and her ability to adapt to whatever I wanted that it eventually pissed me off. I wanted a woman with a mind of her own. High spirited and definitely spoiled, Sabrina had been the opposite of my first wife.

"I don't know how we'd gotten to the wedding ceremony itself. It was like one minute we were discussing marriage, and the next thing I know, we are making an announcement. Sabrina was in love with the idea of a wedding. I wanted her to be happy, and I also wanted her to stick around. I didn't want her to run off to New York." I'd wanted the farm to be enough for her, but I should have seen the signs. We spent a lot of time at her place in Montpelier. As I partially blamed living on the farm for the breakup of my marriage at the time, as Jen and I never had any privacy, being away from it for a while was refreshing. With Sabrina, we had a ton of separation from the farm while doing the costly things Sabrina wanted to do.

"I never had a hint she was unhappy, or maybe I just wasn't listening. When an ex-boyfriend came into town a week before the wedding, I wasn't even concerned. But he'd apparently been making her promises of more, and he was her ticket out of this area. She'd never mentioned to anyone that she didn't want to be a farmer's wife."

I close my eyes, recalling the awkward moment I walked into the bridal room at the church. Her veil removed. Her dress wrinkled. What could be worse than her father walking in on another man up her skirt before the wedding? The thought of it made me sick to my stomach. In order to save his pride, Giuseppe Carrera demanded his daughter face me. I'd paid for most of the wedding when he couldn't afford all the things his daughter wanted.

"His name was Brett." Not that that means anything, but I share it anyway.

"We hate people named Brett," Scarlett whispers in a show of solidarity with me, and I smile as the tension of Sabrina's memory dissolves.

"It was a blessing in disguise."

"I'm so sorry that happened to you." Scarlett's low voice expresses her sincerity, and after her cheating husband, I know she understands.

"Next came Gisela." I decide to skip over the fine details of Gisela's wild sexual tendencies. The things she wanted me to do with her could have been criminal, but I loved them. She was very in touch with who she was and what she wanted in the bedroom, and I was happy to oblige. "Gisela was an artist. Painting was her medium, and she felt she'd found her inspiration at the farm."

Again, Scarlett bristles under my arm, and I press a quick kiss to her shoulder. Her stroking fingertips continue as if coaxing the remainder of my story out of me.

"Gisela was a bit of a Bohemian. Wanderlust mixed with her creativity, and she said the farm fed her spirit but apparently, only temporarily." Gisela's blond hair in lengthy dreadlocks gave her an earthy appearance. She made her own clothing of flowing skirts and loose tops out of natural fabrics. She also wore tons of bracelets and necklaces. "Gisela actually lived in Colebury for a while but spent many days out here, feeding her soul as she said.

She told people I was her spirit animal, and we would get married one day."

Scarlett starts out with a soft chuckle, but her body continues to quake, struggling to contain more.

"Don't laugh," I teasingly warn, as my tone gives away my own chuckle. My head lowers for the back of hers once again, and Scarlett loses the fight against her laughter.

"We didn't know she was actually stealing from people in the community. Little things, but items of value all the same, slowly went missing over time."

The memory of confronting her when I saw her wearing my grandmother's ring made acid boil in my stomach. When I confronted her about it, she accused me of not trusting her, saying I didn't love her enough, and if I did love her, I should have given her that ring anyway.

"The breakup with her was public as she threw my grandmother's ring, which I hadn't given her, back at me, stating I was reserved and standoffish and didn't give her what she needed." Whether she meant sexually, spiritually, or otherwise, I would never know. Gisela ran off one night without another word to anyone in the area. We later learned she'd stolen my mother's china serving platter and a silver gravy boat for whatever reason.

I quiet, recalling a nasty headline once reported about me.

"Mr. Not Quite Right, an article read," I whisper, and Scarlett's fingertips pause.

"Those women don't know what they could have had," Scarlett generously states. "It's their loss, although I'd say you dodged a couple of losers there, Bull. And that article got it wrong. You're perfect."

I smile at her kind words.

"Anyway, I swore off women but quickly realized that wasn't possible. I like women too much," I joke, squeezing at her lower belly. "Blade and Clayton thought they'd be childish dicks and signed me up for MateMe and DatingDairy to get me back out there, proving to myself I could get worthy women." I huff. "I'd only gone on a few dates before I swore it off. I needed more than a profile to assess a person. Women aren't cows to be purchased from a catalog."

I pause, waiting for Scarlett to admonish the full confession, but she doesn't. Her body holds still, but her fingertips continue to rub up and down my arm.

"Well, thank goodness you think that," Scarlett teases, playfully swatting at my arm. "Otherwise, I'm pretty certain I wouldn't qualify under home goods or domestication products."

I snort. "I don't want to domesticate you, Scarlett. You have nothing to worry about. I'm no longer interested in marriage." Well … that isn't *exactly* true. It's just not at the forefront of my thoughts, as it seems to be an eternal *im*possibility for me.

"Would Louisa have been under home goods?" Scarlett says, her voice lowering.

"It was only coffee," I say, reminding us both of the day Scarlett was behind the couch in the Busy Bean Café. The day I learned she was still in town, and I wanted to kick myself because she was so close, and I was unaware. "I'd put you in the lingerie section because you're so sexy."

"Oh, you shop for lingerie often?" she teases, and I laugh but release her. I roll to my back as much as the couch will allow. Reaching for a cushion behind me, I toss it off the couch, providing more space for me to lay flat.

"I sound like a loser," I admit, staring up at the low ceiling and swiping fingers into my hair. Scarlett shifts beside me, almost falling off the couch until I catch her. I tug her forward until we lay face-to-face. Her fingers play with the collar of my short-sleeved shirt.

"I don't think you sound like a loser. You sound like someone who easily gives his heart, opening it wide to possibilities, and has had it trampled on a few too many times. I'm sorry all those experiences happened to you."

Her eyes focus on the buttons of my shirt as she speaks, and her fingers move to my chest, toying with one.

"My mom used to say everything happens for a reason. She died between Sabrina and Gisela, and I think it's another reason I fell for Gisela. She filled more than one void, which sounds heartless on my part."

"Bull, don't try to justify the actions of someone who did you wrong. All those women hurt you, and it's okay to accept that it wasn't you, but them."

I lean forward and press a kiss to her forehead. When those dark eyes finally glance up at me, full of sympathy, I lick my lips. She's so close with her head on my arm, and our bodies lined up.

"If I were to catalog you, I might put you in the toy section." My gaze falls to her mouth. "Sex toys, that is."

She laughs, jiggling against me. "You'd like that, wouldn't you?"

"Would you?" I tease in return, but the heat in her eyes answers my question, and a part of me rises with this teasing discussion.

"Are you considering me a plaything?" Her voice drops as she bites her lower lip in that sexy way she does, letting me know she wants me. With two fingers, I lift her chin so our eyes catch each other.

"I consider you many things, Scarlett, but a plaything is not one of them. You've been played yourself, so you know how much it hurts."

"I do," she whispers, and for some reason, that phrase does something to my chest. However, I dismiss the ache as another part of me surges for attention from her.

"It's so hard not to kiss you." The fingers at her chin drag along her jaw until they dip into her hair at the side of her head. Combing to the back of her head, I give the short strands a little tug, and her breath hitches, causing her lips to fall open.

"I'm sorry, Bull. I don't want to hurt you. I don't want to be like those other women."

I nod, releasing my fingers and smoothing my hand down her

arm, ignoring the sting of being shot down while she presses against me.

"Maybe I'm protecting my own heart," she says. "I'd been such a fool with Shelton. His affair blindsided me, but I'd feel even worse if something started between us and the baby isn't yours."

I nod again as if I understand. It's practical and reasonable, but I'd also like to make my own decision regarding another man's child and the woman carrying it, especially when said woman is in my arms. It's a strange position to be in, that's for certain, but Scarlett doesn't seem to realize I don't care about her ex. As long as she isn't going back to him, I'm here for her and Sprout. But perhaps, she's correct in guarding herself. I don't want to be the one to hurt her as I'll never be in the market to marry again. And I need to tell myself this over and over because the warning bells in my head tell me I'm at great risk of falling for her and wanting something I never get—a wife.

A few days later, I'm driving Scarlett to her doctor's appointment in Montpelier, where we'll be able to hear the baby's heartbeat. While Scarlett and I have discussed potential birth plans and baby names, she tends to cut those conversations short once her eyes start to spark with possibility and hope.

"There's so much that could happen at my age," she'd eventually say, closing the door on any budding excitement. "The *what-ifs* can wake me out of a dead sleep." My chest tightens when she tells me such a thing. I want to hold her each night, comfort her in my bed, and soothe away those nightmares.

There's a touch of reality in her fear, though. Because of her advanced age, as she sarcastically states, she could have had a sonogram at her first doctor's visit when the pregnancy was detected. However, there's some controversy because of Scarlett's age around such a test so early on in a pregnancy, and she opted out of it.

"I was afraid it might harm the baby even though the doctor assured me it wouldn't." Scarlett erred on the side of caution, and I'm grateful. There was also the possibility of not hearing a heartbeat in those first few weeks, and Scarlett didn't want the disappointment of a false negative, meaning no heartbeat when there might be one if she'd only waited another few weeks.

I don't want anything to happen to her or the baby. Even though Sprout, as Scarlett affectionately calls the baby, might not be mine, I can't help hoping—and thinking—that he is. We will also discuss the paternity test during this visit, but again, I don't want to do anything that will put Scarlett or the baby at any additional risk. I've come to some conclusions myself about Scarlett and her ex. I don't care if it's his.

"I want to share everything with you," I reassured her before we left the house for this appointment.

As we ride in my truck, she's uncharacteristically silent. I actually admire Scarlett's ability to talk. She doesn't just chatter, but she's truly inquisitive. She wants to know answers, and she's not just filling silence by speaking. She knows how to be quiet as well, and those moments are just as precious to me. They usually happen when she falls asleep against me while we're sitting on my couch.

Since the night we discussed my former engagements, we've fallen into the routine of cuddling while not taking things to any other level. At times, though, I need to adjust myself, moving back an inch or two from the curve of her backside too close to my front or control the temptation to cup her breasts as my hand skims over her belly, feeling the slightest of changes to her.

Once inside the patient room, Scarlett is asked to undress and lie on the table.

"I can . . ." I point over my shoulder once the nurse leaves.

"If you don't mind . . ." Scarlett mutters as her face flushes.

Our sexual tension isn't tamping down, and each evening is a painful reminder of how much I want her, but I'm respecting her position. Watching her take off her clothes for a routine doctor visit might just push me over the edge, no matter how inappropriate our setting is. The bottom line is, I want Scarlett. She's already in my home, but I want her in my bed. We don't have to complicate things with promises or proposals.

The room was already dim, and when I return, Scarlett lays on the table wearing a cloth gown. She looks nervous, and without thinking, I reach for her hand, giving it an extra squeeze. The technician returns to the room immediately after me and takes her seat opposite me. Lifting up Scarlett's gown to expose her belly, there really isn't much of a bump to her, at least nothing noteworthy, though she's softer in the middle, and her breasts are huge.

"This might be cold," the sonographer warns, squirting some kind of gel on Scarlett's belly before rubbing a special wand over her skin. I'm not up on my baby terminology or even all the tests Scarlett will need, but I want to be here for her. I find myself holding my breath as the technician moves the wand over Scarlett's stomach, then turns a dial on the machine, and an image appears on the screen.

Whomp-whomp-whomp-whomp-whomp.

The room is full of a rapid pulsing sound, and Scarlett smiles as she stares at the fuzzy black and white screen. With my fingers wrapped around hers, I lift her hand and press my lips to her knuckles. She turns her head toward me, blinking as a soft tear slides from the side of one eye.

"You're doing good, Mom," I say to her.

"Mom," she whispers.

"Looks healthy, Dad," the technician states to include me. My mouth falls open to explain our situation, but Scarlett's fingers squeeze mine. I glance at her, and she shakes her head while smiling at me, and my own heart thumps. I soak up the moment, sharing it with Scarlett as we hear Sprout's heartbeat for the first time.

"That was amazing," I say to Scarlett once we're back in my truck. Taking a second to recover, I tip my head back and blink up at the ceiling. Who would have thought another's heartbeat could make mine patter as well? Scarlett has been holding the image the sonographer printed. It's impossible to distinguish anything, so we'll be back in a few weeks to admire the growth and changes of Sprout. For now, it's just a relief to hear a healthy heartbeat.

We decided to skip the paternity test for now. I'm the one who spoke up when the doctor entered and presented the facts to Scarlett. There were risks, like anything in life, but I wasn't willing to take any unnecessary ones. The second the doctor mentioned a risk of miscarriage, I spoke up.

"We won't be having the test yet."

The doctor redirected her gaze to Scarlett. Her body. Her choice. I get that, but the pressure I had on Scarlett's hand must have told her how scared I was for her body and her choice. I didn't want her to take the chance of losing Sprout.

"Maybe we can wait until the next visit." I almost fell over her in relief. Instead, I leaned forward and kissed her forehead, lingering as I muttered my gratitude.

I'm still wound up, and Scarlett's too far away from me, sitting on the other side of the bench seat.

"Scarlett, sweetheart, get over here." The demand gives her the chance to deny me, but I'm really hoping she doesn't. I need a moment with her close to me. Setting the photograph on the dashboard, Scarlett twists and scoots toward me. My arm is extended over the back of the seat, and I wrap it around her, pulling her to me. I inhale her hair, which smells sweet and sugary. Her arms are trapped between us, but Scarlett likes to hug up top, as I call it, so her arms slip upward, wrapping around my neck and bringing her tighter against me. Like this, my nose dips to her neck, and I inhale her floral perfume, mixing with the sugary scent of her hair. My mouth waters, and I can't help myself. I suck at her skin.

The motion is quick, but the suction strong, and Scarlett gasps near my ear.

"You're amazing, sweetheart." I pull back enough to look down at her mouth, and our foreheads meet for a brief second before my lips touch hers. At first, I only intend to give her a tender kiss. We need to celebrate. She's having a baby, and we heard the heartbeat. She needs to be congratulated. But when her mouth opens, my tongue has its own agenda, rushing forward to sweep against hers. Scarlett leans into me, and all thoughts are lost to the touch of her tongue swirling with mine. My fingers fist the back of her shirt as hers curl into my hair at the nape of my neck. She softly tugs, and I lower to her jaw, sucking at the ridge before moving down to her neck. Scarlett purrs, and the next thing I know, I'm leaning her back, lowering her for the bench seat.

"God, Scarlett, I just want to touch you." My fingers move for her skirt, pulling up the material along her thigh. I want her right here in the front seat of my truck.

"Bull," she whimpers as my mouth continues to suck at her neck. "It's broad daylight." Quickly, I lift my head as if I've forgotten what time of day it is or even where we are. We're still parked in the medical office parking lot.

"Shit," I hiss, dropping my forehead to her sternum. Her chest heaves under me as her fingers stroke through my hair. Her touch feels so good, and after weeks without her, I want to be with her again.

"Okay," I mutter, sitting upright and bringing her with me. "Sorry about that."

"Don't be sorry," she says, sheepishly looking over at me while biting her bottom lip.

"Do not look at me like that," I warn, my eyes narrow while there's no bark to my bite.

"Like what?"

"Like you'd let me eat you right here on this front seat."

Her mouth falls open, but she smiles slowly before returning her teeth to that bottom lip. *Dammit.* Broad daylight or not . . .

"Okay," Scarlett whispers, seeing something in my expression. She pushes off the seat and slides herself to the passenger door while keeping her eyes on me for another second. Then she reaches toward the dash for the baby image.

Straining in my jeans, I adjust myself before pressing the ignition button and firing up the truck's engine. We have a good forty-minute ride back to the house, which leaves my thoughts racing. Halfway into the drive, I can't take the silence.

"Whatcha thinking about over there, sweetheart?"

"Too many things," Scarlett states. Is she sorry she kissed me? Is she overthinking what almost happened on this seat? Is she upset I canceled the paternity test? Would she be upset if it turned out to be his? I wait out her silence.

"I think I need a more lucrative job, and I suppose I need my own place."

I don't like the sound of either of those things, but I tackle one item at a time.

"What's wrong with Busy Bean?"

"Nothing's wrong with it, but doesn't it seem strange that I'm working there? I'm a college-educated woman, who had a lucrative job, but now I'm pouring coffee for people and passing out pastries."

"You don't think Audrey and Zara are educated? College isn't the only place to learn life skills. In fact, I might argue there's a lot about life you don't learn in college."

"I'm not disagreeing. I know Audrey actually dropped out of college and went to culinary school, and Zara never went away, but she's been a businesswoman for years. It's different for them. They own the place."

"So?" I pause. "You could own your own business, too."

"That's just it. What would I do? I don't know that I'd be good at running a business. I was a good reporter."

"Are you considering returning to work as a reporter then?" I don't like the sound of that, though I won't hold her back from finding a new job. Would it be wrong to ask her to just be a mom? That was hard work, too, and Scarlett would be just as dedicated to that *job* as any other. Plus, I wouldn't mind waking up next to her every day and returning from a day on the farm to find her in my home.

Scarlett sighs, turning to gaze out the window. "I just don't know."

Taking my own deep breath, I exhale before speaking. "It's okay not to know what you want, Scarlett. Give yourself a little break. You had a high-pressure job, right? You've also had a lot of life changes. The divorce. The move. The baby. Give yourself some grace."

She slowly nods, glancing down at the black and white image in her hands. "You sound like Rita."

"Well, in this case, Rita is a genius." I pause for a beat. "As for finding your own place, I don't like that thought. You do not need to move. I'm not in any rush for you to leave, sweetheart. Where is all this coming from?"

"I don't want to hold you back from finding what you want, Bull. I've been thinking about your past, and it's obvious you're a man who loves and loves hard. I don't want to be in your way of finding it again. I can't keep imposing on you."

"Have I given you the impression that you are?" I am not liking this turn of events. Less than twenty minutes ago, I was ready to take her on this bench seat.

"No." She shakes her head. "I just don't want to feel like I'm taking advantage of you."

My heart drops a little as that's the furthest thing from what's happening. "You aren't taking advantage of me, sweetheart. And you aren't in the way of anything." I don't plan on marrying again, but that doesn't mean I don't want to be around Scarlett. It doesn't mean I don't want her to stay with me.

"I'm just another damsel in distress, though," she says quietly, looking down at her lap.

"Hey. Partners, remember? We're in this together." I reach for her hand, sensing her too far away once again. I'd already told her I won't propose marriage, but we can still be a team here. We can parent together.

An idea forms. I have something for her, and I suddenly know the perfect place to give it to her.

When I pull up to the old trail closed off by a metal gate, my heart palpitates, recalling how someone once stole onto our land and took unwarranted images. However, this route will also take me where I need to go.

"What's this?" Scarlett asks, her eyes slowly sparkling again since our doctor's visit.

"I have something I want to show you." Putting the truck in park, I hop out and unlatch the gate. Returning to the truck, I pull forward and then stop just inside our property before getting back out of the truck to secure the gate once more. I take a look around me as if someone might be spying on us, but that won't be happening again on our land. Re-entering the truck, I drive us forward along the bouncy trail, rutted a little deeper from the rain this past spring. Eventually, I draw near the spot.

"What's that?" Scarlett questions, leaning her head forward and squinting out the windshield to see better. There's no way to miss the singular tree, standing on its own on this low rise of land. I only smile as we pull up and park near the wire fencing protecting it.

"Take a walk with me." Scarlett already has her hand on the door handle and steps out before me. Once I exit the truck and round the front, I take her hand and guide her closer to the large sugar maple.

"Legend has it my great-great-grandfather lived near this tree. His livelihood came from that tree as he used it to produce maple for sweetening. We aren't certain why it's only one lone tree. Might be he chopped down the others, or maybe they died." I shrug. "The family eventually moved closer to our current location, starting with the small home that's mine now and eventually building the larger one where I grew up."

Scarlett tips her head back once we stand under the tree. The sunlight filters through the thick green leaves and reflects off her bright hair.

"It's a brilliant red color in the fall. Because of that color, it's said to look like a giant heart and earned its name as the Engagement Tree."

I walk Scarlett closer to the trunk, pointing out initials in the bark. Her shaky finger reaches forward and traces one set with an arrow between the four initials.

"Those are my grandparents. BE and KC stands for Harland Bull Eaton and his wife, my grandmother, Katherine Caswell." I point at another set of initials with a distinct heart around them and a plus sign between them. "H and E is Harland Eaton, my father, and my mother Rose Newton is the R and N."

Scarlett glances over at me and smiles before a thought occurs and the smile withers. "Did you ask Jennifer to marry you here?"

I softly chuckle. "Actually, I didn't. Some say it's what jinxed my marriage. Didn't ask her in the proper place." My brows pinch as I remember asking Jen in the front seat of my pickup, right before we had sex. It was such a long time ago, so the memory is hazy. I was young back then.

"What about the other women?"

Placing my hands on my hips, I pause before answering. This is sacred ground to my family. What was I thinking by bringing Scarlett here? Am I jinxing us by explaining this place to her?

"I've never brought anyone here," I murmur, squinting up at the leaves whispering in the light summer breeze. Although I sense Scarlett watching me, I don't look directly at her. Instead, I shift my gaze back to the tree trunk. "Sweetheart, I have something to give you and something I want to say to you. Standing under this tree promises you that what I say is true."

"Bull, I don't think we—" Her hand comes up to stop me, and I realize almost too late what she must think.

"I'm not asking you to marry me, Scarlett." *No, no, no.* I won't be going there again.

"You're not?" Her forehead furrows, and her dark eyes lower to our feet. Then she looks up and off to the side. "Of course, you're not." Her soft voice stirs my insides, but marriage isn't what she wants from me anyway.

"You don't want to marry me, darlin'."

"I don't?" Her neck cranes, and she faces me once more. A little crease forms between her brows.

"No," I say, reaching out to press my thick thumb to that divot between her brows. For one, she's already been married and hurt by it. She doesn't need marriage with me to be her partner. There are hints of Scarlett being similar to Sabrina in her need for more —without the greed—and being married to a cow man will not be enough for her. Two, I'm not ever asking another woman to marry me. It just leads to all kinds of trouble. Still, Scarlett's expression is troubling. I'd like to say it's disappointment, but that's me project-ing, and there will be none of that.

"We're celebrating the little life inside you. It's a miracle, a gift, and this is the right place to tell you how precious I think you are. I care about you and that baby." I point at her belly. Scarlett's hand covers her lower abs, and she glances down at what we can't visibly see but know is happening inside her. She's building a human being in there.

Next, I reach into my pocket and lay flat the gift I have for her.

"It seems I missed Mother's Day, and I wanted to give you this." It's a silver bangle bracelet with a mother-child charm on it.

"Mother's Day," she whispers quietly. "I'd forgotten all about it." Scarlett has issues with her own parents and didn't call her mother on the day set aside for such a thing. I should have thought to give her something earlier, but this is all still new to me.

Her eyes fill with liquid as she takes the bracelet from me and rubs her thumb over the charm. "I don't know what to say."

"This tree is life to my family, and you are life to me, carrying that baby. Some say this tree is the heart of this land, and well, it just seems like a good place to take a moment and appreciate what we heard today, Sprout's heartbeat." I shrug, suddenly anxious by my admission. Maybe it's too much. Maybe I'm the only one overwhelmed by what we just experienced. Maybe I'm the one that needs a moment.

"I sound like a sap, don't I?"

Scarlett's been eyeing the bracelet while I spoke, but she looks up at me, her brown eyes as rich as the soil we stand on. "No, it sounds beautiful. You're a good man." Her voice cracks, and I step closer to her.

"Let me be Sprout's daddy then. No matter what or who is the father, let me be the man in his life."

"Bull." Scarlett's voice falls over my name again in a whisper I can't interpret.

"It doesn't matter to me whether Sprout is biologically mine. I want him. I want . . . us to be a team." I swallow, nearly admitting how much I want *her*.

"Take a look around you. See all this land?" I point off in the distance, where we can see the silos of the barn along with the old red structure. "A baby grows into a child who needs to run free. He needs sunshine, fresh air, and a place to roam, just like a calf. I want to give that to you and Sprout."

Scarlett's been scanning the land, but she looks up at me, her eyes blinking. "You are not comparing our child to a calf?" she teases, lessening the tension on her face.

"*Our child.* I like the sound of that," I admit, dismissing her teasing me about cow comparisons. "Let me be the daddy, no matter what." I'm so close to her, I lower my hand to her belly and flatten my palm. Scarlett looks down and covers my larger mitt with her delicate fingers. "Let me take care of you both."

Her head pops upward, and her eyes widen. "Bull, I could never ask you to do that. I just need to find a different job and a new—"

I lift my other hand and stop her words with two fingers over her lips. "You aren't asking me, Scarlett. I'm asking you. If you want another job, get another job, but you also don't need it. I can provide for us. Stay here with me. Live in my house. Hell, make it more your own. It will be littered with baby things soon enough, and that's just fine with me. I want to turn the third bedroom into a nursery."

Scarlett blinks repeatedly, but a few teardrops fall as she looks down at my hand still over her belly. Both her hands cover mine.

"Bull, I don't know what to say. Don't you think it's too much, too fast? It just all seems so crazy. Shouldn't we wait until we know more? From the second we met, we've been like a lit match."

"Maybe we have moved fast. Maybe it is crazy, but I don't need to be Sprout's biological father to love him, Scarlett. And the only thing you need to say is yes to me being his dad. Do it for the baby." I pause a second, reconsidering my suggestion. "Unless you don't like the proposition." I pull my hand away from her stomach, but Scarlett captures it, holding me in place with her hands over mine. Stepping closer to me, she speaks.

"That's just it. I like the proposition too much. I'm afraid to trust it." Her eyes narrow, heavy with concern as she gazes up at me.

"What are you worried about?"

"I'll screw up." Her voice drops. "With you. With the baby. What if I'm not a good mom?"

"You won't screw up, sweetheart, and if you do, well, I'm here to unscrew you."

Her mouth falls open, and I immediately backtrack. "That wasn't the right choice of words."

She chuckles softly at my fumbling, and I pinch her chin between my fingers. As I lean forward, her mouth is only an inch away. "Say yes, sweetheart."

Scarlett licks her lips, and my own mouth waters. "Yes."

Before the final sound completes the word, my mouth crashes hers. One hand slips into her hair while my arm wraps around her waist, tugging her to me. Scarlett's hands are instantly around my neck, her arms coming to my shoulders to pull herself higher on me. Within seconds, I have her back to the tree, sucking at her lips like a sweet maple candy. She gives as much as I take and more, kissing me back with just as much sugar.

My hand slips down to her backside, squeezing as I press her forward against me. Bending my knees, I line us up and lift, grinding the thick wedge in my jeans between her skirt-covered legs.

"Let me celebrate with your body, sweetheart," I whisper to her as I lower for her jaw and her neck. My other hand drops for her skirt and slowly tugs the loose material upward, baring her thigh to me. I cup the underside and lift her leg upward, hitching it against my hip. Surging forward once more, I reinforce what I've said. I'm hot and hard and want inside her.

"God, Bull. It's been so hard to resist you."

"Don't resist." Scarlett's arms are snug around my neck as her body rocks with mine. "I need to touch you, taste you."

"Yes," she hisses, and I drop to one knee. With her back against the tree, I shove up her skirt, which she takes in one hand. My nose runs over her heated center, inhaling the musky scent of her sex.

"You want me, sweetheart?" The damp underwear and sweet fragrance of her already answer my question. Leaning up just a bit, I press a kiss to her lower belly before hooking my fingers in her underwear and dragging them down her legs. She steps out of one side, and my face returns between her thighs, inhaling deeply as I force her stance wider, spreading her legs for me.

"I'm going to worship you," I warn. My tongue lashes forward, licking her like a sugary treat. I can't get my fill, and I latch harder to her clit, my tongue wiggles between slick folds. Her fingers delve into my hair as her hips tip forward. She rocks toward me, and I grip her hips, angling her in a way my face parts her thighs even more. She melts against my mouth, coating my lips in candy goodness, and I lap and lick, eager for every drop of her. Her fingers tighten in my hair, and I pin her back, holding her in place against the Engagement Tree.

"Bull. *Ohmygod*. It's too much. I'm going to . . ." Her legs stiffen. Her thighs clamp my cheeks. She purrs, and I glance up to see her head tip back, resting against the dark bark, which provides a contrast to the brightness of her red hair. The image makes my heart race, reminding me of this tree in full bloom. Her hand releases from my hair as her arms bend back, wrapping around the tree trunk as best she can in this awkward position. She moans in such a way she's disturbing the quiet hill, but I want to hear that sound on repeat. She's the roar of wind over the meadow. The lull of the herd coming home in the evening. She's everything and more to me.

Once I sense she's replete, I slowly pull back, pressing a final kiss to her soaked center. Quickly, I stand, cupping one cheek.

"No more fighting those pregnancy hormones. Whatever this is, just let it be," I plea. My thumb lowers, brushing over her lips, expecting her to argue my suggestion.

"Every night on that damn couch, it's been so difficult . . ." Her voice drifts as her mouth opens and sucks at my thumb.

"Me, too, darlin'. Every night I just want to wrap around you and drag you under me or pull you over me."

"Bull." Her eyes widen as her mouth pops open. Her back is still against the tree. Her underwear still near her ankle, but her hands come to my belt.

"Sweetheart?"

"Today was incredible, and I just want to thank you. I owe you—"

"I don't want you to feel you owe me anything," I state, gripping her wrist to stop her frantic movement. Pulling back from her, I discover her small hands have a firm hold on the waist of my jeans. "I never want you to feel beholden to me."

"Wrong choice of words," she corrects, lowering her eyes to where her fingers take my zipper and tug down the metal closure. "Not beholden. Not obligated. Just—" She stops herself short as she begins pushing down the sides of my jeans and lowers her body between me and the tree. "Just hungry for you."

Her hand is wrapped around me before I blink, and the sharp tug she gives my heavy dick has me losing all thought. With my hands falling forward to the tree trunk to balance myself over her, she's eye level with a precious part of me, licking her lips like she's ready to suck me dry.

"Sweetheart," I hiss as her thumb coasts around the crown and then through the slit, dripping with eagerness. Her mouth opens, and she latches onto me with the force of one desperate to milk me of all my worth. Her tongue swirls and her cheeks hollow, causing a suction like nothing I've ever felt before. She pulls back, but I chase her retreat, wanting to keep the heat of her mouth wrapped around me. Her hands come to my hips, holding me still, allowing herself to bob forward and draw me deep. My knees nearly buckle, and I reach down with shaky fingers, stroking through her hair as she takes me to the hilt, sucking me until I almost see stars in broad daylight.

"I want to finish inside you, darlin'." I groan, wanting to be buried somewhere else in her, feel her surrounding me with the heat of her sweetness. She shakes her head, smiling around my stiff dick before returning to her mission. Within seconds, I'm warning her. It's been weeks of celibacy and sweet torture, knowing she's only a cushion away on the couch or down the hall from my bedroom. I have so much built-up tension it could be embarrassing, but as I break free of the dam, Scarlett digs her fingernails into my hips and tugs me forward, forcing every drop down her throat.

"Sweet Jesus," I hiss as I tip my chin and close my eyes. Quickly, I reopen them to watch her lips around me as I pulse, spilling into her mouth. When it's more than I can take, I pull back, breathing heavily as not an ounce is left. Scarlett swipes at her mouth with the back of her hand, and I lower to cup under her armpit, tugging her upward. "You little minx."

She smiles sweetly, biting her lower lip. While she's pleased with herself, she still holds a hunger in her eyes.

"You want more, don't you, sweetheart?"

She chews harder at her lip, fighting back the confession.

"You give me the truck ride back to the house, and I'll be ready again." I lean forward, pressing my forehead to hers. "I'll fill you in more ways than one."

Her mouth reaches for mine, and I taste my saltiness on her tongue. We kiss for only a minute before I'm pulling back, lowering to restore her underwear, righting my pants, and ready to get her out from under this tree. I'm not as young as I used to be, and I need a few minutes to recuperate, but with all the pent-up frustration of holding out, it's not going to take much. I'm already eager for what we'll do next.

11

NOT ANOTHER DAY

SCARLETT

My heart races with anticipation of what Bull and I will do once we get to the house. He's holding my hand as he drives, sucking at my fingers like a damn candy treat, and it has my insides already swirling. He's so good with his tongue it's a crime, and it's been weeks since we've been together. Images of him over me while slipping into my depths have me on the edge of losing it right here next to him.

We're approaching Bull's home from a different angle of the property. The Engagement Tree. His explanation of the tree's history almost gave me a heart attack, especially when he said he had something to tell me. But just as quickly, my heart felt an unfamiliar fissure as he said he wasn't asking me to marry him. It shouldn't have mattered. The truth is, I'm still married. I shouldn't want to marry again anyway.

Partners.

What Shelton did to me still stings, but with Bull asking to be Sprout's daddy, Shelton's betrayal hardly hurts. It seems silly to me. Shouldn't I be bruised for longer? Shouldn't I mourn and wail and rally against him? Instead, I feel nothing for a man I was married to for fourteen years.

My pinky has more feeling for the man sucking on it than the entirety of my body has for my soon-to-be ex-husband.

I glance down at the bracelet now dangling from my wrist. Bull truly is a sweet man, showering me with gifts and giving me all the sentimental reasoning behind it. Even though he wasn't proposing to me underneath that beautiful tree, his words about life and heart meant everything to me. I'm riding a high I never could have imagined.

However, as we near Bull's house, something inside me shifts when I see a car I'm all too familiar with parked in Bull's driveway. Bull must sense it as well because he lowers my hand, curling his fingers around mine as he places my hand on his upper thigh.

"Who the hell is that?" His voice grumbles.

"That's Dr. Shelton Blake, my husband." My voice drops as I name the man stepping out of his BMW convertible. He's wearing his standard tie and rolled-sleeve dress shirt, looking every bit the male model he could be. If only his insides matched the outer shell of him. Bull slowly pulls his truck to a halt next to the man leaning casually against his sporty car. For some reason, I can't seem to take my eyes off Shelton while I feel Bull's sight pressing into the back of my head.

"Scarlett," he whispers beside me, still holding my hand, which feels like it's going numb from the pressure and tension suddenly vibrating off Bull.

"Let me deal with him," I say, twisting my neck to give Bull a momentary glance and a weak smile. Everything in me wants to tug Bull's hand up to my lips and kiss his knuckles to assure him this is nothing, Shelton is nothing, but something stops me.

Did I conjure up Shelton? Did my thoughts of him minutes after the pleasure with Bull bring Shelton to this doorstep? Of course, that's ridiculous. It's more than two hours from here to Boston. It's also a Tuesday afternoon, and I don't understand what Shelton is doing here. Slowly, I pull my hand from Bull's and slide across the bench seat to exit the passenger door. With a quick glance back at Bull, I slip out the door. As soon as I'm standing on two feet, facing my soon-to-be ex-husband, I hear the heavy slam of the driver's door.

"Scarlett." Shelton exhales my name in relief.

"Shelton, how did you find me?" I hadn't forwarded an address or anything to him when I left. I disappeared the next day and filed for divorce with Rita's help. As I'm divorcing him in Massachusetts, she hooked me up with a lawyer friend of a lawyer friend in Boston. I assumed Shelton would use our personal attorney, Artie.

"Artie has your information. I got your message."

"What message?" I haven't spoken to Shelton since I left. Not one for long bouts of tears or drawn-out pleas, I wasn't going to beg him to come back to me or demand an explanation for his actions. *His* message was received loud and clear—he wanted another woman.

"I received the papers." Shelton glances down at his rolled sleeve, adjusting what's already perfectly folded up to his elbow. Uncertain how to respond as he's simply made a statement, I don't speak. Bull does.

"Scarlett, you okay?" he asks, standing near the hood of the giant truck. At his voice, Shelton looks up and over at Bull as do I. The contrast between the two men is striking. Bull's gray is more distinctly mixed into his once dark locks. His heavier facial covering is an artful mix of dark and light. His skin is tan from hours in the summer sunshine. He's tall and narrow like Shelton, but there's a certain solidness to him. I'm well aware of the muscle definition on him from hard labor. Bull also wears dark jeans and a short-sleeved button-down with pearl snaps. He's completely the opposite of Shelton, and it's everything I love about him.

Well, not love. Not really, right? I can't possibly love a man I've known for such a short time. One who's been extremely kind and good to me, supportive of me, and wants to be involved in my life, my decisions, and my baby's future.

Let me be Sprout's daddy. The words tumble back to me as I return my gaze to Shelton.

"What do you want, Shelton?" My voice is edgy with his presence as is my body.

His eyes shift from Bull to me and back to Bull. "I was wondering if we could talk."

"I think you've said plenty," I snark. "I got your message as well. Loud and clear and due in nine months." Probably more like six months or less, I suspect, for him and his med student lover.

Shelton shifts, stepping closer to me, and it prompts Bull to round the front of his truck, coming to my side.

"Who's this?" Shelton asks, peering from me to Bull. His eyes narrow. Eyes I once thought lit a room and were only looking at me. What an idiot I'd been.

"Shelton Blake, this is Bull Eaton."

"Bull?" Shelton huffs like I must be joking. Only Bull stands taller, crossing his arms, and looks rather imposing, causing my lingering libido to take a little leap. Shelton's visit has just killed Bull's and my plans for an afternoon delight. When Shelton sees Bull stiffen and I don't respond to his laughter, his chuckle dies.

"Nice to meet you." He holds out a hand, cordial and trained in his manners. Bull hesitates. Not that he doesn't have the same manners, but he takes another second to size up Shelton. There's no comparison. If it came down to a fight—*which I don't want to happen*—Bull would win hands down. He could wrestle a cow, and something about that thought has me picturing it with a sense of familiarity I shouldn't have.

Bull eventually reaches forward and offers a shake that's a potential warning to Shelton. My husband's brows rise in surprise as he peers back at me before the two men release hands.

"Could you give us some privacy?" Shelton states to Bull, who in turn looks at me.

"Sweetheart?" Bull questions, the endearment flipping my insides.

"Just give us a few minutes," I say, struggling to find my voice as Bull's eyes say everything. He doesn't want to walk away from me. He doesn't trust leaving me here with this other man. I don't want to hurt him, and I'll explain that to him once I get rid of Shelton.

Bull slaps the hood of his truck and nods once.

"Yeah, I've got work to do." He turns on his heels and steps around Shelton's fancy car, kicking up gravel as he stalks toward the low porch. The front door slams with his disappearance, and my shoulders fall.

I can explain, whispers through my thoughts until Shelton speaks.

"Who the hell is that?"

If there's one man I don't wish to explain myself to, it's the one still standing before me.

"What do you want?" I ask, exasperated by his presence.

"I want you back." The directness of his comment startles me, and both my brows lift so high they ache.

"What?" I had to have misheard him. He can't possibly mean what he's said.

Shelton steps forward, and I take a step back, only I don't have space to move and bump into the side of Bull's truck.

"This thing with Brittney and me isn't working. She's always whining. She's tired. She's crabby." His voice rises as does a hand for his hair, swiping it back in frustration. "She isn't you. I miss you."

I huff. "Why?" If he missed me so much, he should have come to me and said as such, *before* he dipped his scalpel into someone else's heart. He could have said he wanted to spend time with me. He could have planned a weekend away, or heck, even a vacation, which we both desperately needed and hadn't taken in years.

"I haven't had sex in months."

My mouth falls open. He cannot be serious.

"Brittney never wants it anymore, and honestly, she's getting fat."

"She's pregnant," I defend, although I owe the woman nothing.

"That's just it. I don't think I'm cut out for fatherhood."

My arms cross over my midsection, my own belly protruding just the slightest bit. My heavy breasts truss upward with the motion, and Shelton's eyes fall there on my body.

"You look good, Red."

"Don't call me that," I snap, but he's licking his lips like he does. His eyes smolder as he narrows in on my enlarged breasts. I recognize all the signs of him wanting something from me, only he's not coming anywhere near me.

"Please, Strawberry. I want us how we used to be." His use of my childhood nickname bristles up my spine, and his statement doesn't settle well with me. He's not saying take *him* back, forgive *him*. He's not even saying he loves me. He only wants sex.

"I'm pregnant," I blurt. As much as I didn't want to tell Shelton, the words tumble out like a shield of protection. He stumbles back like I've struck him. His hands flare out at his sides before bracing him against the edge of his sporty convertible.

"With him?" His voice drips incredulous as though it's unbelievable I'd choose to sleep with someone else *after* he did the same to me.

"It could be yours." It's a possibility. Still, I realize the second I say the words they're bitter and choking. I don't want this child to belong to Shelton. I don't want anything more to do with him.

"That can't be." The doubt in his voice drives my desire to be rid of him deeper.

"We slept together the night before I left. The night before I learned you were with another woman, probably in our own bed. The same bed you slept in with me." I step forward, all my energy turning into a need to slap him, and I've never hit anyone in my life.

Slowly, Shelton smiles, a devious grin appearing on his pretty face before it registers that he's possibly gotten two women pregnant at the same time. The smile quickly fades. "This cannot be happening."

As if sleeping with a med student and getting her pregnant while still married to me isn't scandalous enough, the idea of having two women pregnant by him sounds worse.

Shelton tips his head, and his eyes narrow. "You're lying." His voice grows tighter as his fingers curl against the edge of his convertible.

My mouth falls open. "Why would I lie about being pregnant?"

"Scandals are what you live for, and you want to hurt me."

"Are you kidding me right now?"

"You're saying this to get back at me. I don't want to be a father, and I'm upset about Brittney's pregnancy. You're trying to scare me off, but it's not going to happen." He presses off his car and steps up to me, crowding my space. He lifts one arm and secures his hand near my shoulder over the open bed of Bull's pick up. "There's no way you are pregnant, *sweetheart*." He hisses the term Bull used, but I will not let him taint it for me. "You're too old."

"You son of a bitch," I snap, pressing at him, pushing him to move away from me. While Shelton isn't as solid as Bull, he's still strong, and he hardly flinches at the pressure I put on his chest. Using the truck as leverage, he tugs himself forward, pinning me with his body to the side of the large vehicle. His face dips for my neck, and he mutters near my ear.

"We were always good together like this. Your fiery spirit mixing with my big dick."

I gag over the dirty words that would have turned me on at one time. My hands press harder at him, struggling with his nearness but not feeling truly threatened by him.

"Well, your big dick dipped into someone else, and it's not coming anywhere near me again."

Shelton shifts as if grinding against me will remind me of how good we once were. He should have remembered all those times before he decided to dally with the dollop under his instruction. My hands push harder at his pecs, and the strangest thought occurs to me. It doesn't feel right touching him. His isn't the firm chest I want to run my hands over. His aren't the arms that I want to hold me. And his big dick isn't *that* big.

I've had bigger, better, and someone with more heart behind his worth.

"Get away from me, Shelton," I demand, pushing at him once more.

Thankfully, he puts distance between us, but he doesn't release his hold on the truck. "Are you really pregnant? Is it mine?"

Holding a figurative stake for his heart, I do what years of entertainment news has taught me to do.

I lie. *Maybe.* "Nah. It's his."

Shelton pushes off the truck, no longer stumbling but placing more space between us.

"You really know how to wound a guy," he snarks, and my eyes widen. "Are you listening to yourself?" I bark as the question mixes with a laugh of disbelief.

"And here I was ready to take you back," he says as if I should be grateful for the offering.

"It should be me taking you back, Shelton, not the other way around. I'm not the unfaithful one, and I don't want you back."

"Because of him," Shelton states, his voice tensing again.

"Because of you, Shelton. It's over. We're over." As soon as I make the statement, I realize we had been over long before his infidelity. We weren't connecting like we once had. We weren't those young, hungry people, eager to please each other while high-strung on our careers. We'd separated emotionally long before we physically had. If we had noticed sooner, if we had seen what was happening *before* . . . Well, I can't predict the past. We didn't recognize what was happening to us, and it led to this.

"I hope you're happy." His tone lacks any sincerity and comes out as pure sarcastic malice. He points at me as he says, "You did this to us. There's no turning back."

"No, Shelton," I say, saddened by the truth. We both had a part in our demise, so I won't take full responsibility. Shelton is clearly insane if he can't see his role in our failed marriage.

"You'll be hearing from my lawyers." The divorce papers have already been served to him, but he's just trying to have the final word. His threat hits me only moments after he's back in his car and stirring up gravel as he exits Bull's drive.

My concern isn't for me. I don't want anything from him other than the baby I'm carrying, which might be his, and he'll be in the fight of his life if he tries to take Sprout from me. Then again, Sprout could be Bull's, and Shelton would never be the wiser for it.

UNPACKING

SCARLETT

When I enter the house, Bull isn't present. Assuming he went out the back door, I don't think he could have gone too far as his truck is still out front. For a moment, I soak up the guilt of lying to Shelton. I'm not really a devious person, and lying to him doesn't settle well with me. I really do need to know the truth, if for no other reason than my own sanity. I'd feel better if the baby isn't Shelton's.

However, there's another concern on my mind. I don't like the possibility that all Bull wants from me relates to the baby. The thought hints at why I didn't press kisses to Bull's knuckles or try to reassure him of my status with Shelton before exiting his truck. Bull is definitely concerned about me ending my marriage, but what's upsetting to me is we aren't discussing the start of a relationship between us. Where do I fit in his life? Is it really just parent partners with benefits? What do I really want from him? I've always been an independent woman. Can I rely on him?

I'm not asking you to marry me, Scarlett.

The sting of his words rings like a gong in my head. I was the one who panicked for a minute, interrupting him because I was worried he was going to ask me to marry him. But I'm a living contradiction. I want to be with Bull, only I want it to be for us, not just the baby.

With that thought in mind, a knock comes on the front door.

"Scarlett Russell?" the deliveryman inquires once I open it. I glance around him to see the moving service van in the driveway, and my heart skips a beat. "We have a few boxes for you."

I smile as he hands over the electronic signature pad.

"We can bring them inside the door for you."

"Wonderful," I say, smiling back at him. What are the odds that my things would arrive on the day of Shelton's visit? I didn't have many belongings remaining at the apartment, but I do own more clothes, some books, a couple of awards, and a few personal effects. I loved my desk and a comfy chair in my home office, but I was willing to part with both items. I don't want any reminders of my old life, especially as I'm undecided if I'm returning to it. Once I moved to Bull's as a more permanent residence, I called my former cleaning service and asked Vonda to pack up my things. She'd easily recognize what was mine, but I also submitted a list of items just to be clear. After scheduling a pickup date, I paid the moving service in advance and prepped Vonda to pack on a day Shelton was out of town.

There aren't many boxes, and I have the movers place them in neat piles near the door. After tipping the men, a weight feels lifted from my shoulders.

"You're truly stuck here now, Scarlett," I say to the piles, but I don't feel stuck. I feel liberated and right where I belong. Whether Bull wants me or not, I don't feel as untethered as I first did upon arriving in Vermont.

With the stench of Shelton in my nose and his presence lingering against my body, I decide to take a shower. I need to wash away Shelton's nearness and his hurtful words.

You did this to us.

When I first left Shelton and called my parents, thinking they should know where I was, my mother accused me of the same thing. I hadn't satisfied Shelton. I hadn't given him a baby. I had been too career driven. There was no concern for me and how unsatisfactory Shelton had been toward me. He was the one who hadn't wanted a baby. He was equally driven in his career. I wish my parents could have had my back, and I silently vow to Sprout I will never be a parent like them.

I glance down at the mother-child charm dangling from my wrist. Mother's Day. I'd ignored it, choosing to bypass a phone call and send my mother a floral arrangement instead. She texted me, demanding I call her, but I'd ignored her request. I used to meet my parents once a month, which I considered a courtesy where I would check on their health, and they would berate me for little things in my life.

"This is all your fault, Scarlett. A man wants to be the center of your world." My mother had said when I told her Shelton and I were divorcing. Shelton had been the center, but in hindsight, that might have been a part of our problem. I put his needs first. Not that I'd known how much I wanted a baby until I was having one, but I hadn't considered it on a deeper level, giving in to Shelton's argument that it wasn't the right time until it felt as if too much time had passed.

How dare he call me old. I'm forty-two. That's not ancient, and it's a hit below the belt, considering he knows I lost my job due to my age, *and* he took a younger woman to bed. Then again, I shouldn't expect Shelton to be considerate. He wasn't in our bedroom or our marriage.

The thought saddens me, but not from a sorrowful point of view. It's more from the fact, I've been missing out. One night with Bull Eaton showed me all I'd been longing for physically, and what a truly compatible sexual partner could offer. The memory heats my cheeks as I stand under the hot shower spray, upset that Shelton ruined our afternoon. Technically, Bull and I have only had sex twice, and my body craves his despite the split in my heart.

When I return to my bedroom, I'm only wearing a towel as

seems to be the custom between Bull and myself, teasing each other in terrycloth as we cross the hallway. I've just entered my room and reach for a lotion bottle when I turn with a start. Bull's leaning against the doorjamb, focusing on his shirt which he's holding in his hands. His body glistens. He must have been working in the sunshine, expelling energy. Shelton certainly put a damper on everything.

"I'm so sorry about that," I say, opening the lotion bottle and squirting some into my hand. Bull doesn't look up at me. His position reminds me of a sexy cowboy on the cover of a romance novel. Chest gleaming, body leaning, and his thumbs hitched in his pockets while his shirt dangles from one hand.

"I saw him press you up against the truck and kiss you."

I gag. "He did not kiss me. He just . . . moved in too close." Hastily, I rub at my arms, smoothing in lotion before tugging at the curled knot of the towel over my breasts.

"What was he doing here?"

"He said he wanted me back until he learned I was pregnant."

Bull nods in response, keeping his gaze downward. His chest flexes as his hand clutches the plaid material tighter. I want him to look at me, but he doesn't, so I cross the small space and cup his face, pressing against his jaw so his eyes meet mine.

"Bull, honey, I'm not going back to him. He's an idiot. He said he'd take me back, but instead, it should be the other way around. I should want to take him back, and I don't. He should be apologizing to me, but he wasn't."

"What if he had apologized? What if he'd recognized the error of his ways?"

"That'd be a small miracle, but even if he did say he was sorry, there's nothing to go back to. We're over. We were over long before he cheated. I just didn't see it until what happened happened." I shudder to think how much longer I might have lived in the dark about our marriage. Perhaps Brittney's pregnancy was the wake-up call I needed. Or maybe my own pregnancy is.

I step back for the dresser, reaching for the lotion once more and smoothing some on my other arm.

"And he said nothing about the baby?" Bull can't comprehend the thought of a man not wanting a child.

"Shelton isn't interested in being a father." At least not to my child, which hopefully isn't his child.

"Maybe you need to back up and explain everything to me."

I turn and step over to him, noticing his feet are bare and his jeans are dirty. I press at his thighs, so he'll let stand between his legs.

"He told me Brittney was getting fat, so I told him I was pregnant. I just sort of blurted it out. Then he accused me of lying, making up the story to turn him off. He wanted to have sex with me." I chew my lip, nervous about offering up this information, but I don't want any secrets between us, and I don't want to lie to Bull about Shelton's reasons for being here. Bull's head pops up at the confession. "When he asked for clarification of the truth . . . if the baby was really his . . . then I lied and said it wasn't. That's when he said everything was my fault."

I glance down at the shirt still in Bull's hand. He sets it on the bed next to him and reaches for the hem of the towel at the top of my legs. He tugs me closer to him, spreading his legs wider to accommodate me between them.

"You know that's not true. This isn't one of those Screwup Scarlett things you've mentioned. This was all him, and he's a fool for looking elsewhere."

"That's sweet," I whisper.

"I'm not trying to be sweet. I'm being honest. His mistake, though, is my reward because it brought you to Vermont. It brought you to the Gin Mill and Green Rocks, and a night I never want to forget. It brought you right here." He tugs at the material again, and I clutch at the twist near my chest. If he pulls the towel once more, I'm going to be naked before him. Unfortunately, I sense Bull's earlier desires have dwindled a bit, as have mine after Shelton's visit.

"I'm grateful to be here," I remind Bull because I truly am. He's done more for me in the last month than Shelton did in our entire marriage. It's a sad reality.

"What's with the boxes downstairs?"

"Those are the remainder of my things. I had the cleaning service pack them up and ship them to me. I hope you don't mind that I had them sent here. I'll move them out of the way." I should have done that before I showered.

"You shouldn't be lifting things." An edge to his voice punctuates the words.

"I can manage," I snark, growing edgy myself. "I should get dressed." I spin around, but as my back comes to him, his arms wrap around my waist, tugging me to his chest, and I stumble onto his lap.

"For a moment there, I thought I'd lost you. I saw him lean into you, thinking he kissed you. Then I saw the moving van going down the lane. I thought you were already gone." His arms tighten, and my hands cover his forearms, stroking over them.

"I wouldn't do that. I wouldn't disappear like that."

"You still might leave." A million questions rest in his tone.

"If we learn the baby isn't yours, you'll want me to go anyway."

Bull stiffens behind me, squeezing me tighter into his chest.

"Why would you say that?"

"Because it's true. If Sprout isn't yours—"

"You don't think I want you? What do you think earlier was? In my truck. By the tree." His mouth presses to my neck as he speaks as if the words can seep through my skin.

"You got caught up in the excitement of the heartbeat. We both did," I admit, as I'm just as guilty of wanting Bull to take me on the front seat of his pickup despite the parking lot and equally guilty for what we did by the tree. That beautiful *fricking* tree and its romantic stories, plus all his pretty words about heart and life.

I'm not asking you to marry me, Scarlett.

"I wasn't caught up in anything but you. I told you I don't care who the father is. I want Sprout, but I also want you." His arms flex around me a second before he continues.

"I like you. I like how your scent lingers in the bathroom after you shower, and you laugh at my jokes. You get excited about watching movies, and you want everything explained during a hockey game. I like your smile and how you chew your lip when you're horny and how . . . Just, dammit, Scarlett. I wake up looking forward to seeing you, and I want to go to bed with you in it every day that ends with day and turns into a night. I care about the baby, but this isn't only about Sprout. This is about you. Us. I don't want you to leave."

My heart beats so fast in my chest, I'm certain he can hear it through my back. My body trembles at the fierceness of his tone, the sincerity in it, the intensity of it.

"I'm not leaving."

His breath hitches behind me, and his mouth comes to the exposed portion of my back. Suction kisses work over my shoulder blade, and my knees give a little, lowering me to his spread lap. I rest in the crook of his legs while his lips continue to suck at my skin. A soft tongue licks along the curve of my shoulder blade before he nips me, and I squeak. He lifts an arm at my waist for the knot of the towel and tugs it free.

"I should shower," he mutters as his teeth continue to nibble at my shoulder blade. The only response I can give him is a soft purr. He tugs the damp towel from between us, and I sit naked in his lap. His hands coast up my sides before both come forward to cover the bump of my belly. His nips turn more aggressive, and he shifts behind me to get to the curve of my neck just above my clavicle. With a sharp bite from him, I bend forward, pressing my backside into the seam of his jeans, and groan. The noise spurs him onward, one hand dipping lower on my body, forcing my legs to spread while the other hand remains flat on my belly, holding me in place over him.

"We were interrupted," he mutters, strumming his fingers

over my sensitive folds. I tip my head back for his shoulder. "No more thoughts about him."

"Fine by me."

Bull slips a finger into me, destroying all my thoughts of anything but him. His finger easily slides back and forth as I'm instantly wet for him.

"Slide your legs over mine."

I do as he says, but my legs are shorter than his, and my toes can't touch the ground. "I'm going to fall," I warn as I struggle to sit over his thighs with my legs spread wide open. His finger hasn't lost a beat, adding a second to the first.

"I'll never let you fall," he says, and a million more promises linger in his words. His mouth works more intently at sucking my skin along my neck and down my shoulder. His teeth scrape over the ball of my shoulder while his fingers slip in and out of me, making a soft suction sound.

"Bull," I warn, as my thighs tremble and my toes point, desperate for support as they dangle inches above the ground. He scoots himself back on my bed only a few inches, not breaking his rhythm. His heels hook into the low frame, lifting my spread thighs and opening me in a way I've never felt so exposed. It's wild and wonderful as his fingers work me and his mouth kisses me. I glance up to note how we sit within the small frame of the mirror over the low dresser opposite the end of the bed. Unable to help myself, I watch as Bull fingers me, and his mouth sucks at my skin.

After another minute, his eyes catch mine in the reflection, and he pulls back. He keeps his focus on me in the mirror, his deep voice ruffling my hair. "You like watching?"

"I like watching you," I admit. "I like watching us."

"Sweetheart, I need to be inside you," he says to me through the mirror.

"I'd like that." His fingers release me, and I cry out at the absence, but he works at the button and fly of his jeans, shifting me only a little to lower his pants and underwear to his thighs.

"I really should have showered," he mutters.

"You smell like sunshine and hard work." And all man. Scooting back a bit more, he keeps me reversed to him, and I shift my legs, so I balance on my shins.

"You naughty woman," he teases, holding himself upright and dragging his tip through my slit, moistening himself before guiding my hip to lower me and take him in.

"Jesus," he hisses behind me, holding me still a second. I can't say this is a position I've experienced before. I'm on my knees, straddling him, my back to his front, but my God, I'll do it again.

"Eventually, I'll be too fat to do it missionary," I say for some reason, and Bull chuckles behind me.

"We're going to practice all kinds of positions, sweetheart. Missionary is the least of them. And you won't be fat. You'll be beautiful."

My lower belly swirls with the anticipation of all we'll do. Or it might be that Bull lifts me only a little and then slams me back down on him. He guides me to draw him deep and then lift to the tip, threatening to release him. It's a teasing game of torture, and I love it, but I need more.

"You touch yourself?"

"I . . ." I don't know how to answer him. Do I admit that all these weeks of wanting him has left me with a heavy finger work-out? Do I tell him he's been the center of every fantasy? Do I confess how even the slight nearness of him has had me so worked up, some nights I think I'll hardly make it to bed before I combust?

"Do it. Now." His command sends a thrill through me, and I reach for the tight nub, working it frantically as he slides me up and down his thickness.

This is a big dick, I want to scream to the mirror, briefly recalling Shelton's words. I only peek at our reflection for a second because the scene is too much. I'm a woman gone wild at forty, and I'm falling for the man behind me.

"Bull," I groan, getting so close.

"I can't wait to feel you explode all over me, milking me with your tight—"

"If a cow reference comes next—"

"Pussy," he mutters, and I break, shuttering with the release. A noise echoes in the room, and I realize I've been screaming out his name like a prayer of gratitude. Falling forward, I brace a hand on the bed between his thighs as he hammers into me, thrusting upward as I fall back down over him.

"Sweetheart," he hisses once before stilling me. I look up at the mirror again, and his face strains behind me. A vein stands out in his neck. His fingers dig into the fleshy part just above my hips. His eyes are closed, but the lids pop open, and he catches me watching him. With a slow smile on his lips, he leans forward, sucking at my shoulder while his sight remains on mine through the mirror. "You're the most beautiful woman I've ever known."

The compliment is a heavy one, said with honesty and confusion, as if he's startled at the truth of what he's said. I blush. Not from the position we're in but from his sincerity.

"You're so sweet, Bull Eaton."

"And you're delicious," he mutters, dragging his teeth over my shoulder once more before pressing a kiss to the raked skin. "And now I really need a shower."

He chuckles, forcing himself to jiggle inside me, and we both feel the rumble from our joined attachment. I lean forward a bit more to release him, and Bull laughs.

"You are one dirty momma," he teases.

"I will not be calling you dirty daddy," I say, shivering with the thought. Bull helps me to shift off him, and we both scoot to the end of the bed.

"Just as long as I'm still Sprout's daddy, you can call me anything you want." He brushes back my wild hair, partially air-dried from our romp, and presses a quick kiss to my lips.

As Bull exits the room, I reach for the towel dropped to the floor and wonder if I can ever call him mine.

13

INSIDE HER OR INSIDER

BULL

More than two months have passed with Scarlett in my bed every night. Her body is beside mine, and I outline her changing shape as she lies on her side. The "baby bump," as she calls it, is present, but a simple glance at her and you still can't tell she's pregnant. She's taken to wearing some of my T-shirts as dresses or summer smocks, also her word, as she continues to work at the Busy Bean. Our hours remain early, with me milking cows starting at four in the morning and her shoving off to work by five thirty. I'd love for her to quit the coffee shop and work around the farm more as we can always use the extra hands. She doesn't need to work for money. I have plenty to take care of her, but she continues to like the job even if she isn't trained in baking pastries or making coffee.

"It's early," she mutters in front of me as her back presses against my chest. My hand continues to skim over her hip and toward her belly again, just feeling the heat of her skin. Summer's warming up, and the open windows let in cool relief in the dawn hours.

Scarlett gave me a leather wrist cuff with a single silver washer on it with *Sprout* engraved in the metal. It's a father-to-be gift. I don't wear it while I work, worried it will get caught on something and snap, but I slip it in my pocket every day and return it to my wrist as I return home. It tickles against her skin, and I lean forward to suck at her neck.

"Bull, babe, whatcha doing?" Her sleepy voice hints having sex might be the last thing on her mind, but I can't seem to get enough of her. I'm like a sex-crazed teen around her, and I've been questioning if her pregnancy hormones are somehow contagious. I wouldn't say I have a pregnant woman fetish, but something about Scarlett and her changing body turns me on.

"Thinking of you," I whisper to her sleep-moist skin. "But it's early. Go back to sleep for a bit." I'm ready to get out of bed when her hand catches mine over her belly, and she moves it upward under her T-shirt to cover the heavy swell of one breast. Scarlett already had nice tits, but their growth is just as mouth-watering as everything else. Filling my mitt, I massage the one. At times, she's told me they are extra sensitive, almost aching, so I'm gentle at first, cupping the weight, smoothing over her hardening nipple. With her fingers over mine, she forces me to pinch her.

"What are you doing?" I tease as she purrs while I stroke and tug at the ripe tip. Shifting her to her back, I lift the T-shirt and latch onto her, sucking as much as I can. She overflows my mouth, but I leave no inch untouched, licking at her, slurping at the globe, wondering what she'll taste like when the baby comes.

"Is it wrong that I want a taste once you lactate?"

"Are you comparing me to a cow again?" she mutters, a quiet chuckle mixing with her irritation.

"It's just such a marvel to me, and as milking is my business, I want to experience it."

"I've heard about this kind of thing," she says, stroking over my hair while her eyes remain closed, and I continue to swirl my fingertip around her nipple.

"You're going to be beautiful while you nurse." Scarlett's eyes slowly open. "I can't imagine I'll ever see anything more beautiful than a mother feeding her babe."

"That's a cow reference again, isn't it?" she hisses, turning her head to the side, but I capture her chin and bring her face back to me.

"It's a compliment. You understand what an incredible gift you have. You can grow a life inside you. You can feed that baby from your own body. It's an amazing wonder."

"Some women find it a curse."

"Really? I get the whole period thing feeling like a punishment, but do you hate being pregnant?" Scarlett's quiet as her hand lowers over her exposed belly.

"Actually, I'm enjoying it more than I thought I would." Her fingers spread, continuing to marvel at her own ability.

"That's my baby in there," I say, leaning forward and pressing a kiss to her belly.

"Bull," she whispers. She's cautious, concerned I'll change my mind if we find out it's not biologically mine. She's worried my hopes are too high, but she doesn't understand that my heart has fallen in deep. I'm in love with her and the baby. A few weeks back, when her ex showed up, she worried I was all in for only Sprout, but it's not just the baby. I want all of her.

My fingers circle the bump of her abs before lowering to stroke over the coarse hair near the apex of her legs. Her thighs spread automatically, anticipating where I'm headed, and I don't want to disappoint her. I never want to give her a reason to second-guess her decision to stay with me. My hand slips forward, curling over her before two fingers thrust inside.

"Babe." Her back arches as her head tips back. She's so wet and ready for me, but I'm taking my time. In the quiet of dawn, I just want to tease her and drag this out a bit, take her sweet and slow. Scarlett and I are pretty hot when we come together, and we've experienced things in a lot of unique spots in my home. Over the back of the couch. Against the wood stove chimney in the kitchen. Even on the staircase once. Of course, with her changing shape, we'll continue to be creative, so I want this moment.

As I slide in and out of her wet heat, she's dripping, and I'm so stiff. I'd blame it on the morning, but it's all Scarlett. She does this to me.

"Sweetheart, I want to feel you around me." Sensing what I mean, Scarlett rolls toward me, ready to climb over me, but I press her back. "I'll be careful," I tell her, knowing we both worry about squishing the baby. Scarlett researched it when I was concerned I'd hurt her, and she told me I wasn't coming anywhere near the baby. Folding up to my knees, I position Scarlett's lower body, slipping a pillow under her backside to tip her upward. Holding myself in place, I drag my dick, which is hard enough to hammer nails, through her slit and coat the tip. I love that being pregnant means we can go without anything between us, and briefly, I wonder if Scarlett will consider a second baby even though she hasn't had the first.

Eventually, I slip inside, taking my time to fill her, drawing out the tension. She hisses as I get to the hilt. Her legs are pressed against my pelvis. We're as close as two humans can get, yet it almost doesn't feel like enough. She's crawled into my soul, and I want to live in hers, but I fight back those thoughts, reminding myself that admitting such things is too much. I won't be making any verbal promises. I'll be keeping all my feelings to myself.

Pulling back, watching as I spill from her body until only the tip remains, I take a breath and surge forward, filling her once again. Staying steady, I repeat the motion as Scarlett's head rolls on the pillow, her bright hair glowing in the dimness of dawn. She's so beautiful. Her hair reminds me of the Engagement Tree when it's in fiery bloom come fall. The heart of this land. She's the heart of me.

Taking my time, I pull back and thrust forward, drawing out the sensation until we're both panting with the need for more. Angling higher on my knees, Scarlett moans.

"What's this?" Her voice squeaks with the change in position, allowing my shaft to rub against her clit as I move forward in this position. Her eyes spring open and widen. "Bull?"

The hitch to her voice tells me she likes this, and the tension in her body hints she's close.

"I told you, I want to feel you. There's no better sensation than when you come and I'm inside you."

Her arms stretch over her head, reaching for the slats of my wooden headboard. Fingers curl around the wood strips as she moves her hips in a way that matches my dance over her, and she breaks. Her legs tighten at my hips. Her head tips back. She's a goddess like this, all curves and arches, giving in to the power of us coming together. With that thought, I release the tension I've been holding back. Her orgasm sets off mine, and I spill into her, pulsing as she clenches. If she wasn't already pregnant, she would be from this.

Lowering my hands to brace myself on either side of her shoulders, I stare down at her, still inside her. There's so much I want to tell her. How happy she makes me. How much I love her. How thrilled I am she's having this baby, but I keep it all locked up tight.

"Feel good, sweetheart?" I ask, knowing there's no way she doesn't, but what I really want to know is if she's satisfied with me. Could she ever fall in love with me? Could she want more with me?

That night, dinner is almost ready at the main house, and I'm expecting Scarlett any minute. Joey has the television on in the den, and I've wandered in to see my favorite niece. When Canyon showed up with her a few years ago, our world turned upside down. Our mainly male household didn't know what to do with a girl on the edge of becoming a teen. Thank goodness Carly took over the female matters, although I'd like to think Canyon has a good handle on these things. His love of women over the years certainly should have prepared him to raise one, which leaves me wondering how I'll be if Sprout turns out to be a girl.

"Whatcha watching?" I ask as Joey sits on the couch, her feet up on the ottoman. The television screen comes to life with blaring music and the spinning title of KTEL. The program is titled *Insider*. Admittedly, I haven't investigated the place where Scarlett told me she once worked. She doesn't talk about it, dismissing her former employer as a modern-day gossip rag full of spoils about the rich and famous. It's definitely not my thing. I'm not up on pop stars, movie star marriages, or even the greatest hits in music.

"It's summertime in the city, but what about the neighboring countryside? Who's missed some of our favorite stories? Ever wonder what happened next? In tonight's segment, we have updates on some of our most requested stories, turning old news new again."

The square image in the upper right corner immediately has the hairs on the back of my neck lifting. Despite it not being full-screen, I already recognize the picture as well as what the headline reads. As if conjuring it larger, the square blows up to fill the monitor, and the headline appears.

Bovine Bridegroom turns Dirty Dairy.

"Turn this shit off," I hiss to Joey, but she's transfixed by the image. The remote is in her hand, but she doesn't change the channel, and the train wreck begins as a familiar-sounding female speaks.

"In a special interest story about our New England neighbor Vermont, this tale doesn't hold the happily ever after of Julia Roberts in Runaway Bride. *In fact, it's quite the opposite. You've heard always the bridesmaid, never the bride, but what about the repeat groom? Sources say this hunky dairy king has been engaged and left at the altar on more than one occasion."*

The image focuses on the backside of a cowboy, covered in muck, but zooms in to highlight the tight-fitting jeans.

"Who could leave a man like that?" the feminine voice questions, a hint of both sarcasm and attraction in her voice. Closing my

eyes, I don't need to see the rest of the scandalous special segment, but my ears remain open, and it's then that the familiarity of the voice registers to full recognition.

"Looks like this bovine bridegroom has taken to the fields. Perhaps he's found love in other places, although that's not legal in most states. Just what are they doing in Vermont?"

As my eyes slowly open, I watch as the cowboy in question is bent forward, rocking in a way that didn't seem inappropriate in any manner until this shitshow aired and interpreted the motion as thrusting into a calf. Eventually, the cowboy is caught hitching up the poor thing, which was stuck in the mud, caused by days of rain and a flood of the backfield. In the video, the thickness of the muck sucks at his boots, and he falls over, tumbling with the baby cow. The medium-sized animal lands on top of the poor sucker. For a moment, the calf rocks, his own hooves stuck once again, and the position is nothing more than a mess. But this no-nothing show spins its own web.

"Poor cowboy can't even get the cows to come home with him."

That babe unsticks himself and stumbles out of the mud, leaving the cowboy in a heap, covered in muck. When he rolls over and presses upward, the backside angle is caught again.

"Looks like our dairy king is out of luck, or should we say muck, with even his own animals. Oh well, here's hoping he catches the next one."

There's a chorus of chuckles before the video shrinks, and the screen shows a group of reporters—and I use the term very loosely—crammed together in an office cubicle.

"Updates?" The original male announcer stands with his arms over a mid-waist cubicle wall.

"Last check-in, the Bovine Bridegroom has sworn off women," a male reporter states.

"But a quick search of Dating Dairy shows an image of someone strikingly similar to the cow king," adds another person.

"The best way to confirm likeness might be a view from the backside." The female lowers her eyeglasses, pulling them forward and back like a trombone. Despite the glasses and the longer

length of hair, there's no question who she is. She's the woman who reported the whole damning scandal on the video. *"Wowza."*

"Jojo, turn it off," I demand. Her head turns as if she'd forgotten I was behind the couch. Then her eyes shift to my side, narrowing at who she sees.

"I knew you looked familiar," my niece states. As if in slow motion, my neck cranes, and I gaze at Scarlett over my shoulder. Behind her stands my brother Blade.

"I can explain," she offers weakly. The words crash into me like the ramming of a steer. I've heard that phrase before.

"Putting aside the personal humiliation for a second, did you know that story damn near cost us our farm? People didn't want to do business with us."

I stare at Scarlett, whose mouth opens but thankfully shuts just as quickly.

"MoosHaveRights2, an animal activist group, got that video and investigated. Somewhere, your reporting suggested that mud was shit our milkers were walking through, dragging their teats in the muck, making them unsanitary producers. We had to have multiple inspections and hormone tests, which the FDA is very strict about, proving we weren't doing anything to alter our milk after collected. We also had additional health inspections of our cows, our barns, and that backfield, all at our expense."

"I'm sorry," she mutters.

"Sorry?" I snap, exasperated at the weakness of that word. "This is the kind of reporter you were?" As soon as I've asked, I raise a hand because I don't want an answer. "Do you have any idea how mortifying that was? It looks like I fucked a cow."

"Bull," my brother warns, shifting his eyes to Joey still seated on the couch. Ignoring him, I continue.

"Your *Insider* team didn't do their homework, or they'd know that mud was caused by heavy rains and a flooded field. Cows are not the sharpest of animals and slow to move in the mud. I was trying to move them along. That calf followed its mother but got stuck. Cows will leave their babes behind. I had to wade through that *sh* . . . muck to get him out of there. Ever pick up a calf when you're ankle deep in sucking mud, Scarlett?"

I don't bother to wait for an answer. "I'm strong, but calves are heavy, especially if they're stuck as well. You have no footing or leverage, and when I lost my boot in that crap, we tumbled over, and he fell on top of me. My last resort before he trampled me into the mud was to push him over. Luckily, he found solid ground and scrambled off."

I heave a deep breath before I continue.

"MoosHaveRights2 wanted to go after me for animal abuse as it looks like I tossed that calf off me after he humped me." I cup both hands behind my neck. "Or was it I humped an animal? Despite your disgusting bestiality claims, I care about my animals. I would never hurt them, but you wouldn't know that, would you? Only looking for a story, weren't you? As if digging into my love life hadn't been bad enough? Making a mockery of my misery wasn't enough for you. Is that what you're doing here?" My heart races at the sudden possibility. "Are you here to *investigate* me again? Are you looking for more on the Bovine Bridegroom?"

Everything in me tells me not to believe it could be true, but I'm so wound up by the images and her voice reporting that bullshit.

"Here's your inside scoop from someone who knows him best." I slap at my chest hard as I reference myself. "It was the man left at the altar angle you wanted first, right? Well, he'll never be in that position again. He'll never be a groom. He'll never be anywhere near a wedding. Not ever. He will not be left behind. He's no longer on those dating apps because he can't trust anyone. And as for the cows on my land, you keep your nose out of a business you don't understand. This isn't Dirty Dairy, or whatever the fuck you think you'll call us next. This is my property, my family, and you won't find your follow-up story with us."

My chest heaves as I watch tears stream down Scarlett's face.

With thick lashes, her makeup is a river of black down her cheeks. Her head lowers, and her hands clench together, making her look repentant, but I have no forgiveness in me. That fucking cockamamie story they cooked up when it was a slow day in the newsroom caused a scandal—*a real scandal.*

My heart races so fast I turn back to the couch, bending at the waist to place my hands on the back of the furniture to catch my breath. *This cannot be happening.* I could not be such a poor judge of character again. I brought a woman into my home who nearly decimated my family and me with preposterous reporting and lies.

Glancing up, I realize we've gathered more of an audience. Canyon stands near the entrance of the family room from the front hall, and my dad stands beside him.

"I'm so sorry," Scarlett repeats behind me. The words tremble in her faltering voice, but I close my eyes. I can't look at her right now. How could she report such a thing? How could this have been her career? How could she destroy the lives of people she didn't even know?

We should keep our distance. Is this how she'd done it?

Closing my eyes is a mistake. Behind my lids, I see two things —a mixture of the woman on the screen, chuckling as she tugs at her glasses and the woman who was under me this morning, filling my heart with her tenderness as we joined as one. I shudder and quickly reopen my eyes, focusing on my hands curled over the back of the couch, veins extended with my anger. This is worse than being divorced, left at the altar, or a broken engagement to a thief. This is my heart being ripped out of my chest as the woman I thought I loved, who I brought into my family, who might be carrying my kid . . .

I spin to face her, and my insides twist like a snowstorm, cold and out of control. "I think you should leave."

Blade gasps beside Scarlett, and she slowly nods, looking up at him with dark, tearstained cheeks. Her lids blink before she looks back at me, but I instantly turn away. Shifting to my right, Canyon has his head lowered as well, shaking it side to side in disbelief. I find my father staring at Scarlett, his eyes full of concern.

"Don't look at her," I snap. Does my father not remember all that happened? We almost lost this place. People didn't want our milk. The slaughterhouse didn't even want the cows we had to sell to cover the legal costs. Farms tied to MoosHaveRights2 didn't want to sell us new heifers at first because they were skeptical of our practices. Generations of dairy farming were almost down the drain by a careless story.

Dad's eyes shift and narrow at me. In the background, Scarlett's sandals tap on the hardwood floor as she exits the room, and I watch as my dad disappears into the front hall. Left in silence, my brothers remain as the quiet support they've always been. The dairy king's men were ready to put my heart back together again. Only this time, I'm not certain they can.

14

GOSSIP GIRL

SCARLETT

I trip over my own feet as I stumble down the gravel lane. A pebble gets stuck between my toes, and I try to bend forward to remove it, struggling with the added weight and bulge of my belly before jiggling my foot in the sandal. I flap my ankle around until the small rock flips free, and I can continue forward.

I recall the story as I walk. The reason the Eaton name sounded vaguely familiar returns to me. The report was three summer's old. We'd gotten word of a man who'd been stood up at the altar similar in fashion to the *Runaway Bride*. Three times he'd been left behind, and we wanted to know why. Based on his picture, I remember the girls in the office wondering what could be wrong with him. He was good-looking, solidly built, and had a glint to his eye. We'd come up with several hypotheses as to how a man such as him could be alone, and none of the possibilities were flattering. We didn't know the truth—that behind the image of a handsome silver fox was a good man who'd had bad luck with women.

It was a fluke that our investigative team arrived after the rainstorms of that spring and captured the images of Bull fumbling in the field with his cows. *Frolicking* is how the cameramen had captioned his video. We laughed, wondering unfairly what they were doing in the meadows of Vermont. I recall feeling uncomfortable reporting such a suggestion as the fine-assed cowboy was humping his animals, but it was a slow summer season, and I remember thinking the story wouldn't be viewed by many. It hadn't, actually. The statistics showed it was one of our least watched episodes, but something happened over on social media, and the video went viral. Perhaps it's what Bull said; an animal activist group got involved. We didn't follow up. Without a direct interest in the television airing, we moved forward.

I'm so ashamed.

The story made a revival all these years later due to the social media sensationalism. Lex wanted to try a new segment, highlighting old news with follow-ups. We sat around in office chairs, and he reported out former stories, flashing snippets of them before we commentated. We filmed an entire series about eighteen months ago, intending to use the news flashes as this one was used as a filler. I'm a little surprised the network would play a video with me in the picture, given I no longer work for them, but they hold all the rights to what they've produced, present example included, even if I'm currently not employed by them.

My pace slows as my feet grow heavy, the weight of what just happened pressing me down. Bull will never forgive me, and I don't blame him. Reporting on the average person never made me comfortable, but then again, mega-stars are just people too, and it shouldn't have felt right to expose their dirt either. I'd always had a twinge of guilt covering divorces when the husband cheated with a nanny or reports of a woman losing her child before birth. *How is that newsworthy?* It's not. It's private, and a good reminder that I no longer have what it takes to report such sensationalism.

As I continue down the gravel drive to Bull's house, my thoughts race. *What will I do?* Rita is my first thought. Bull will not want me at his place, and I'll need to call my best friend once again for support.

"Scarlett, hold up." A deep male tenor behind me stops me in my tracks, and I turn to find Bull's father coming down the lane.

"Harland?" I walk toward him, wondering if something else happened after one of the most humiliating moments of my life.

"Hang on," he says, drawing closer to me, moving faster at sixty-something than I am.

"Harland, are you okay?" He's my first concern as he's breathing fast when we catch up to one another. He reaches for my hand extended toward him.

"Let's walk a bit," he says to me, waving out an arm, turning us back in the direction of Bull's home. We begin in silence, and the anticipation of what he has to say rattles my weary bones. The evening is warm, and I'm suddenly exhausted. With the tension between us, I break first.

"I'm so sorry, Harland. I never meant any harm to your family or the farm." I wish I could explain myself better. Saying it was my job feels like a weak and unworthy excuse. I don't have a good reason for what I've done or what the network did.

"Darlin', I've never met a person without regrets, and anyone who says he doesn't have any is lying." He softly chuckles. "Everyone makes mistakes. Bull's made at least three, named Jennifer, Sabrina, and Gisela. Might even be a few more in there I don't know about."

I offer a weak smile, recalling my own major mistake named Dr. Shelton Blake. Somehow, my error seems so much bigger than anything Bull could have ever done. He deserves someone better than me. Better than Jennifer, Sabrina, Gisela, and now Scarlett on his list of women who have scorned him.

"It's what you do about a misstep once taken that's the real lesson. Once you learn the wrong you've done, what matters is the next steps you take to make it right."

I nod to agree as I look up at the dirt path before us. In some ways, I've just learned a valuable lesson. Reports such as the one the network made have consequences. It's a lesson taught to a child but not necessarily understood until you're standing in the middle of a poor decision. It occurs to me that Harland is patient and calm as he speaks to me. He isn't scolding me or accusing me of wrongdoing as my parents would.

"I don't know how I'll make this right." My eyes scan the lane and the pasture fenced in beside it. Somewhere off in the distance is that romantic tree, and Bull could have lost all this because of the network's false reporting.

"Things happen on farms. Sometimes, it's misinterpreted. Typically, it doesn't make the news, but . . ." Harland shrugs.

I find little comfort in what he's said as the initial story wasn't really about the farm but a man who'd headed to the altar more than his fair share of times.

"I've hurt him," I whisper. "I've hurt all of you."

Harland sighs heavily. "That happens too, darlin'. It won't be the last time, but hurt comes in waves." He swipes his hand up and down like the rolling hills around us. "So does forgiveness."

"I don't think he'll forgive me," I whisper.

"First, you'll need to forgive yourself." Harland's squinting, his gaze focused somewhere off in the distance. "You'll need to accept what you did, realize what's done is done, and then take steps to do right by it."

While I understand what he's saying, I don't know how and say as much. "I don't know what to do." Apologizing will never be enough.

"I think it's about time you learn more about this land and how we operate, seeing as it holds our future, and so do you."

He continues to gaze forward when I turn to look at him. "I might be old, but I'm not blind. I know a pregnant woman when I see one. With life churning inside her, she has a certain glow about her. You have that same dazed, dreamy look my Rose had when she was carrying the boys."

"The girls I work with call that dopey look pregnancy brain as I'm a bit forgetful at times."

"The girls at work know you're pregnant before the family?" Harland chides another slap of hurt in his tone.

"I had morning sickness at work. It was difficult to disguise as Audrey and Zara have both had babies."

Harland nods. "You and Bull keeping it a secret for some reason?"

"No, sir, but there are some . . . complications surrounding my pregnancy, and I think we just wanted to be certain of a few things before we shared with everyone."

"You feeling alright? Taking your vitamins and such?" His concern comforts me. His simple questions are more than my own parents have asked. Then again, they don't know I'm pregnant yet unless Shelton told them, which I doubt he did.

"It's nothing physical. Sprout is doing great."

Harland makes a funny face, scrunching up his nose and forcing the crow's feet near his eyes to fold. "Hope Sprout isn't really the name you're giving my grandbaby. It was difficult enough when Rose wanted to name Blade after a piece of grass." He chuckles, and my smile grows.

"Bull's been around the block some. Is the complication his reckless desire for love? Are you questioning your relationship status?" The question surprises me and sounds rather social media-ish. Does Harland know something I don't? Is Bull unhappy with me? If he wasn't before, he certainly is now. I have no doubt he'll want nothing to do with me after this mess. He'll decide he doesn't want the baby after all if we learn it's not his.

"I'm not certain what Bull and I were, but after this, I have no doubt he'll want me to leave." My chest aches. We had something. Two people cannot come together the way we did and not have something building between them. I can't be alone in how I feel about him, but maybe I am. I certainly was alone in what I thought of my marriage. Maybe I'm just a bad judge of character. Maybe I can't interpret people like I think I can.

"Bull's angry," Harland interjects. "He just needs time to cool off. My boys are lovers. They got that soft spot from their mother. I've seen him fall in and out of love so many times that it's like watching a child on a seesaw. Eventually, the ride gets old, though, and a man wants to stop playing around. He needs to figure out what he really wants. I'll say this, his eyes never followed a woman around a room the way his follow you. I'm not certain he's ever smiled the way he does when he sees you. He was too young in his first marriage. Desperate to prove himself with his second attempt. Not certain about that third bird, but you, Scarlett, you're the four-leaf clover he's been looking for. Don't give up on him yet."

Harland must be confused because it will be Bull who walks away from me and not the other way around. Not only is this breaking his heart but it's also hurting his family's livelihood. Inspections? Lawyer fees? Loss of business? Our little story went too far, and I need to make amends. I need to make things right.

The next morning, I'm up when the cows rise, or at least I think that's what a dairy farmer might say. Harland walked me the remainder of the way to Bull's place, and I returned to the guest room for the night, so I didn't hear Bull if he came in. However, when I climb down the stairs, groggy from a restless night of sleep, I find the under-cabinet lights on in the kitchen. The coffee pot is full with a mug next to it. Bull's been leaving a mug by the machine every morning as I can't reach where he places them on the highest shelf in his cupboard. The gesture hits me like an arrow in the chest. He's still such a sweet man.

After slipping into a pair of old Wellies near the side door, I strut down the lane, ready to swallow my pride and learn more about this farm I'm living on. In the dark quiet of the early morning, it's peaceful, and I take a deep breath of fresh air despite the hint of cow manure. I enter the large white structure housing the Eaton herd and hold back a wave of nausea at the animal smell.

"What are you doing here?" Blade says.

"I'm here to help milk the cows," I state, putting on a brave face while having no idea what I'm getting myself into. If I had visions of hand milking some hundred-plus cows, Bull quickly dispelled the fantasy a while back, giving me a tour of the place where a complicated-looking machine rivaling the coffee maker at the Busy Bean actually does the milking. Bull and his family still need to do plenty of other things to move the process along, like steering the animals into position, sanitizing their udders, or teats as I've been corrected, and then hooking the machines up to milk.

"What the hell?" Bull says from behind me, and I spin to face him, feeling small compared to his booming voice and large presence, but my breath also hitches as it's so good to see him, even if it's been less than twelve hours. He looks as tired as I feel.

"I'd like to learn more about the farm," I admit, trying to stay strong, but my voice cracks. He glances away from me for a second before turning back with a shield over those midnight blue eyes.

"It's not safe in here for you."

"Why not?' Blade comes to my defense. I'm ready for Bull to tell his brother about toxoplasma or animal infection concerns while I'm pregnant, but he and I already learned cows make the safe list. Although we've both assumed his family doesn't know I'm pregnant, his dad clearly does, leaving me to wonder if the others have their suspicions.

"She's . . . it just isn't," Bull catches himself. "We don't need help."

"We can always use help," Blade interjects again.

"Not from Scarlett." The words are a sucker punch to the gut. Bull has written me off as unacceptable to be near his precious herd.

"Blade, could you give us a minute?" I ask, glancing over my shoulder.

"I've got work to do," Bull mutters, turning for the door, but Blade's circling me, glaring at his brother.

He mumbles to his eldest brother, "Be nice." Then he slips through the door, leaving Bull and me alone.

"I've got to get to work, and you should still be sleeping." He isn't looking at me as he speaks but staring toward the door as if he's longing to make a break for it. He can't get away from me fast enough.

"I didn't sleep much last night," I admit, missing him behind me, his arms around me. Shelton and I never slept close to one another, and I've grown accustomed to the warmth of Bull.

He huffs in response.

"Harland knows I'm pregnant," I say, and Bull turns back to me.

"Did you tell him?" His voice rings incredulous as though I've betrayed him once again. It hurts that he thinks such a thing of me, but it's not without reason. I shake my head.

"He said he just knew." I recall his kind words about glowing. "He also mentioned it might be a good time to start learning about this place on a deeper level as I'm carrying its future." My hand covers my lower belly. *Does Bull still want this?* I'm wearing knit leggings with some stretch and one of Bull's T-shirts that fits almost like a dress. I'm warm, but I didn't know what to wear.

"You might not be." The strike hits its mark as Bull glares at me. After all his professions of wanting to be Sprout's daddy no matter what, the words hurt. I should have known. My gut told me to wait. Don't get involved with him. Stick to roommates.

Before I speak, I take a deep breath, fighting the pain in my chest. "Maybe we should find out sooner rather than later." Bull has pushed for us to wait until the baby is born before taking a paternity test. While I want him to be Sprout's daddy in every way, I also want to know the truth. I don't want to feel like I'm still holding onto a piece of Shelton. After all that has happened, it's time to learn the truth because I'm the one suddenly wading in muck, stuck up to my knees in love with a man who hates me.

"How?" Bull snaps.

"I'm sixteen weeks along, and I can have an amniocentesis." I should really wait until I'm twenty weeks when I have another ultrasound, but I don't want to put this test off any longer.

"What's that?"

"It's a genetic test. As I'm considered at risk due to my age, the test detects possible birth defects like Down syndrome and spinal bifida, but it can also determine paternity. We just need to swab the inside of your cheek for your DNA."

"Birth defects?" Bull questions. "But you're healthy."

"Healthy as a cow." The saying is *healthy as a horse*, but Bull doesn't even crack a smile at my cow-comparison joke, and I swallow. "Anyway . . ."

"What about the baby?" Bull huffs, crossing his arms. "You can't just draw blood from him."

"The amnio uses a large needle to extract cells from around the baby. The sample holds Sprout's DNA."

Bull's arms fall apart, fists forming at his sides. "Is that even safe?"

"Women have them all the time. There's a risk, just like with everything else, but we need this." I swallow around the lump in my throat. "We need the truth so we can move on from the unknown."

"The truth," Bull huffs. "I didn't think you dabbled in truth."

I take the sting of his words, understanding he's still angry.

Bull stands taller, his expression hardening. "You'd like that, wouldn't you, though? To know the truth means you can move on."

I bite the inside of my cheek to fight the words ready to lash back at him. I don't want to move anywhere. I don't want to be anywhere but here with him, but I understand he can't accept I made a mistake. A horrible, horrendous, ridiculous mistake.

"I think we both deserve an answer," I say, glancing down at my feet, wiggling my toes in the large rubber boots. *Whose are these anyway?*

"Sounds like you've already made up your mind." Bull turns for the door, tugging it open and leaving me in someone else's shoes. I'm not liking the feel of them.

My eyes are red-rimmed and swollen from more tears by the time I get to the café. There's work to be done, so I keep my head down, but I'm not fooling Roderick or Zara once she comes in. The morning rush is steady as it always is, and I'm more a bumbling barista than ever, especially when a customer makes a comment.

"Aren't you that woman reporter from that television program?" Glancing over at Zara, I don't know how to respond. My bosses know the truth as I'd put it on my application, but I'd assured them it wouldn't ever be an issue. *Who would recognize me?*

"Would you like anything else?" I ask, ignoring the gray-haired woman's question.

"You were on that show last night." Her friend snaps her fingers to help her think faster. "The one reporting on our sweet Bull." Her eyes narrow as full recognition takes over.

"That will be ten thirty-two," Zara interjects, attempting to move these ladies along as there is a line.

"He had such a rough go of it. No lady luck," the second woman tsks while the first nods to agree.

"But that wasn't nice of you to report on him when he was stuck in the mud," the first adds. For a moment, I wonder if Rita and I will be like this one day, admonishing salesclerks and berating baristas like two grouchy old women. I nod to agree with their assessment—it wasn't nice of me—hoping it will appease them and force them to move on.

"Bovine Bridegroom? Who came up with such a name?" the second asks. *I did.* A lump forms in my throat, and I swallow back the distasteful memory.

"Rude," lady one states.

"Rude," lady two adds, nodding at me with a scowl on her face. At any second, she's going to tell me I should be ashamed of myself, and I'll continue to agree with her. I'm deeply ashamed. Thankfully, they turn away with coffees in hand but continue grumbling as they take a table together.

"Need a break?" Zara mutters beside me, but I shake my head. I need to face what comes my way because I did this to myself, and I did this to Bull.

My breaking point comes when Louisa enters. She's on another coffee date, and her head pops up in recognition when she sees me behind the counter.

"You," she mutters, slipping her arm into the elbow of the man standing next to her. She smiles falsely at me, her grin too large.

"Louisa," I state, recalling her name.

"Poor Bull," she whispers through a false smile. Her date ignores her, placing their orders, which thankfully Zara pours. I ring them up, addressing him with the total. After he pays, he picks up both mugs and turns away from the counter. Louisa's hand slips from his arm, and she leans forward over the countertop.

"He would have been better off with me," she whispers. "No one wants to be second best." Her eyes roam my body. "Or even fourth in line."

I grit my teeth as she walks away and then I turn for the coffee machine, grabbing a towel to clean off the nozzles Zara just used. Funny how Louisa would have been in that exact position had she dated Bull.

"Break. Now." Zara gently pushes me aside and points at the kitchen where I enter to assist Roderick in his baking. I don't need a break. I need to keep working. What is that old saying about idle hands? *Idle hands are the devil's workshop.* We need that on our chalkboard beams.

Silently, I walk up next to Roderick. It's summertime, and a favorite of mine is a good old-fashioned blueberry muffin, but our resident baker can never do simple. Instead, he's making berry burst muffins, which is a delicious blend of berries in the batter, making the classic muffin explode like a firework in your mouth. The seasonal pastry is appropriately named.

"I heard about the report," Roderick says, stating the obvious without naming the program. He's working beside me as I scoop the muffin batter into the cups for baking. "I typically avoid that kind of sensational stuff because of Brian. I didn't know you were famous."

"I'm not," I snap, too sharply. I might have won some awards, but in hindsight, they feel superficial. What have I done with my life? Reported on rumors about other people, while the good people around me worked hard, producing things like the treats in this café or, in the case of Bull and his family, milk, an American staple with a multitude of health benefits.

Roderick nods once. "Want to talk about it?"

Despite shaking my head, I answer. "He hates me," I whisper, feeling fresh tears blur my vision once again. *How can I keep crying?* I thought this emotional stuff disappeared at the end of the first trimester.

"Hate is a strong word, honey, and I doubt that's how he feels. Maybe sad. Maybe hurt. Rejection is a hard pill to swallow." Roderick knows all about rejection from the ignorance of his parents and the bullshit of a former lover. He's referring to the original topic of Bull as the Bovine Bridegroom. His initial rejection was our folly. We chased his story because of the twist in the circumstances with no thought to the heart of a man left behind. What was wrong with us? Where was our compassion for his heartbreak?

"I've hurt him," I admit. "And I'm so embarrassed."

"Then you say you're sorry."

"It's never that simple," I state, and Roderick nods.

"Sometimes, a simple apology really is enough."

If only.

"Hey," Audrey calls out as she enters the kitchen and her cheerful tone addresses me. "What are you doing back here?"

"Zara sent me in here." Audrey's brows pinch in question, so I explain. "People were talking about me."

Her brows lift. Perhaps she's the only person who doesn't know what's happened. I give her the shortened version, and Audrey takes in my story.

"This community can really stick together. When I started working the area, trying to collect produce and products for the restaurant company I worked for in Boston, Griff told every farmer within a fifty-mile radius not to sell to me."

Is she kidding me? "Why would he do that?"

"Because he wanted fair market value, and he didn't trust me. Yet." She winks. "Give Bull time. He'll come back around." Her confidence in Bull's emotions does nothing to assure me he'll forgive me. Wanting fair prices isn't quite the same as scandalizing Bull's past relationships or turning the dairy into mud.

Zara waltzes into the kitchen as Audrey finishes her story and offers additional advice. "Ignore people. Bunch of busybody know-nothings. When I was a teenager, everyone around here called me a slut."

"You were a slut," Roderick teases, winking at her.

"Yes, well, we all grow up and grow out of our phases. Just give people time, but most of all, give Bull time. He deserves it." It's a reminder this all blew up only last night.

Time. At this point, we only have to wait for the paternity test. If Bull isn't the father, he won't want to spend any more of his time with me anyway. If he is the father, he'll have a lifetime to hate me.

15

90-DAY GUARANTEE

BULL

The following day Scarlett had off from the Busy Bean, but I'm quick to exit the house once again. I'm still angry over what we've learned. Why didn't she tell me? Did she not recognize me? Was the story so inconsequential to her that she didn't recall it?

I wish I had answers, and I hate that I miss her in my bed. This is the exact reason I didn't want to get involved with someone again. The Bovine Bridegroom does not need more heifer heartbreak. Scarlett was supposed to be a one-night stand, but I don't fault her directly. When I found her still in Colebury, I could have walked away. I should have walked away. I shouldn't have turned back for that damn café wanting to talk to her, wanting to know more about her. *One and done.* Why can't I adopt Canyon's philosophy?

Of course, now there's the added complication of Sprout.

Swiping a hand through my hair, I stalk into the barn. The sun will be up soon as it's summer, and the heat is already heavy. I enter the small office inside our dairy barn to find Blade and Canyon already present. Canyon is on the computer while Blade is flipping through a catalog. Our insemination technician will be here soon.

I'm pouring myself a cup of coffee when the office door swings open.

"Good morning, Eaton brothers."

"Scarlett," I hiss after she greets the room. Her false cheer blinds me. I've been trying to avoid her for the past twenty-four hours, but even with the forced smile, I can't take my eyes off her.

"Where can I help today?"

"We're working fence repairs," I mutter, making it clear this work is not for her. We have Clayton and Blade on milk duty this morning.

"Look." Scarlett sighs, swiping a hand through those loose red curls I love to fist in my fingers. "As long as the three of you are together, I just wanted to say again how sorry I am. We didn't think. It's not an excuse. Our ignorance isn't even worthy of an apology. We were misinformed, and that piece shouldn't have ever been a story."

Canyon glances over at me, waiting out my reaction. Taking another deep breath, she carries on. "Bull already knows I have a history of screwups." Tears well in her eyes, but she rapidly blinks them away. It's a good thing because I hate when women cry, especially when it seems sincere instead of a ploy. When I glance away from her, she continues. "I'm not making excuses for myself. I've done you wrong, your family wrong, and I'm just so sorry I hurt you."

My head lowers as I feel her eyes on me.

"I'd like to learn more. How a dairy farm works. Educate me on the process. Maybe there's something I can do around here." Her arm flails out. "I'm a selfish city girl, and I hadn't considered how milking happens. I mean, I know milk comes from cows, but I didn't know the hard work behind the process, or the real people, doing honest work. I'm sorry I was so shallow."

When no one speaks, each of us avoiding eye contact, Scarlett babbles on.

"I figured putting me to work would teach me a lesson. Let me get my hands dirty and put my back into things and—"

"You can't work here. You're pregnant," I blurt, unable to hold back my concern for her despite my anger. "You shouldn't be putting your back into anything."

Blade's head shoots up, wide eyes looking at Scarlett while Canyon turns his gaze to me. His mouth falls open before clamping shut. When Scarlett licks her lips and bites the lower one, I need to look away again. Silence lingers.

"Fine." Her voice lowers, defeated. "I know where I'm not wanted. I'll just get out of your hair." With that, Scarlett exits but the quiet tone of her rejection echoes in our small office.

"She's pregnant?" Canyon blurts out the second Scarlett exits.

"When did that happen?" Blade adds.

"No thanks to you," I mutter to both of them. "Remember that one night you dared me to ask her for a drink?" Canyon slowly smiles. However, it's still possible that's not the night Scarlett got pregnant, and I hate to think about such things. The emptiness in my stomach fills with an unsettling feeling. As much as I don't want to consider it, the truth is she might be carrying that city schmuck, doctor dick's baby, and maybe a paternity test sooner rather than later is a good thing. But it's not going to change my mind. I want that baby, and I'm concerned about this test to determine the father. I don't want her putting herself or the baby at risk.

"Are you letting her leave?" Canyon asks, shifting his gaze to the door.

"What do you want me to do?" I snap, exasperated by this entire situation. She hurt us. She hurt the farm. And she hurt me, but can I really fault her for doing her job? *Yes*, I decide. *I can.* What a shit job she had.

"I don't think you should let her run off," Canyon adds, turning for the window which Scarlett just passed, heading for the lane. Her bright red hair bobs as she hastily walks away.

"Why? Fuck her," Blade says.

"Hey," I mutter. That's a little strong.

"We almost lost the farm," he reminds me. It isn't *exactly* true. People closest to us believed in us and not the slur of walking our cows through their own shit or producing unsanitary milk. We struggled with a few buyers, and there was the hassle of the inspections, but some of it was stuff we might have encountered on any other day. MoosHaveRights2 is a bastard of a group finding fault in the oddest of ways, and we still don't understand how they got involved other than illegally sneaking on our land.

"You know I wish I'd known about Joey from the start. Her mother might be a bitch, but I still wish I'd been there. Known my child existed from day one." Canyon's voice lowers as he reminds us all of his history. He didn't know he'd gotten a groupie pregnant until a ten-year-old showed up on the scene without her mom. It was complicated and changed everything for Canyon. "I don't think you want to miss out on this."

Glancing up at the window, I stare at the now-vacant drive. Did I really want Scarlett to go? What if the baby is mine in every sense of the word? Hadn't I already told her I wanted Sprout no matter what? I'd meant it, but I was still angry.

"Well, if you ask me, good riddance," Blade mumbles.

"No one asked you," Canyon interjects before I can speak. "And you wonder why you're alone," Canyon continues, rubbing in the perpetual bachelorhood of our brother.

"Fuck you," Blade says, turning back for the cow catalog he's been flipping pages in but not reading. Canyon ignores our youngest brother and turns back to me.

"She's not a groupie," he says, keeping his eyes on me. "She's not looking to gain something by being with you or blabbing to the world she slept with you."

"Isn't she?"

Canyon tilts his head. "You don't really believe she's here for a second scoop, do you?"

I'd like to think not, and within a heartbeat, I realize I don't. Scarlett might be a lot of things, but devious just doesn't seem like one of them. Plus, there's nothing exciting to report. There wasn't anything worthwhile in the past either. So I got dumped, and it hurt, but it happens. Maybe not three times, but it still happens to everyone. Even Scarlett had her heart broken by her husband. In some ways, that sounds worse because the commitment to love and honor her was already in place when the cheating occurred. He should have been faithful to her, keeping his promises of loyalty. For a second, I'm grateful I haven't made those kinds of promises myself to Scarlett.

"If only women came with a ninety-day guarantee," Blade says, flipping through the cow catalog. "Although she did sound sincere. I mean, she could have started sobbing and wailing, pouring on the waterworks, but she stood here, head up, and said she was sorry."

My lips twist, contemplating what Blade said. She did sound contrite, but it takes more than an apology to make things right. I've heard I'm sorry too many times in my life.

"Wish someone had apologized to me," Canyon adds, recalling once again a daughter showing up without explanation or apology for keeping the truth from him for nearly a decade.

"It's also a little ironic that the best woman to cross your path in . . . *forever* . . . is the one you're pushing away," Blade mutters, flipping another page of the catalog without looking up. "But no one asked me, so what do I know?"

"Two seconds ago, you said fuck her," I remind him.

Blade's brows lift. "Yeah, and now, I'm thinking, as you already did, and she's carrying your child, you can't just let her leave. Plus, people change. See, I just changed my mind."

"That sounded so stupid it almost made sense," Canyon says, rolling his eyes at our brother. "Bull, get out of here. Go after her. At least talk to her."

When did he get to be the rational one about women? His rule of one night only started this whole thing. *One and done.* Of course, I can't remember the last time he's been out and done such a thing. And one night with Scarlett was never going to be enough.

"Fuck," I groan, yanking my cap off my head and swiping fingers through my hair as I turn for the door.

"Scarlett," I call out, hoping she'll slow her pace. She's traveled pretty far in the time it's taken my brothers to reprimand me. Jogging down the road, I holler for her again. Unfortunately, she's at her little sports car, slipping in and backing out of the drive by the time I near the house. Blocking her exit down the lane, Scarlett stops before me, and I round to the side of her BMW.

I'm not certain what I'm supposed to say to her, and when I see her face, my tongue freezes even more. She isn't sad. She isn't angry. She's resolute as if she's just had enough. Like me, who has had breakup after breakup and then this scandal, Scarlett's had a shitstorm of events in the past few months with losing her job, finding out about her husband, and getting pregnant with a virtual stranger. She looks *finished,* and nothing scares me more.

"What do you want, Bull?" The sharpness of her question startles me. What do I want from her? What have I wanted from any of the women in my past?

"Where are you going?" I ask instead of answering her. She slips on a pair of sunglasses.

"I need some . . . retail therapy."

Is that a thing? "What is that?"

"Look, I just need a day alone, I guess." She doesn't look at me. With her eyes forward and large sunglasses covering them, I can't read her well enough to answer my biggest question: *Will she be back?*

"What time will you be home?" The need in my voice annoys me, and I hate its presence.

"Home?" she mutters, turning to face me with those oversized glasses blocking her eyes from my sight. She pauses on the word, hesitating over it as though it's unfamiliar to her. Does she not view my house as her home? Is she going to leave? My eyes drift lower even though I can't see her belly. What about the baby?

"I don't know when I'll be back," Scarlett states, turning her head away from me again. "But I'm not leaving. I know you feel I've failed you, and I admit I have. But I'm asking for a little faith in me. I won't be going anywhere unless you make me leave. Do you want me to go?"

Her determination to stay surprises me, and I don't know what to make of it. I also don't respond to her question, and without looking up at me, she puts her car back in drive, and I push off the roof. Sticking around says more about her than running away, and admittedly, Scarlett's facing us Eatons head-on.

I watch as her car disappears, still worried she doesn't mean what she's said but telling myself to believe she'll be back. We just need some separation for a day . . . or two. Kicking at the dirt, I make my way back to the barn and throw myself into a long day's work.

Do I want her to go?

It's a recurring thought as I work the post hole digger into the packed dirt where I need to replace a strip of fencing.

Can I trust her? Like Canyon asked, do I really think she's here for a second scoop? I don't. I'm not certain why Scarlett's in my path, other than the baby, and Sprout weighs heavily on my mind.

The baby is our glue. *Parenting partners.* Is that all I want from Scarlett? I've said I'd never ask her to marry me because that only leads to disaster, but at the moment, I can't imagine things getting worse than they already are.

When I was with Jennifer, it was young love and twentysomething lust that drew us together. Or maybe it was Jen's complacency and willingness to give in to whatever I wanted. Her need to be a mother was her strongest ambition, and we were kids who couldn't seem to survive troubling marital issues like infertility. Scarlett and I are past those younger years of indecisive decision-making. I'd like to think we could act more adult in problem-solving. *In good times and bad.*

Sabrina had been a relationship of sex and companionship. She filled a void for me, which wasn't fair to her, and probably explains her search for something deeper with someone else. She was also greedy, which Scarlett is not. Sabrina wanted material things from me more than she wanted me. *For richer and poorer.*

Finally, Gisela's wild desires lead to something out of control. Her reckless behavior and artistic ideals just didn't match who I was. Again, she filled another hole, but then she stole from me, and it was easy to let her leave. Scarlett hasn't stolen anything but my heart, and once more, the fissure inside aches. *To love and honor.*

Why have I always fallen so quickly? My mother would mockingly say I was a lover. I wanted a wife. I wanted what I witnessed between my parents. I wanted someone to warm my bed, hold my hand, and laugh with me. However, I've come to learn wife is more than just a label, and marriage is more than a decree. It's something that needs a commitment to survive. Something that isn't greedy but needs communication and understanding with compromise in the mix. It's something that includes recklessness and creativity but boundaries of trust. A true marriage involves a soul mate as a wife, and I thought Scarlett might be it for me.

We differ in so many ways, but most of those differences endear her to me. She's lively and vibrant, filling the quiet that's consumed me for years. She's generous with her time, spending it with my family and me, and I've missed cuddling with her on the couch. Finally, she's sexy in all kinds of ways she doesn't recognize in herself, like the way she smells, how she's willing to let me do what I want with her body, or how she purrs when I enter her. Scarlett and I are compatible in one area that surpasses all the others, and I can't deny sex is a huge part of communication for me.

Touching her allows me to tell her how I feel when words escape me. When she touches me, I feel the same is true of her. She's communicating how much she appreciates me, how much she likes living with me, and how much she wants to be near me.

Am I misreading all the signs once again? My history proves I'm not good at interpretation.

"Heard you had a fight." Dad's words break into my rambling thoughts. I hadn't heard his truck pull up.

"Yeah," I say, no sense denying things as I slam the post hole digger into the dry dirt again. Fence repair is typically a two-person job, but no one wants to work with me this afternoon.

"Want to talk about it?" The question startles me as my dad isn't one for communication. That was Mom's jurisdiction, and on a day like today, I miss my mother. She'd know what to say or what to do, or just remind me that things happen for a reason. Maybe discovering the truth about Scarlett and her involvement in that news story is a sign that things aren't meant to be between us.

When I don't answer Dad, jabbing the hole digger at the ground once more, he speaks. "Your mother was a feisty woman, too. Ran me in circles at first. Like to think it was that red hair." He chuckles softly, and I recall my mother's faded rust coloring. "But I think it was her heart. She was well-intended."

My arms thud on the hole digger as it hits a solid patch, and I still, turning to face my father. "How was reporting that shit about us relevant to anything?"

Dad shrugs. "It wasn't. Not the personal bits or the parts about our farm. It was hurtful but not spiteful. Damning but not intentional. Scarlett didn't set out to harm us. She set out to do her job. The overzealous activists are the ones who really hurt us. That's the thing when what we do in life involves passion. There's a risk. Doing what feels like the right thing to one might be the wrong thing for another. I'm not saying I agree with Scarlett's employment or even her motives, but it's not my place to judge her, nor can I condemn her for what she thought was right at the moment."

As my moral compass isn't perfect, I understand what Dad is saying, although I don't like it. "That's where consequences come in. Think before you act. I recall a certain someone saying that often." I tip a brow at my father, who easily dispensed that advice when I was younger.

"If you want to discuss consequences, perhaps you should have thought before you acted with Scarlett." It's the first and last comment my dad will make on my decision to have a one-night stand.

"And at the time I offered that advice, I was hoping it might rub off in other decisions you've made with women, but did it?" He pauses for effect, knowing full well it didn't stop me from leaping before I looked. "You've always been so eager to have someone at your side, but it can't be just someone. It's a certain someone. And now, she's here."

I glance back at the handles of the hole digger.

"You're in a bit of a pickle with Scarlett. There's a reason there's a saying about learning to love. It's a lesson. It takes time and energy. I'm not saying Scarlett needs to be your wife. She doesn't even need to stay on this farm if you don't want her to, but she's going to be part of the rest of your life. And I'd be sad to see that baby of yours gone. I'd actually miss Scarlett, too."

We haven't explained the possibility Sprout might not be mine. It still doesn't matter. If Scarlett wants to know for her own peace of mind, I understand, but it's not going to change mine. I want that baby. In my soul, I feel that Sprout belongs to me, and so does Scarlett.

"I respect that you're rightfully upset, but just remember, making her leave can have long-term effects. She might never come back."

And that's my biggest fear. If I don't trust Scarlett, how will she trust me to take care of her and the baby? If I don't have faith in her intentions now, what's keeping her with me? Why would she stay by my side if I can't stand by hers?

"This is just a fucking mess," I mutter, slamming the hole digger one more time into the packed dirt, twisting it to loosen the soil.

"If it isn't messy, it's not love."

My head shoots up at my father's words. Jennifer slipped away easily. Sabrina fell right through my fingers. I should have run from Gisela, but Scarlett . . . she's not going to be so easy to let go. And the truth is, I don't want her to leave. I just don't know how to get past what's been done.

Dad slaps me on the back and turns for his truck, leaving me to continue this two-person job alone.

"Thanks for your help," I mutter, referring to the post digging, but accepting I also mean his advice. If I push Scarlett away, there's no reason for her to come back to me.

"Seems you can dig your own hole without any help," he sarcastically says, waving over his shoulder.

Have I dug a hole? Why does it feel like things are suddenly my fault?

16

BIG BURGERS

SCARLETT

Rita and I enter The Mountain Goat, a bar just outside Tuxbury. Zara told me how she once managed the place since it's owned by her uncle Otto. He still owns it, but it's under new management. Rumor has it, it still serves a decent cheeseburger, and I need one the size of my head to stave my hunger and lose myself in my misery. Although it's a tavern, Rita accompanies me to the local favorite to commiserate through food love.

"I've really fricked up this time," I say to Rita as we sit across from one another in a booth.

"You really had no idea?" Rita isn't judging me. She's just curious how I could have forgotten such a report and not connected Bull's name with the Bovine Bridegroom I invented.

"We never said his name in the reel." Most likely because we didn't have his permission to run the story. I'd have to go back through files I no longer have access to in order to find out how we got the information about Bull in the first place.

Was it an anonymous tip? Was it something one of our interns read while searching the internet for outlandish stories? How did this story cross our desks and earn our interest? I didn't always question what I reported when I should have done better, been better, but I'm determined to get answers—correct answers.

Should I have recognized that now-familiar, firm backside which I so foolishly ogled on the update segment?

"I'm a horrible person," I say to Rita.

"Yes, you are," she agrees, gazing at me through those fun, red-framed glasses. She sips her cola after speaking, and my mouth falls open. "What? Isn't that what you want me to say? You want me to tell you I agree with you. Does that make you feel better?"

"No," I admit.

"Then stop beating yourself up. You've had your twenty-four-hour grace period to pity yourself; now it's time to rectify things with Bull. If that's what you want." Rita sits back in the booth and stretches her legs so her construction boots land on the edge of the bench seat next to me. She's working on her passion project this summer, building homes for those in need, and I really admire her commitment. I don't have passion. I don't have commitment. *Gah, I'm self-deprecating again.*

"Yes, I want to make things right with Bull."

"So you're sleeping together again, correct?" As my sole friend in the world, Rita knows too much about me. "I'd suggest sexy lingerie and a night of heavy apology sex for starters."

"Rita." I choke. "I'm pregnant. My body is like a misshaped pear. That's not sexy, and I don't think Bull will come within ten feet of me. He's not just angry; he's furious. Like never want to see someone again angry."

"If that's really true, why are you still living with him? He'd have kicked you out if he felt that way."

Admittedly, what she says seems true. Bull did not rush after my retreat this morning to tell me to get the heck out of his house. Instead, he cautiously asked me when I'd return as if he was worried I wouldn't be back. Then again, maybe he just wanted to know my timing, so he could kick me out when I returned. Or better yet, he could toss all my things on the lawn before I arrived home again. Maybe I should have done those things to Shelton. I should have burned his clothes and lit our mattress on fire. Honestly, Bull doesn't seem to be the type to react in such extremes, though, and I'd already been back to the house to find all my belongings still intact.

"I have the damsel in distress syndrome, and apparently that's Bull's thing." Recalling what Bull's told me about his previous relationships, I fit the mold. Although, I'm not certain I see the distress in the women of his past. Jennifer sounded weak-willed and unsure of herself other than her desires for motherhood. Sabrina sounded needy, greedy, and unworthy of Bull, and that Gisela woman sounded like a kinky whack who stole from him.

"You do need a bit of saving. From yourself," Rita adds. "Look, we all make mistakes. Every person in the world makes them. Some of the stuff you reported on him might be unforgivable. I don't know. I don't watch that kind of thing. Sorry, cookie. But I know you. You aren't that malicious. You aren't in distress. You're pregnant, and that makes you forgivable in several ways. But let's go back to making things right with Bull. Just explain yourself. It was your job, Scarlett. Maybe you should have left it long ago, especially if your conscience was catching up to you, but you can't beat yourself up for what you should have done. I've done hundreds of risky, unnecessary, and downright stupid things while drinking. Some, I dare say, might be unforgivable as well, but I can't go back. Moving forward is a huge part of my recovery. Acceptance of what you cannot change. Courage to change what you can. Wisdom to know the difference."

I sigh, knowing Rita's had a rough road even if she appears put together. More guilt consumes me that I hadn't been here for her when her life crumbled. She was so good at pretending she was all put together, I hadn't had a hint of her struggles.

"Accept this happened."

"But Bull needs to accept I never intended to hurt him."

"And he will, in time."

"What if he doesn't?"

Rita pauses, looking at me over the worn-wood table. "You said he wants to be the baby's dad. He doesn't care about the label of biological father, right?"

"Yes."

"Then Bull will come around."

For Sprout. Not necessarily for me, but for the baby. Everything for the baby. I should make a plan in case Bull does want me to leave. I could do this on my own. Plenty of women are successful single mothers. I'd dealt with Lex's daily tantrums, Shelton's needy behaviors, and the whims of superstars. I should be able to wrap my head around raising a baby alone.

Only I don't want to be alone, and I don't want to leave Bull. I want to be with him. Plus, if I leave, then I really am like the other women in his life. I'll have left behind a good, kind, decent man who wants to be good, kind, and decent to my baby. I owe him. He deserves to see that one woman has staying power, and that person is me. Like I told him earlier, he needs faith that I won't go anywhere unless he asks me to leave. It's *his* choice.

Bull would be the father of my dreams to my child, and maybe one day, he could open that big heart of his to me. If only he could forgive me and give me a chance to prove to him that I'd be here for him like he's been for me. I love him, dammit. *Oh, my goodness*. I'm in love with Bull.

However, I cannot settle for less than him loving me. I've already done that with Shelton. Still, I don't want to give up what Bull and I already have, what he's already given me, even if it is only a sliver of who I know he can be.

Our burgers arrive and true to their reputation, they are large, juicy looking, and smell delicious. In addition, a side of greasy, salty fries that would make me retain water and my ankles swell fill a plate between Rita and me, and I am going to devour every bite. Picking up the heavy burger, I moan around the first taste. It's grilled perfection, or maybe I was just that hungry.

After leaving the farm this morning, I'd spent time at the tractor supply shop, purchasing flowerpots, an array of midsummer flowers, and wrought-iron hurricane candleholders. With tips from the service clerk in the garden department, I filled three pots to overflow with red geraniums, blue salvia, and something dainty and yellow I couldn't recall the name of. *Pregnancy brain.* I arranged the two candleholders, filling the bottom with sand and adding a thick pillar candle to each. The final touch was a welcome sign. The inside of Bull's home was homey, but the outside needed to say *come in and stay a while.*

I wanted to brighten Bull's day—and every day ending in day —when he returned to his house to find the new things decorating his porch. It wasn't a gesture of apology as much as a statement. I wanted to stay a little longer.

"The offer still stands for you to move in with me if you need." Rita has been generous with the suggestion, but I don't want to walk away from Bull. If he wants me to leave, that's a different story, but I want to stick it out with him as partners, like he said. Although I'm beginning to hate that word.

I also owe it to his entire family to face them and their farm. The first place I felt I could do better was learning more about the dairy.

"Well, look what the cows brought home," Rita teases, and I turn in the booth to see Canyon and Blade enter after a set of women. I swallow the bite of burger, now a lump in my throat, and turn back to Rita.

"Excuse me a second," I say, sliding out of the booth. The women have gone left, making it clear they didn't enter with the brothers, who only held the door open for them. When I approach the younger Eatons, they still, crossing their arms and spreading their legs as if they are taking a stance and blocking my exit. The position is similar to bodyguards I've had to talk my way through in order to get into a club and scope out who was hanging out with whom inside. But I'm not that person anymore.

"Hi, guys." I give them a weak wave. "Can I buy you guys a beer or dinner maybe?" I point toward Rita. "My friend and I are just having a burger."

Blade doesn't say anything while Canyon takes a second to assess me. "You doing okay, Scarlett? Feeling okay?" His eyes lower for my belly, and my hand falls there out of habit.

"I'm good, Canyon. Thanks for asking." I peer around him, obviously looking for the third part of this brother trio. He couldn't be home waiting on me, could he?

As I glance around Blade, he shifts right, preventing me from seeing the door.

"What . . ." *the frick is this?*

"How about that beer, Scarlett?" Blade asks, his voice straining as though he's protecting something or rather someone.

"Sure," I say, dragging out the word. "Join Rita and me." I step aside so Blade can pass me, and as he moves forward, I slip behind him, heading out the front door of the Goat, and find Bull in the parking lot in Louisa Miller's arms.

⑰
STOOD UP

BULL

I'm so tired.

It's been a long day after fighting with Scarlett, fixing fences, and reflecting on my dad's advice, and the last thing I wanted to do was go out for a beer. In fact, I'd been hoping to sit at home and wait on Scarlett. She'd obviously been back as my front porch was decorated like something out of a home and garden magazine. Flowerpots. Candleholders. A welcome sign. The burst of color was all Scarlett, and my insides did a little line dance of relief.

"She planted flowers." Canyon clarified after picking me up and taking an appraising look at my front porch.

"Well, she put them in pots."

"What's the difference? It's a sign of permanence," Canyon stated as we drove to the Mountain Goat, a less touristy, more for locals spot owned by Otto Rossi. Speaking of permanence, though, Scarlett's car was not parked by my truck despite the fact she'd been back.

"Just a quick beer," I warn my brothers as we pull into the gravel lot of the bar. As Canyon is the driver, I trust him to exit us early tonight. Only as soon as we are crossing the lot, the crunch of running feet over gravel catches my attention, and before I can turn around, two arms wrap around me from behind. Two female arms.

"What the—"

"Bull, I haven't seen you in for*ever*," Louisa Miller whines at my back. The truth about Louisa and me is I've known for*ever* that Louisa had a crush on me. She wasn't even subtle about it, and something told me to stay away from her. When I saw her that time in the tractor supply store, and she flirted hard, she'd somehow worked us into a dinner date. Eventually, I'd chickened out of dinner with Louisa, opting for a coffee date instead. After my one-night stand, the guys were pushing me to get back out there, and I'd proven I could do it—spend one night with a woman and walk away. However, I hadn't really proven anything. Or maybe that the universe is talking, hinting that the one-night stand had more in store for me than one night. I hadn't been able to forget Scarlett, and now we had months to learn about each other because she was having a kid.

We would be joined for eternity as parents. It was a commitment I separated from marrying her. But my fear was, if Scarlett left, another man would step in, sweep her off her feet, and want to take care of her and Sprout. I did not like that idea, not one bit.

"Hey. Louisa," I stammer, working at the arms wrapped around me like a coiled rope. Instantly, I smell the alcohol wafting off her. She'd arrived with two friends, and I nod at them once I have Louisa free from me. One of her friends says they'll head inside for a table.

"Just give us a second. I'll be right in," I tell Canyon, whose eyes narrow at me before leading Blade behind Louisa's friends.

"Louisa, I'm sorry I didn't call again." It's a long-overdue apology after cutting our coffee date short and ghosting her afterward. Caught up in Scarlett, I hadn't given Louisa another thought. I've had a lot on my mind. Still, wanting to do the right thing, I needed to apologize for my behavior.

"You could make it up to me," Louisa flirts, reaching for the button closure of my shirt and giving it a playful tug.

"Louisa, I'm with Scarlett."

"After what she did to you?" Her playful expression shifts as if she's fighting something distasteful in her mouth. She actually pouts, reminding me of her young age.

"Yes." Despite what Scarlett has done to me, I'm still with her, if she'll still have me. Cupping Louisa's shoulders, I press her back from me again but quickly release her. Her eyes glance up at my face.

"Well, that happened fast." The bitter undertone is not settling well with me. Louisa and I shared one coffee, and I don't owe her an explanation about my complicated relationship with Scarlett.

"It was great to see you again," I say, trying to remain polite while cutting off the conversation.

"If you'd ever like to get coffee again, or anything else. We could have a drink inside . . ." She points over her shoulder to the front door. Swaying on her feet, I'd say she might have had a few already.

"Louisa, I don't think that's a good idea." Coming here tonight suddenly feels like the worst idea, and I'd be turning on my boot heels for the truck if only I'd driven.

"Friendship hug, then," she squeals. Throwing out her arms, she steps into my space and wraps them around my waist again. Natural instinct has me giving her a tepid pat on the back before looking up to find Scarlett watching us.

"Scarlett?" I did not see her car in the lot. Then again, I hadn't thought to look. Releasing my arms from Louisa, she slides to my side, keeping her arms around my waist.

"Oopsy. She caught us," Louisa mewls like a spoiled teen, and the color in Scarlett's face turns to ash. She turns back for the door while I rip myself free of Louisa, no longer feeling sorry about that coffee date gone wrong.

"Scarlett," I call out, following her retreating back. Once inside the dim-lit bar, my eyes need a second to adjust from the bright evening outside. Scanning the place, I easily find Scarlett by that gorgeous hair and step over to the booth where Rita sits across from her.

"That is not what it looked like," I blurt.

"Uh-oh," Rita mutters, lifting her cola and taking a long sip from the straw. She glances at Scarlett across the table, who is not looking up at me. Half-finished burgers rest on their plates. I'm interrupting their dinner, but I need to explain myself to Scarlett. Rita reaches for her purse. "I should give you two a minute."

"Don't go," Scarlett whispers across the table to her friend. "I haven't seen you in weeks." Scarlett hasn't seen her friend because she's been with me, but right now, I don't trust that she won't run before I can say what needs to be said. Finally, Scarlett looks up at me, her face still washed of color.

"Just let us finish our meal. We can talk when I get home."

Home. At least she still thinks of my place as her home.

I nod, biting my tongue as I turn for another booth two down from Scarlett and Rita, where my brothers sit. Practically throwing myself on the bench seat, I cup my head in my hands, and a beer slides between my arms.

"What the heck happened?" Canyon asks, and I give him the quick rundown of Scarlett seeing me with my arms around another woman.

"You know you don't owe Scarlett anything," Blade states, back on the screw Scarlett bandwagon. "It's not like you're married to each other."

My arms fall to the table with such a sharp thud my beer wobbles in the glass. "We're parenting partners."

"What the hell is that?" Blade asks.

"You aren't going to marry her?" Canyon questions at the same time.

"Of course, I'm not marrying her. We all know how proposals work out for me."

"But this is different," Canyon reminds me. "She's pregnant with your kid."

Maybe. I close my eyes, feeling sick inside. Maybe Scarlett's correct. Maybe I'm too ambitious to want a baby that might not be mine. The second I question myself, though, I know I'm wrong. Sprout is mine. It's something I feel in my bones.

"I don't need to marry her. Scarlett's still . . . been through a lot lately. We don't need to rush." Canyon's brow furrows as he's watching me while Blade mutters, "Oh no."

Glancing up, I notice Redd Bottom making a beeline for our booth with Dillard on his heels.

"Gentleman. How's it hanging, Bull?" He chuckles. "We got to see your mucky backside on television again. I never can look away from a man working his cows." His salacious voice implies every nasty word he isn't saying.

"Got time to watch television, Redd?" Blade interjects. "Business must be bad this year." Redd's expression sours at Blade's slur. Redd makes statues out of wood stumps. The man is dangerous with a chain saw. It's an art form, but I have no idea how he makes a living off it. Redd's been known to use his art as an excuse not to help out on his family's land.

"My wood's got nothing to do with leisure time," Redd defends.

"I bet your wood doesn't get any leisure," Canyon snarks to his beer as he lifts it for his lips. Blade snorts, and Dillard guffaws behind Redd.

"Did I see you with Louisa Miller in the parking lot?" Redd inquires, and I slam my glass back to the table.

"What do you want, Redd?" Blade interjects. Thankfully, he's on the inside of the booth, or he'd be attempting to stand and drag Redd to the parking lot.

"Excuse me." All heads turn to Scarlett, who's standing just off the edge of the booth. Redd does a double take, and I know the feeling. He's stunned by Scarlett's beauty. Those wide brown eyes. That fresh, bright hair. Her creamy skin. Damn, she looks so good.

"Scarlett Russell." She holds out a hand, and Redd swipes his against his jeans before reaching for hers.

"Redd Bottom." Scarlett chokes and looks to us to confirm he's not kidding. His name sounds like a cherry-colored ass. "How can I help you, pretty lady?"

Scarlett points at the seat beside me. "You're blocking the booth. I'd like to slide back in by my man."

Blade chokes. Canyon lowers his glass, and I sit up straighter. *What?*

Redd steps back, and Scarlett slides in next to me, catching my eyes for only a second before glancing back up at Redd.

"So, what are we discussing?"

"The dairy king and Louisa Miller in the parking lot," Redd says, sounding proud of himself for putting me down.

"Oh, dairy king," Scarlett whines, drawing out the term in a teasing voice. "And with Louisa Miller in the parking lot. Did she use jumper cables? This sounds like a hint in the game *Clue*."

Scarlett pauses, batting her lashes while she insults Redd, who stands still. Her hand lands on the back of my neck and plays with the hairs tickling my nape. "But I like that dairy king comment. However, that program should have come up with something more original. Like rough rider, for the way he takes me in bed."

What? I choke. Blade snorts, and Canyon just stares at Scarlett while she squeezes at my nape.

"Or even pussy pleaser." She purrs like a kitty cat and shimmies her shoulders, squeezing her hands together before her chest. "Because he loves to cuddle, and he keeps me satisfied."

Fuck. What the hell is she playing at? And why am I getting hard listening to her?

Her hand returns to my nape as if she's claiming me, and Redd does not miss the motion.

"Yeah, well." Redd swallows, fighting the effect Scarlett is having on him as her brown beauties laser up at him, and she continues to smile. "Bovine Bridegroom takes the win."

"It did. That's why I came up with it. I love alliteration."

Redd's eyes narrow, and I'm not liking the turn of this conversation. *She* came up with that label? Her hand drops to my thigh, squeezing at my leg.

"But we made a big mistake in naming Bull. We missed all the other delicious terms for him, and I'm lucky he was able to escape all those other women because now it's my turn." Scarlett looks at me over her shoulder, tightening her grasp on my thigh. "I've named myself Sticking-around Scarlett because I'm not letting Bull get away."

Scarlett gazes back up at Redd. "That makes me the future dairy queen, I guess. Or would it be bovine bride? Perhaps I'm just a cowgirl to my cowman." Scarlett leans forward as if she's about to impart a secret to Redd. "But I don't want to share my favorite position on Bull with everyone."

She fucking winks at Redd, and his mouth falls open. If he isn't frustratingly turned on by now, the man is a monk. He blinks, fighting her spell and turning deep red to match his name.

"Well. I—" His stammering causes Scarlett to give a little wave with her fingers while the heat of her other hand seeps through my jeans like a possessive claim on me.

"Have a nice night, boys."

Redd steps away from the table, and I watch his retreat. Dillard glances back over his shoulder and gives the table a thumbs-up as if he's proud of us.

"What the hell?" I blurt.

"Damn, I knew I liked you," Canyon states.

"Let me out of the booth. I see someone I know." The strain in Blade's voice gives away all the sexual tension built up in him, and I hate to think he'll sneak off to the restroom for a moment alone at the expense of Scarlett.

"I'm sorry. Was that over the top?"

Canyon laughs, and I give in to a chuckle. "I heard what he said, and Rita mentioned he's one of those wankier guys who peaked in high school and can't let go of the long-gone status." Rita's assessment hasn't been incorrect.

"And I'm sorry about the bovine bridegroom title, but it was creative." She smiles sheepishly at me. "But who was that guy?"

"He's no one," I dismiss.

"His family's property borders ours, and he's been after sharing land with us for years. He's an ass," Canyon adds. I shake my head to agree.

"I'm sorry he spoke like that to you because of me," Scarlett says, lowering her eyes while her hand still remains on my upper leg.

"It's nothing," I admit because it wasn't the worst of things.

"But it was still because of me, and I'm sorry. Again, I'm so sorry."

I nod once, knowing we need to talk, and I want out of this bar.

"Finished with your dinner?" I ask, twisting to look over my shoulder and back at her empty booth.

"Yeah, Rita said she had to see someone about her charity work."

"Let's step outside," I suggest, and Scarlett nods to agree.

"Will you need me to drive you home?" Canyon questions, narrowing his sights on someone across the bar. He's really asking if he can stay a little longer.

"I can give him a ride," Scarlett says, and Canyon turns back to her.

"Now that we all know you like to ride the bull . . ." His teasing voice falls away, and Scarlett laughs, covering her face.

"It was too much, wasn't it?"

Actually, it was perfect. Scarlett stood up for me. Not that I can't defend myself but calling me her man was nice to hear. Having someone take my side was also nice. Recalling what my dad said earlier, though, it wasn't just someone, but a *certain* someone, and that made it all the better.

18

THEM'S FIGHTING WORDS

BULL

Once we step outside, Scarlett stops by the trunk of her car. Crossing her arms, she faces me.

"You remember that my husband cheated on me with another woman, right?" She pauses. The playfulness of inside is forgotten, and my early position recalled. "I want to believe I can trust you."

My mouth falls open. "Says the woman paid to lie about others." My bitterness returns, swirling inside me with a mix of conflicting emotions.

"Bull, I know you're hurting, and after what I witnessed in there with red ass, I understand even more. But I'm going to break this down for you. First, I do trust you. You've allowed me into your home, haven't taken advantage of me, and provided for me, which also encompasses care and concern for Sprout. But I don't ever want to see you in the arms of another woman again. You need a hug, I'm your woman."

My mouth falls open to protest, but Scarlett continues.

"Maybe you shouldn't trust me." Her voice turns distant as her fingers fist in the material at the sides of her dress. "Trust is earned, and I've done nothing to prove myself to you. But here's what I have done. I've been in your bed every night, giving you my body and my—"

What? What else is she giving me?

" . . . my faith in you, that you're a good man wanting to do the right thing."

My shoulders sag at the answer, and I find it's not what I'd hoped she'd say.

"I hate the way that man just spoke to you, and I hate that it's because of me."

I shake my head with a bitter chuckle. "Scarlett, forget Redd. He's a nuisance, but he's harmless. It's only words."

"But you shouldn't have to listen to such things."

"I don't." Most days, I ignore Redd because he's just as she called him, a red ass.

We stand in silence for a moment. She looks up at me while I avoid her piercing gaze as though she's reading me and coming to some conclusions.

"Being a man of honor, I know you'll understand that I need to know the truth about Sprout. Finding out the paternity of Sprout is more about me than you."

"How?" I question.

"I need to know he has nothing over me. I don't want him to think he has any right to our child, and a test will prove he doesn't. And if the test proves he is the biological father, I need to prepare for battle because he will not go near our kid without one helluva fight."

I scratch at the back of my neck, dumbfounded by the conviction in her voice.

"Does he need to know? He doesn't want you, Scarlett, and I don't mean that to be hurtful. He'd only use Sprout." I don't know that man, but I know enough to sense he'd only use his child as a means to an end.

"I don't want to tell him. I already told him Sprout wasn't his, but I need to know the truth for me. I need to have proof it isn't Shelton's. I'd feel better knowing I'm not hanging onto a piece of him. But notice I said *our* child because in my heart, Sprout is yours. There's a difference between being the father of a child and actually being a dad to a child. You'll be Sprout's daddy in every sense of the word if that's what you want. That's my gift to you. We promised to be partners, and unless you'd like to renege that offer, I'm staying put. If you don't want me in the house, I can move somewhere close, but I think Vermont is the best place to raise our child. *Our* child. And this is where you live."

She waves out a hand at me. Her eyes blink a few times, and I notice her swallowing hard before she continues.

"You don't want to marry me, and I get that. It comes from fear, Bull." Her voice softens. "Fear of being left behind. Fear of rejection. Fear of not being good enough. But I wish you could turn that fear into faith because I'm standing here, Bull, telling you that you are good enough. You are worthy of love. You are not going to be left behind by me. I accept things as they are, so I need you to accept me as I am. I made a mistake, a huge mistake, and I'm asking you to forgive me for it."

She harshly swipes at the tears leaking from the corner of her eyes.

"Bull, you've done more for me in the past few months than Shelton did in years of marriage. I fricked up, but I won't give up the goodness you've done for me. I won't pretend it didn't happen because it did. You're good for me. We're good together, and together is how I want us to be in whatever form that takes."

I stare at her as her chest heaves, and she brushes another tear off her cheek.

"I'm done now," she says, crossing her arms and looking off in the distance.

Stumped by all she'd poured out to me, the only thing I can think to say first is: "Did something happen with Shelton?" When did it come about that she might have a custody battle with him?

"He called me this afternoon."

The words are a sucker punch to the gut, and I step closer to her.

"What did he want?"

"He wants me to come to Boston."

"Over my dead body," I growl. Gripping her upper arms, I beg her with my eyes not to leave.

"Which is what I told him."

Scarlett told me how he wanted sex with her, and that's why he'd shown up at the farm. He wanted her back because he was a horny bastard. However, he cannot have his wife back. He cannot have Sprout. They are mine.

I lean forward, pressing my forehead to the top of her head. *God, I've missed her.* Instantly, one hand falls to her belly, and her hand covers mine. The thought of her leaving makes me sick. If she went back to Boston, would she think the farm wasn't enough for her? Would she fall in love with the city again and decide Vermont was too quiet, too peaceful, too . . . anything other than the city? Would she want her old life back?

"Stay with me," I whisper to her.

"I'm not going anywhere unless you go with me, Bull."

———

Once we return to the house, I just need a minute, and I use checking on the cows as an excuse to get time to collect my thoughts. Scarlett certainly laid a lot on me in the parking lot at the Goat. First, her feisty spirit had me rocking a hard-on even as she schooled me with my fears. She was right about everything she said, but I'm still not certain I agree with her.

I want to be good enough.

I want to be worthy of her love.

I want her to stick around.

I take a long walk in the summer evening before returning to the house. Momentary panic seizes me when Scarlett isn't in the guest room, but then I find her curled up on my bed. Standing beside it, taking a long minute to observe her, I fight the questions in my head. Should I ask her to marry me?

She said she understood why I haven't and accepted how we are, but is it really enough for her?

"Bull?" she questions, her voice foggy. "You okay?" She offers no explanation for being in my bed.

I'm not going anywhere without you.

"I'm good," I say, finding I partially believe myself. I have a few things of my own I'd like to tell her, but her sleepy state tells me now isn't the time.

"Come to bed," she whispers, and my chest caves when she holds out a hand, wiggling her fingers for me to take. Pressing a knee to the bed, I lower to my side, facing her. For a long minute, we stare at one another.

"Tell me what you're thinking." Her soft voice encourages me to speak my piece.

"I'm not going to say it didn't hurt having all that shit stirred up again, but apology accepted."

"Really?" Her dark eyes dance in the dim moonlight coming into my room.

"As much as I didn't like having my private life blasted through the public like that, I can't change the past. I don't like what's been done, but it happened, and I can't go backward. It's over."

Scarlett swallows, and her voice drops as she says, "Thank you."

"But I have some conditions of my own. I never want you to work for that rag or any other thing that reports in that manner again." Scarlett can be strong willed, and I expect her to fight me on this concession, but she acquiesces easily.

"I promise. I'll never go back to work for them again."

Taking another moment to watch her face, she chews at her lip, waiting me out as if she knows I have more to say. As if she knows I need a minute. As if she knows me, maybe better than I know myself.

"It's hard for me to trust people," I admit, as she called me out earlier. "It hurt when Jen left even though there wasn't much between us anymore. I hated feeling like a quitter. And it stung to stand at that altar waiting on Sabrina, only for her not to show and then finding out it was because of another man. As for Gisela, well, even after spiraling out of control, it was hard to accept I'd made such a wrong assessment of her."

Sighing, I roll to my back, unable to face her any longer. "How's that saying go? Fool's rush in. I've been the biggest fool of all. I leap before looking all the time. I did the same thing with you. What's more foolish than a one-night stand?" Turning back to her, I catch her eyes. "And here we are."

"Are you saying we made a mistake?" Thickness fills her voice.

"No." I shift my body to mirror hers. "But . . . I've gotten ahead of myself once again." How do I tell her all the feelings I have for her? I'll jinx myself by admitting I want more from her. "Just know that I heard what you said, and I'm still here for you and Sprout. I still want us. Parenting partners."

Even though I termed it myself, I'm getting sick of the concept. It's not that I only want to share in parenting with Scarlett, but I want to share my life with her. I want to be a part of what she does, and where she lives, and who she wants to be in the future.

"As for the paternity test, I understand why you want it. I don't like it. I hate that it is another risk, but we need to rule out Shelton." I'm refusing to believe he's the father, and if we find out otherwise, I'm prepared to tackle that when it happens. I'm not giving up Sprout without a fight either.

"Okay, Bull," she agrees softly, reaching out to cup the side of my face, stroking over the heavier scruff I have by the end of a day. I inch closer to her, and she wraps her hand around my head. I'm not certain if she's pulling me closer or I'm leaning in, but just like when we crashed together in the restroom of the Busy Bean, our mouths meet, and all the conflict inside me seems to subside. This woman is my future. This woman is my home. This woman is my family.

Lost in the tenderness of her mouth underneath mine, I don't want to talk anymore. Slowly, Scarlett tips to her back, and I lean over her breasts, keeping our mouths fused as one.

Quickly, Scarlett pulls back and glances down at her belly.

"What?" I question, following her gaze. Her hand covers her stomach, but she reaches for my hand and pulls it to below her belly button. "Is that . . ."

Scarlett slowly smiles as my eyes widen. "Sprout doesn't like it when I'm on my back."

"Was I hurting you?"

"No, babe. You would never hurt me." The truth in her words and the trust in her voice have my mouth meeting hers once more, hoping to swallow her faith in me as I work on my faith in her. My hand still presses to her belly, and Sprout rolls again. Quickly, I pull back, staring down at my fingers, spreading over the T-shirt she's wearing to sleep in. My T-shirt. But I want to feel her skin underneath my palm. I want to feel our baby playing kickball inside his mother.

We both watch our hands over her stomach another second, and my heart races. There's new life under my hand. A new life with Sprout and Scarlett, and I need to get over my fears to accept what she's giving me. This is what I've always wanted.

"If Sprout doesn't like that position, maybe we need to get you off your back," I tease.

"Want me on my knees instead?" Fire sparks in her eyes. Is she flirting with me? That connection we have ignites, and I tug at her hips, drawing her over me.

She straddles me, and my hands sweep under her T-shirt, pushing the cotton material upward to expose her to me in the soft glow of the night. She's wearing this skimpy bikini underwear, saying it's the most comfortable for now, as it rests just under her growing belly. With a sharp tug at one hip strap, the material snaps, and Scarlett shifts so I can move the strip of fabric to one side.

Her naked center rests over my jean-clad legs, and the heat of her seeps through the denim.

"You ready for me, sweetheart?"

"Always for you," she whispers as I lower my hand between her thighs and test her warmth. She's wet and willing, and I easily slip a finger into her. She rocks over it like she'll be riding me soon enough, but first, I want to watch her dance. Sliding her hands up her breasts, cupping them and pressing them together, she's a vision.

When I add a second finger to the first, she gasps. The angle is different with her straddling over me and those fingers upward in her, but she continues to move, running her hands up her chest and lifting her hair. I'm enjoying the private show as her lids lower, but her hips rock faster.

"You're so fucking beautiful, sweetheart."

Her hands fall to her belly, and her face turns away from me as she licks her lips.

"None of that," I tell her, lifting a hand for her chin and forcing her to look back at me. "Motherhood is only making you sexier."

"God, Bull. You say the sweetest things."

"Don't want to be sweet with you right now, though," I admit as I want to strip her of everything. Not just her clothing, but her heart and her soul. I want it all to be mine, along with this beautiful body.

My fingers move faster, and Scarlett matches the rhythm, working her body as she swallows them into her. The sound of her excitement becomes the harmony to her movements.

"Bull . . . *ermygawd* . . ." Her hands fall to my chest as she bounces up and down before she stills, clenching over my fingers, thick within her. Her head falls forward while she comes fast.

As soon as she's done, she's fumbling with my jeans, working the button and yanking down the zipper. I sit up with her attention on my pants and tug my shirt over my head, tossing it off to the side of the bed. Falling back, Scarlett wiggles my jeans down to my knees before leaning over and taking me in her hand, holding me at the base and squeezing my stiff shaft.

"Sweetheart," I mutter before she leans forward, swirling her tongue around the seeping slit and then circling the crown of my head before opening wide and drawing me into the warmth of her mouth. I hiss.

She glides over my length, taking me to the back of her throat before slipping to the tip again and sucking me off with a pop. Opening once again, she swallows me again, swirling her tongue and hollowing out her cheeks until I can't take it anymore.

"Fuck, Scarlett. I need to be inside you." She releases me from her mouth but strokes up the hard length as her body moves higher up mine. Positioning herself at my tip, she waits just a beat, dragging me through her wet folds.

"I'm not certain I can go slow," I warn her, the anticipation of filling her pushing me to my limits.

"Rush in," she whispers, releasing me and slamming her body down to mine. The thrust is so quick. The angle is deeper. She's practically kissing my balls with that sweet pussy of hers, and my eyes roll back in my head. "Grip the headboard," she commands of me, and I reach over my head, curling my fingers around the wooden slats.

Then I'm fulfilling my namesake, bucking up into her as her hands fall to my chest again. She's following my lead, letting me fill her with sharp surges. My hips are wild, working off all the anger, all the fear, all the emotion of the past few days. She's here with me, my heart says. She's letting me into her body, as she told me. Now, if only she'd let me into her heart.

Not allowing that thought to take over, I thrust into her, and she meets my motion, rocking her body over mine.

"Bull." Her breath hitches as her clit hits the spot, and I sense the urgency in my name on her lips. She's ready to go again.

"Give it to me, sweetheart," I say. "Give it all to me." Give me a life with you, and I promise I'll make it all good.

"Oh. God. Bull." She stutters through her orgasm, breathless as it hits her. She doesn't scream so much as open her mouth wide and ride out the sensation. In an instant, I'm filling her, going off like summer fireworks inside her. She holds still while I pulse within her, giving her my all.

When I'm finally replete and emptied of all that I have, I reach up for the back of her head and pull her down to me. Finding her mouth, I kiss her hard, pouring the rest of me into that kiss.

Be mine forever.

They're words I can't say, though I think them all the time. She will be mine as we parent together, but it's not going to be enough.

"God, I've missed you," I admit to her mouth still over mine. It's been less than two days, and I missed her in my bed and in my arms. I missed how easily we worked together seamlessly as though she's been here my entire life.

"I've missed you too, honey." No words sounded sweeter, but I don't want her to miss me. I want her to know I'm here with her on every day that ends in day and all the nights as well. "I'm not going anywhere, Scarlett. Thanks for rushing in with me," I say.

"Happy to oblige anytime, partner," she teases, drawing us back to that first night when she called me that. Her head tips to the side, her cheek pressing over my heart, and a fingertip draws over my chest as I wonder if she'll ever call me something else— like husband perhaps.

19

ACTIONS SPEAK THE LOUDEST

SCARLETT

Three days later, Bull squeezes my hand as the amniocentesis procedure is done. For those few days, we've been shy around one another, still feeling a tenderness from the tension once around us. At night, though, we find our way back together in Bull's bed.

"The doctor will call you with the results," the technician says. Bull already swabbed his cheek and sent it to the necessary labs. My doctor explained how things would work with the baby's sample.

"You might experience some cramping or light spotting, but that's normal. Any concerns should be addressed with your doctor." I've been fortunate so far in my pregnancy. Other than the swelling of my hands and feet, which dissipates typically once I lie down and lift my legs for a bit, I've found the pregnancy easy. At least compared to the horror stories I've read about geriatric pregnancies. The label still makes my blood boil.

"Shouldn't be more than a week." The technician continues to discuss the lab results. "But normally, it only takes about three days."

As the technician cleans off the instruments, Bull helps me sit upright.

"Let's get lunch," he offers. "And how about some retail therapy?" He wiggles his brows. Bull thanked me for the flowers on the porch, telling me the decorations made the place look welcoming, which was exactly what I wanted.

Once I'm dressed, I find Bull waiting for me outside the room. As we're in Montpelier, and it's a beautiful summer day, we find a place to park and stroll around the area. My hunger is always bigger than my stomach can handle, but a turkey club calls my name. I've been told to watch my diet, especially as I'm at risk of gestational diabetes, which could result in permanent diabetes at my age.

At my age. Always my age.

I'm feeling strangely positive about the future results of both the genetics test and the paternity test, and I'm excited to finally know the elephant in the room will have an answer. As we stroll through town on our way to a diner, a baby store looms ahead of us. When we near the shop, it hits me again.

I'm having a baby. At my age.

"Should we go inside?" Bull asks. Staring at the display window, I note the little clothing intended for a miniature human. I'm due in the winter, so the summery outfits aren't appropriate for my newborn once he or she arrives. Still, everything is so tiny.

"Okay," I whisper, beginning to sweat from the reality of what's ahead for me. I'm going to be responsible for a little person, and I really don't want to screw this up. Will I be nurturing and open-minded? Will I be able to take care of someone other than myself? Can I give unconditionally when I'm sleep deprived, leaking from my breasts, and still overweight a little bit? These are all things I've read about happening to new mothers. Sleepless nights. Days without showers. Breast leaks. Sore nipples. Stretch marks. Weight retention. The list goes on and on.

Entering the store, I find it's a sensory overload of cribs, baby apparatus, and doll-size clothing. Bull looks out of place as he squeezes his large body through the displays.

Eventually, he stops next to a white crib near the back. "We should make some decisions because I want to start working on the nursery." Bull's already mentioned turning his upstairs office into the baby's room. We've discussed neutral colors and baby bedding, but staring at a beautiful white crib puts things into perspective. Soon, it's not going to be just Bull and me.

"Scarlett?" I hear Bull's voice, but my eyes roam the displays around us. The responsibility to feed, clothe, bathe and love a little person overwhelms me. Diapers and changings. Breast pumps, bottles, and baby bibs. Mini-bathtubs and baby-safe soap. How will I keep my child safe from things that aren't material, like people gossiping about him? Protecting him from a bully? The possibility of someone hurting him?

My heart races at all the things I'll never be able to control and scare the ever-living crap out of me.

"Sweetheart?" Instantly, firm arms surround me, pressing me into his chest, and my cheek rests near his heartbeat. "Are you feeling okay?"

"I'm going to be a mother," I say, my voice no more than a croak. A firm palm strokes up and down my spine.

"Yes, you are," he proudly states, calmly as can be while his heart beats rhythmically under my ear.

"I'm going to have stretch marks and sagging breasts. I'm going to lack sleep and smell like dirty laundry. I'm going to feed my baby, from those sagging breasts, like a cow." My voice rises, but Bull only chuckles, the vibration rumbling against my cheek.

"It isn't funny," I snap, but Bull continues to stroke my back. "I don't know what I'm doing. I'm not going to know what he wants when he cries or how to breastfeed. I've never changed a diaper in my life, and I don't know anything about developmental milestones, or teething, or feeding. Then he's going to grow up. He's going to go to school where other kids can be cruel, and he's going to fall in love with a woman who might hurt him, and no one is going to love him as much as me and . . ."

"Scarlett, sweetheart. Slow down." He holds me tighter in his arms. "Breathe." His chest rises and falls, taking a deep breath and exhaling slowly. "Follow me, sweetheart. Breathe."

As my heart hammers away, I try to do as he says. Closing my eyes to the overload of baby things around us, I follow his lead.

Inhale. *Exhale*.

Inhale. *Exhale*.

"It's going to be okay. You're going to be great, and we're going to do everything together."

Together. How strange will it be to share this experience? Even when I was with Shelton, we were two separate entities. He was the doctor. I was the reporter. We crossed paths but easily went in separate directions to further our personal drive and strengthen our careers. We did not come together.

Yet here is Bull. He held my hand when I told him about the pregnancy and the possibility it might not be his child, and he still wants the baby and me. He had me move into his home, and he's provided safety, comfort, and a loving bed. In his own way, I believe he loves me. Maybe he can't say the words. Maybe he doesn't think he needs them or believes in them, but everything about Bull Eaton says he's a man who loves, and loves deeply, and the way he does it is with action and deed.

"Keep breathing with me," he says, drawing me back to him. He settles my racing heart, easing my concerns. I need him, and it hits me. He's that someone I didn't know I needed in my life until he's standing here, holding me in a baby store while I go into panic mode about my future. He's going to be the rock I lean on, and I can only hope my need for him feeds his need to be needed.

Because that's what Bull wants most. He needs to know someone will stay with him, stand by his side and want his support, and as I told him the other night, that someone is me. I meant it all metaphorically the other evening. I said it to stand my ground and stand up for him, but I really feel it. At this moment. In this store. In his arms.

I need Bull more than I've needed anyone in my life, and I'm okay with that feeling. I'd like to tell him I love him. I'd like for him to tell me he feels the same way about me, but I've lived with those false words from a husband who cheated on me and parents who didn't believe in me.

I won't be that kind of parent. I won't be that kind of wife . . . or lover . . . or whatever Bull wants to call me.

Squeezing him in return, I whisper, "Thank you."

He chuckles softly against me. "For what, sweetheart?"

"For you being you. For all you do for Sprout and me, and all I know you're going to be to both of us."

A kiss comes to the top of my head, and I want to look up at him. I want to return that kiss, but I can't let go of him. Not yet. The backs of my eyes prickle, and I'm afraid if I glance up at those midnight eyes, I'll break. Right here in the store, I'll cry like a baby and tell him how much I love him. How much I appreciate him and need him by my side.

"I think you're you, too, baby," he whispers to my hair. "And I really like that about you."

He's so sweet. I don't exactly know what he likes about me, but he's still so sweet.

"Hi there. Is there something I can help you with?" a salesclerk greets us, and Bull's head pops off mine. Still, he keeps me tucked into his chest.

"Can I answer any questions for you and your wife?" The salesclerk has a soft voice and glancing over at her, I see her smiling as she addresses Bull. I pull back, ready to correct her on our status, but Bull tucks me back to his chest.

"We're interested in this one," he says. "And do you have any bedding with little yellow ducks on it?"

This time, my head leans away from his chest, and he peers down at me.

"Yellow ducks?" I question.

"Isn't that the one you were looking at on the internet with Rita?"

My mind blanks for a minute, and I want to blame pregnancy brain until I recall the first time Bull heard I was pregnant. When he came into the Busy Bean Café, and he *overheard* me mentioning it to Rita while we scanned baby products on the internet.

"That's correct," I say, surprised at his memory. Bull leans forward, pressing a quick kiss to my lips before pulling away and addressing the salesclerk.

"Then baby ducks, please." Baby ducks and a burly cowboy. *When did my life get so complete?*

20

PARENTAL DISAPPROVAL

SCARLETT

My mother calls the day after my freak-out in the baby store, and because I'm riding a strange new high of emotion for Bull, I answer my phone. Bull's gone to the dairy barn while I'm on my way to a maternity clothing store in Burlington, a little over an hour from Dunham. While I'm only slightly starting to show, I'm curious about maternity wear and think I might need some more stretchy materials soon.

"Scarlett Joanna Russell, where are you?" There isn't any concern in her tone but a screeching demand to know my location as her voice filters through the Bluetooth. "It's been almost five months since we've seen you."

While I'm used to visiting with my parents once a month for a torturous lunch date, I've missed the last few due to my move to Vermont, which I find I must remind my mother of.

"I'm in Vermont," I state.

"Still?" Her shrill voice doesn't surprise me, but what does bother me is the fact she cannot believe I'm still where I told her I'd be. "What about Shelton?"

"What about him?" I snap in response.

"He's your husband, Scarlett. When are you coming home?"

"Mother, we're getting divorced."

Her gasp tells me she wasn't listening to me when I told her I'd be filing such a thing months ago. As I travel the highway through the countryside, I ignore the subtle hardening of my belly or the pain shooting up my spine. The technician said these things were normal.

"What do you mean you're getting divorced?" my mother questions.

"I can't believe I need to spell this out for you. Shelton cheated on me. I've already told you this. He slept with a medical student. He got her pregnant, and he plans to marry her. Which he can't do unless he divorces me."

"What's this talk about divorce?" my father projects next through the line.

"Dad," I groan, gritting my teeth through another tightening across my belly.

"Scarlett, you need to come home."

Considering his words, I realize Boston is no longer my home. My home is here in Vermont, with Bull, with our future.

"Dad, I am home."

"At your apartment?" Mother asks, and I realize I'm on speakerphone with them.

"No. My new home in Vermont."

"You're living there?" she shrieks again. I'm forty-two years old, and I do not understand what is so difficult for them to understand about this concept. I've moved. I'm getting divorced. And there's one more thing I haven't mentioned to them.

"Oh, and congratulations. You're going to be grandparents." I smile to myself, chewing my lip as I tell them the news. It's the first time I've really broken the information to others. Audrey and Zara found out through my initial vomiting at work and Bull blurted it out with his brothers, so this feels different.

"You're what?" The shock in my mother's tone shouldn't surprise me, yet it hurts. This is what they wanted. She told me I should have had a child. She told me I worked too hard. Although, those things were in reference to my life with Shelton.

"Strawberry, you must come home." My father's use of my childhood nickname pierces my heart. They were tough parents to please, tough parents to love, but they were the only parents I had. I wanted their approval. I wanted their love, but most of all, I wanted their support. "You and Shelton need to be together so he can take care of you."

"Dad, he left me for another woman. He impregnated her."

"Pfft. You're his wife. He needs to be with his child," Dad states, and I couldn't agree more—if I was to remain his wife, if he was the father of my child, and if I wanted him. But none of those things are true.

"I'm not going to be his wife much longer. And it's not his child," I tell them because I've made a decision about that paternity test. Despite its results, it won't matter. Bull is the man for me and our child.

"Did you have an affair?" Mother gasps. *Is she listening to herself? Does she hear what she's asking me?*

"No, Shelton did."

The other end of the line is silent for a second.

"Scarlett, first it was journalism school where you ended up working for that rag of a company for too many years. Then it was Shelton who you could not keep satisfied." My mouth falls open at this remark from my father. "But this . . . this is just incomprehensible. How could you do such a thing? You're a married woman."

Not for much longer, I want to remind them again, but it's like banging my head on this steering wheel my hands have white-knuckled. It's not going to make the car move faster, or the reality of my situation seep into their brains any better. And it's definitely not going to make them more sympathetic.

"Mother, Dad. I'm not in love with Shelton. I'm in love with—"

"Love," my mother trills again. "What does love have to do

with anything? Come home, Scarlett. You can go to marriage counseling and rectify what you've done with your husband."

I'm so angry I can't find the tears I should be crying over their accusations and their disappointment, but with the pain shooting up my spine and the trickle of something between my thighs, I've had enough.

"I'm sorry you can't listen to me. I'm sorry you can't hear what I'm saying, and I'm sorry you'll miss out on a grandchild. I'm your daughter." I feel the need to remind them.

"But Shel—"

"Goodbye, Mother. Dad."

I'm not exactly certain where I am, but I pull to the side of the road and rest my head against the steering wheel. Rubbing a hand at the left side of my belly, I grit my teeth against the pain. I'm so angry I can hardly breathe, and again, I wait for tears that do not appear for them—my parents. I'm forty-two years old, and I've just had the epiphany of a lifetime. I'll never be who they want. I'll never conform to their desires for me. And they'll never know the incredible gift I'm about to bring into the world because I don't need that kind of toxicity around my child.

"Come on, Sprout. Be good for Mommy." At my words spoken aloud, along with the future label, I burst into tears for an entirely different reason. Something is wrong. Something is very wrong.

With shaky fingers, I dial Bull's number, waiting for it to ring through the Bluetooth. My belly contracts again *hard*, and I let out a hissing groan as Bull answers his phone. Before he speaks, I do.

"Oh God, Bull. It hurts so much."

21

BATHWATER CONFESSIONS

BULL

"Scarlett, where are you?"

The agonizing sound in her voice rips me in two as I stand outside the dairy barn. She should have stayed home to rest, but she was so persuasive, kissing me one more time every step to the door before I left this morning. She had the day off, and I'd have liked nothing more than to crawl back into bed with her, but the cows called.

Just going to do some personal retail therapy today. I didn't question what that meant as she distracted me with cock-hardening kisses.

"I'm somewhere outside Burlington." Her voice strains as the sound of her teeth gnashing fills the phone.

"Burlington?" I hiss. My heart races as Blade steps outside.

"What's wrong?" he mouths, but I shake my head, swiping fingers into my hair. She's almost an hour away.

"Scarlett?" Her sudden silence unnerves me.

"It really hurts, Bull." Tears fill her voice.

"Sweetheart, please. Get to a hospital or an urgent care. Drop a pin on your phone, and I'll find you. I'm on my way." With the location finder, I should be able to track where she's at as I'm already jogging to my truck. Stepping into it, I start the engine, and the phone clicks over to Bluetooth for hands-free driving.

"Sweetheart? Honey, talk to me. Tell me what happened." As Scarlett explains the situation with her parents, irritation fills her voice, and the rising anger concerns me. I can hear her gritting her teeth through the pain.

"Never mind. Don't think about them. Get to the urgent care." I can't search my phone to help her find a location near her while I'm driving, so I pull over for a minute. Finally giving her an address, I demand she go there and pull back on the road. "Just stay on the line with me until you arrive at the medical center. We don't need to talk."

As I drive too fast down the backroads, I will myself not to think the thoughts wanting time in my head. I will not allow my thoughts to go to the negative place where dreams are lost.

"You're going to be okay," I assure her as she grunts again. "You're the strongest woman I've ever known."

Scarlett hisses, and I hear a blinker through the phone.

"I'm here," she whimpers, indicating the immediate care facility. The pain in her voice is so raw my insides split, and I continue my white-knuckle driving.

"I'm on my way, sweetheart."

When the line goes dead, everything in me seems to shatter, and I holler at the empty road before me, sending up a prayer for all to be well in the end.

Arriving in the small town just outside Burlington in under forty minutes, I find Scarlett resting in a room, hooked up to an IV.

"Sweetheart, I'm here," I quietly tell her, swiping a hand over her head once I reach the side of the bed.

"Bull, you really came for me." The doubt in her voice almost shatters me again, and I see her release a long breath as if she'd been holding it the entire time she'd been here. She curls toward me, and a sob escapes her. I wrap my arms over her as best as I can without knocking the IV line.

"Shh," I attempt to soothe her as her body shakes and her quiet sobs rattle underneath me. "Tell me you're okay. Tell me everything." *Tell me Sprout is still well inside you.*

"The doctor said it was dehydration. Along with the previous day's procedure and the stress of what happened with my parents, I had false contractions."

"And Sprout?" I swallow around the question.

"He's fine. He'll be happier once this fills my system." She glances up at the bag hanging beside her. Her eyes are red-rimmed, and her cheeks, void of color, are stained with tears. Continuing to stroke over her hair, I brush it off her forehead.

"Where were you going in Burlington?"

"I wanted to look for maternity clothes." Her eyes still glisten.

"Sweetheart, I don't want you going anywhere without me."

"I'm fine now. Better even. It was just a little stress and too little fluids." I want to address the stress part but decide it can wait. Cupping her hand with both of mine, I pull it up to my lips, close my eyes, and set my mouth against her knuckles. My heart still hammers inside my chest. I swear I might need the bed next for the heart attack she's given me.

"We're getting a hotel for the night," I tell her. "No argument." We'll leave her car here overnight, and I'll return tomorrow with one of my brothers once I have Scarlett home. Home. In my house. Where she belongs.

Quietly, we wait out the drip and her discharge with strict orders for rest the remainder of the day. The urgent care doctor will pass along what happened to Scarlett's regular doctor, where she'll need a follow-up in a few days.

After her discharge, we stop at a pharmacy where I run in to buy basic necessities, a random assortment of snacks, and a package of underwear at Scarlett's request. Finding a quaint bed and breakfast, I'm grateful for the midweek vacancy.

Leading Scarlett up the creaking stairs of the older inn, I can't take my hands off her.

"I'm not an invalid," she admonishes, but I'm not letting her go.

"You're following my orders now, sweetheart."

"And suddenly, you're a doctor?" she teases.

"Yes, and I'm not past examining every inch of you once you're better."

"I'm fine." She sighs. "Just worked up."

"We're going to unwork you."

The antiquated room with a four-poster bed and an old fireplace appears to please Scarlett. She climbs up on the bed while I drop the bags with our measly wares on a rocking chair in the corner.

"How about a bath?" I can't seem to sit still and need something for my hands to do. Before she even answers, I'm entering the bathroom and filling a large clawfoot tub. Next, I return to the bedroom to help Scarlett undress despite her protests.

"Scarlett, dammit. Let me take care of you." I need to do something as I've been coming out of my skin the past couple of hours. Sensing the strain in my voice and my nearness to breaking, she sits back as I remove her sandals and massage each foot a second. Guiding her to stand, I slip her dress upward and marvel at the swell of her belly, which is more apparent when she's naked before me. Her hand coasts over the bulge, and mine meets hers.

"Any movement?" I hold my breath.

"I think Sprout's resting. He's had a workout this morning." Her weak voice does nothing to settle my concerns. In her bra and underwear, I lead her to the bathroom and then remove the final pieces exposing her larger breasts and a soft patch of curls at the top of her legs. The changes to her body only increase my attraction to her, and I'm grateful there's more change to come. She's beautiful while pregnant.

Helping her into the tub, I hang onto her as she lowers into the steamy water. I'm still unsettled, but Scarlett calmly sits upright, swishing her hands back and forth through the warm liquid.

"Bull, I know I'm getting bigger, but do you think you could join me?" Her dark eyes plead with me, and I read the fear of her thoughts equal to mine. It's going to be a tight fit in that tub, but I tug my shirt over my head.

"Anything for you, sweetheart." Quickly, I strip the remainder of my clothes and wedge myself behind her. I warn my body to behave as Scarlett does not need to be worked up in any way. As we melt into the warmth of the water, she leans back against my chest, and I massage her shoulders.

"I want you to tell me everything, but only if you can stay calm about it."

Scarlett begins her story of the upsetting phone call, and I find I'm the one struggling to remain quiet. Silently, I seethe. Her parents have unbelievable balls. The betrayal from the people who should have loved her unconditionally is incomprehensible, and I'm disappointed in the couple I've never met. A couple who will be my child's grandparents. For a moment, I'm grateful once again for the parents I had. While I know their marriage wasn't perfect, it was pretty close, and they were amazing role models. For all the trouble I'd been and put them through with my relationships, they never judged me. Their support meant everything to me over the years.

"I'm forty-two years old, and they can reduce me to a fourteen-year-old child in a heartbeat. I feel like I've been caught stealing or kissing."

"As long as you're stealing kisses from me, I don't care what age you are. Nor do I care what they think of me. What they did to you is wrong, Scarlett. You see that, right? You didn't do anything wrong."

I don't like that they accused Scarlett of having an affair or even the hint of nefarious relations with me. While I can't say Sprout was conceived in love, he was definitely conceived by two people who want each other, who care for one another, and who will be here for him every step of the way.

Scarlett shifts, struggling to twist a bit in the tub between my thighs and her changing shape.

"Bull, honey, why are you so good to me?" Her hand cups my jaw. "You say the right things, and you came for me today."

Because I love you.

"Anything you asked, I'd do for you, Scarlett. I care about you, and I care about our baby." My hand covers her belly, waiting on a little kick to let me know things are okay in there. While technically she didn't ask me to come to her today, I'd never let her suffer as I felt she was earlier. I'll always be there for her and the baby.

"Thank you for today. And all the other days ending in day that you do things for me." Her sincerity stirs my insides as her thumb swipes along my jaw.

"Sweetheart, I don't want to tell you what you can or cannot do with your parents, but you've got to let go of your feelings about them right now. Especially how easily they upset you." I can't believe these people don't see the incredible woman sitting before me. Well, I wouldn't want them to see her now, naked, but why don't they see her beauty, her kindness, and her determination. And I'm especially concerned that they aren't accepting of the gift she's going to give them. My dad is thrilled to be a grandfather again. I'm the one who should be thanking Scarlett for all she gives to me.

"I learned a valuable lesson about my parents today. No matter how much I want their approval, I will never have it." Her head drops, and her hand lowers for my chest. I quickly pick it up and press a kiss to her palm.

"I understand they are your parents, and you might want to please them, but you don't need them, Scarlett. My family adores you, and I swear they'll love Sprout."

"I don't want to be a parent like them," she sadly states, and I sense her doubts similar to her meltdown in the baby store.

Tipping up her chin so she looks at me, I assure her, "You won't." I have every bit of confidence she's going to love Sprout, and any other child she might bear, wholeheartedly. Reaching up for her cheek, I lean down for a quick kiss. As I pull back, Scarlett follows me, latching back onto my lips and kissing me back more insistently.

"Easy, girl." I chuckle against her mouth, anxious by her urgency. Ignoring me, she shifts to her knees and returns to my mouth, hungry for me. Her tongue hesitantly comes forward, drawing mine against hers while her hands cup both my cheeks. I'm trying to be good, telling my body to be still, but my dick has a mind of its own, reacting to her between my thighs.

"I can't get close enough." She giggles, and my hands coast up and down her back while she straddles me, adding to the sweet torture of her nearness.

"Sweetheart, you cannot sit on me like this right now. You have to move off me."

Leaning forward, she teases me as the center of her rests over my stiff length. "I want to move on you."

"We are not fooling around. You just had a scare that scared the hell out of me. I don't want to hurt you."

"You won't hurt me. I just need to be close to you." Her voice softens, and dammit, I can't turn her down.

She leans forward to kiss me again. At first, her lips are slow and soft, drawing my lips into hers. Her hips rock in a tantalizing dance over my lap, stroking her folds along the length of my thick shaft. I'm instantly hard for her. Her tongue swipes at the seam of my lips, and I can't hold back. My palm flattens on her back, and my tongue surges forward to meet hers. The kiss turns more intense once again.

"Slow," she murmurs against my mouth.

Giving in to her command, I follow her lead as she returns to kissing me tender and sweet while she rocks with lazy drags over my stiff length. Her pussy coasts over my dick, stroking me with her lower folds while the water in the tub sloshes around us. Her hands clutch my shoulders as her eyes close and her head tips back, losing herself to the slow rhythm she's working over my body. My hands rub up and down her lower back. I love watching her. She's lost in her head, but that head is filled with me and this moment.

I want to be all of her moments. I want her heart full of me, too. Leaning forward, I press a kiss just above her left breast. Then I drag my tongue down the swell and circle the nipple before opening my mouth to suck at the heavy globe. Her tits are amazing, and I hungrily lap at the one. My eyes glance up at hers as I twirl my tongue around the spreading areola and over the peaked nipple. She slowly smiles without opening her eyes, and I move to the other breast, giving it equal attention.

As I lean back, her eyes open, her dance unbroken.

"I want you inside me," she whispers. Our eyes hold, and my thoughts whisper how I want nothing more. I want to be inside her body and soul. I want to live in her heart. *Please don't break mine.* The fear feels unwarranted in this position but also overwhelming. I try not to consider I might have lost Sprout today. I could have lost her. It's extreme but not without reason. She is older and pregnant, but these are thoughts I try not to dwell on.

"I don't want the baby to get worked up."

"The baby likes orgasms," she says, and I softly chuckle.

Reaching between us, she tilts up on her knees and positions my tip at her entrance. With my hands on her hips and hers moving to the edge of the tub for balance, she lowers, taking her sweet time to draw me into her heat. Then she moves in a way that her breath catches.

"Am I hurting you?"

"Never," she whispers, her eyes full of lusty pleasure before her lids lazily close a second. "You feel incredible." Her hips rock, rubbing her clit in a way so it hits my pubic bone, giving her the friction she desires.

My name hitches on her lips as she moves quicker, and I tap into her, thrusting my hips upward just the slightest bit. Her mouth gapes open. Her head tips forward. She's a goddess over me.

"Look at me," I demand. I want to look in her eyes when she falls apart, when she releases everything over me buried deep inside her body. The water rocks in the tub as we move, but we can flood this room for all I care. I don't want her looking away from me, seeing me when she comes undone

"Bull, I love . . . being with you." Her hesitation gave me hope she would say something else, and I lean forward to take her mouth until her kissing rhythm becomes sporadic. I swallow back imaginary words. Words she didn't say, but I feel from her. There's no way she doesn't love me in some manner. We can't be this connected without it. It can't feel so strong, so right, but I've been wrong before.

Falling back against the tub, I watch her move until she stills, holding herself down as I fill her to the hilt. I marvel at her, attached to me, over me, swallowing me into her as she comes undone. Overwhelmed by a mix of emotion and intense physical connection, I go off myself, giving her every part of me. Take my seed, my soul, my everything.

Bone tired and completely drained, it's as if all the blood has been sucked out of my body.

"Let's get out," I suggest as the coldness of the water seeps into my weary body. Keeping my hands on her, I help her stand and then rise myself. I'm worried she'll slip and fall in the large tub, so I don't stop touching her. Once we step out, I quickly reach for a towel, wrapping it around my waist as Scarlet reaches for one for herself, but I take it from her.

"Bull," she groans as I wrap it around her, working the material over her body to dry her.

"Just let me pamper you for a little longer." I swipe at the water droplets along her shoulders and down her arms, taking extra care between her thighs and around her legs. Her eyes follow my every motion. Once I'm satisfied she's dry, I secure the towel at her breasts as best it will fit and lead her to the bedroom. Scarlett climbs up on the bed.

"You know it was torture living with you at first when you walked around in only a towel." Her sated eyes scan over my chest and down to the towel tucked at my waist.

"I have no idea what you're talking about," I tease, standing to my full height and holding my position as she admires my body once more.

"It must have been an adjustment for you as well having me live in your house," she questions, her voice dropping a bit.

"Every day was hell." I teasingly chuckle. "But I think you're what that house was missing." *What I was missing.* "Just because you're you."

Scarlett catches my eyes and gives me a sheepish smile. "Yeah, I think you're you, too."

"Snacks?" I offer, pointing at the bag on the chair.

She shakes her head. "I'm tired, but we don't have a change of clothes."

"We don't need clothes," I tell her, tugging my towel free and allowing it to drop to the floor. Her mouth falls open a second, and a gleam fills her eyes again, but I give her a warning glare. "You need to rest. Let's nap. Then I'll find us a meal. We have the rest of the day and night to just chill."

"The rest of our lives actually," she says, wiggling out of her towel, and I find myself just as hungry for her once again.

"What do you mean?" I watch as she tosses her towel to meet mine and tucks her legs under the covers. She's sitting upright with her swollen breasts on display. Her belly enhances in her seated position. Impending motherhood agrees with her so much.

"No matter what those results say, Bull. You're Sprout's dad *and* his father."

"Scarlett," I whisper.

"I don't care what we learn. If the results say otherwise, something opposite of what I hope, we can tell Sprout someday. Some other time. But this is ours no matter what." The fierceness in her voice makes her statement definitive. She chooses me, no matter what. Her hand glides over her belly in a loving caress, and I crawl up the bed, peppering kisses over the growing bulge. Her fingers move to my hair as my mouth meets her skin on repeat.

"Thank you. Thank you so much, sweetheart." I can hardly contain the happiness welling inside me. "I promise I'll do everything I can to make you happy."

"I already am," she whispers, and everything in her eyes tells me the truth. She's right where she belongs, with me before her. Dragging her down to her side, I lay beside her body to kiss her before we curl into one another and take a much-needed nap.

22

ALMOND MILK AND FULL MOONS

BULL

"She feeling okay?" Canyon asks after I explained what happened the other day to Scarlett on her trip to Burlington. His concern for my girl is a reminder I have something he wished he'd had—the experience of his child before Joey was born. I'm grateful Scarlett is giving me this chance. I'm grateful to be a future father.

We're at the main house for dinner. It's been a bumpy number of days for Scarlett and me, and I'm happy to be sitting down to a meal and hope for some normalcy. Dinner is ready, and the dining room fills. After the family takes their place at the table, Dad addresses Joey.

"Joey, perhaps you'd like to—"

"Harland, if I may, I'd like to say grace tonight." Scarlett's already told me she isn't religious even though she was raised Catholic. I've not known her to pray for anything, so her offer surprises me as well as the others.

"Okay, darlin'." Dad nods.

"Thank you for this wonderful meal before us and for bringing this family into my life. I'm undeserving of their devotion but grateful for their forgiveness," Scarlett says, pleased with herself. I reach for her hand, giving it a squeeze.

Plates are passed, and the pork chops are served.

"I think it's time we initiate Scarlett into the family. We need to find her something to do around here," Dad teases, winking at her. It's been suggested she help Carly, but never be put in charge of cooking a meal.

"She could milk the almonds," Blade says straight-faced, and I chuckle.

"You produce almonds here?" Scarlett asks, looking around the table.

"We don't grow almonds," I state, shaking my head.

"She has tiny fingers and could easily squeeze them," Blade continues, pinching his thumb and forefingers together and then tugging at the air to imitate the impossible. "*Eek-eek. Eek-eek.*" His noise matches the exaggerated drip of almond milk coming from imaginary almonds.

"Would you stop it?" I chuckle. Teasing her means they accept her, but after the stunt she pulled before Redd Bottom at the Goat, I'd hope so. Scarlett really put on a show for me, for us, proving her skill at reporting false news as acting. However, nothing was false in her actions, and the fierceness of her words later in the parking lot told me it wasn't an act. Her spending nights in my bed—*our bed*—proves that Scarlett does care for me. She's sticking around like she said.

"Is that how you get almond milk out of almonds?" Scarlett holds her face perfectly still, and for a second, I think she's serious. Hopefully, it's another sign of her acting ability.

"You don't milk almonds," Joey interjects, rolling her eyes like Scarlett cannot possibly be that gullible.

"Bet Bull has something you could milk," Blade mutters.

"What the—?" I cut myself short because of Joey's presence at the table but narrow my eyes at my youngest brother as he lifts his glass of milk to disguise his smile.

"What's he mean?" Joey asks. Blade snorts, forcing milk

within his glass to ripple around the edge. He's such a child sometimes.

"Nothing," Canyon, Carly, and I say collectively.

"I know where milk comes from on a woman. Is Uncle Bull going to have to milk you?" Joey glances over at Scarlett. Horrified, she then gazes down at herself. Canyon closes his eyes, and Blade stares at our niece.

"Oh God," Joey mutters, covering her small chest with crossed arms like a giant X. "May I be excused?"

"Please," Blade mutters, almost begging Joey to leave the room.

"You started this," I warn him as Canyon tells Joey she needs to eat her dinner, but she's already slipping from the table.

"You all scarred her for life," Carly warns, dismissing herself to follow Joey. Once the girls are gone, I reach over and smack Blade on the back of the head.

"What? Was the almond milk too much?" he teases, mocking himself with a hand on his chest.

"No wonder you're alone," Canyon mutters, shaking his head.

"I'm sorry about that," I say to Scarlett whose face remains pink.

"She thinks I'm a cow, doesn't she?" Scarlett's lower lip trembles. Knowing how sensitive she is to the comparison, she's still so cute. I can't help myself and lean over the table, cup the back of her neck, and tug her toward me for a quick kiss.

"If you two are gonna be like this at the table, I want to be excused now," Blade teases. Ignoring him, I keep my hand on Scarlett another second.

"You aren't a cow, sweetheart." Our foreheads meet before I release her and sit back. "She could have compared you to an almond."

Scarlett's mouth falls open before she giggles, and I look up, meeting the eyes of my dad at the opposite end of the table. He stares back at me with a knowing look in his eyes.

"A certain someone," he mutters, and I peer sideways at Scarlett.

A certain someone makes forgiveness and love worthwhile.

Four nights later, the sky is a deep blue color, not quite dark but illuminated by a beautiful moon. It's a giant yellow-orange ball hanging low in the sky and reflecting the Earth's surface.

"It's so beautiful," Scarlett says from behind me. I hadn't heard her approach as I stand just off the edge of the patio outside the dining room. The temperature is cool this evening despite the earlier heat of the day, and she wears a blanket draped over her shoulders. Slipping up behind me, she wraps her arms around my waist and kisses my shoulder blade. For a second, she rests her head on my back before pulling away. "What are you doing out here?"

I glance up at the bright lunar circle. "Just . . . thinking." I can't really define what I've been thinking other than staring off at that moon and letting my thoughts wander. An itch under my skin warns me the ball will drop, the other shoe will fall, and all that feels good in my life will disappear. I'm not a pessimist, but everything feels too good to be true.

Scarlett is in my home, in my bed, and in my heart. Like that glowing moon, she's warmth inside me I don't think I've ever felt, despite a young marriage, a broken engagement, and a reckless relationship in the past. None of those women compare to Scarlett. She's just like that vibrant moon in a distinct shade of orange-yellow, brightening my life even when I have dark thoughts.

"Bull Eaton, tell me what's on your mind."

She slips up to my side, staring up at me as if she's been speaking, and I haven't heard her.

"Wanna take a walk?" I ask, and Scarlett nods.

"A moonlight stroll," she teases, slipping her hand into mine.

We walk across the field behind the house. It's not used for grazing or planting as this half-acre is all mine.

As we near the edge of the property with a wooded strip, Scarlett points up at the trees. "Is that a fort?"

Glancing off to where she points, I find the old platform my grandfather built for us boys when we were young. We'd come down the lane from the main house and steal off to this spot that belonged to our father. It's been reinforced over the years but left as is for too long. Joey came along too late to want a fort, and as she had trouble adjusting to farm life at first, the last thing she wanted was a fort in the trees.

"It is," I admit. Scarlett leads us in the direction of the old structure. Releasing my hand, she walks hastily to the tree's trunk and places her foot on the bottom rung of wood that makes a ladder up the tree.

"Hold on there, pregnant lady. We won't be climbing any trees in your condition." I catch up to her and wrap my arms around her, tugging her back to my chest.

"I just wanted to see if we could see the moon better up there," she says.

"The moon will keep rising, and it's going to shift, growing smaller as it climbs in the sky. We'll be able to watch it just fine with our feet on the ground."

"I don't think I've ever watched the moon," she says, and I tip my head, so she looks up at me over her shoulder.

"No stargazing?"

"It's kind of difficult to see the stars under city lights." It's a reminder that Scarlett comes from a different world than me.

"Do you miss it?"

"The city?" she questions immediately but shakes her head. "I like Vermont."

"Well, Vermont likes you," I tease but feel incomplete with her answer. *Is living here enough for her?*

"Mmm," she purrs, tipping her head back and glancing up over the trees again. I lead us back to a more open spot in the field but keep my arms around her. We stand in an embrace, chest to chest, with our heads tipped upward.

"I've always felt the moon gets a bad rap. Like when something happens, people always say, *is it a full moon or something?* As if something that beautiful caused all the trouble in the world."

"But a moon does cause things to happen like tides," she reminds me.

"And births," I add.

"What?" She looks up at me, and I explain.

"A few years ago, there was a study about cows and how full moons seemed to trigger birthing. Humans were also a part of that study."

"Goodness. The comparison to cows never ceases," she teases, tipping her head back again, looking up at the sky and the moon behind her. Her neck elongates, and I lean forward, sipping at her throat, running my tongue along her neck, and nipping at her chin before pulling back.

"Hmm," she purrs again, slowly bringing her face back to me. "Full moons also bring out the wolf, right? Or is it that they encourage vampires to bite?" Her eyes sparkle despite their dark color.

"Can't say I know much about vampires, but wolves don't really howl at a full moon specifically. They just howl. It's a mating call or a warning sign."

"Mating?" she teases, giving me a goofy grin. "Ow-ow-*owul*."

"Scarlett." I laugh. "You're crazy."

"For you," she says, and I smile to match hers before leaning forward to kiss her, long and deep. She makes me want to howl at the moon, beat my chest, and scream to the heavens: *let her love me.*

As I pull away from her, she steps out of my embrace and lays the blanket on the grass. "Let's sit, and you can tell me more about the moon." Her smile reads mischievous, but I follow her down as we lay on our backs. Scarlett shifts to her side a little, taking the pressure off her spine, and places my hand over her belly. Sprout rolls around inside her.

"Hope he's not getting any ideas to come early."

My head turns, catching her eyes. "You're still feeling okay, right?" I don't want anything to happen to the baby, but I also don't want anything to happen to her. I hate to feel as if I'm prioritizing, but if she lost the baby now, I'd give her another one. We'd try again. I won't quit on her like I felt I quit on Jen. We'd just start over.

A sense of losing Scarlett when we were miles apart while she was suffering near Burlington and I was on my way to her really put things in perspective for me. I will do nothing that might risk losing her. I will not jinx what we have by proposing or asking for more. I don't want us to lose where we're at or where we're going. I will keep my emotions in check in order to keep her by my side.

"So tell me more, moon-master," she teases, interrupting my thoughts.

"Well, the word month comes from the term moon because of its phases lasting almost thirty days. Each month has a specific full moon name, did you know that?"

"I didn't," she admits, turning her head from mine to gaze up at the sky again. "So what moon is this one?"

"It's late July, so this is the Buck Moon. It was termed by Native Americans for male deer who begin to regrow their antlers at this time. Sometimes, it's also called the Hay Moon because it occurs around hay harvesting or a Thunder Moon because of all the thunderstorms that can occur in the summer heat."

"That's so interesting," she says, still staring up at the sky as it turns darker as a backdrop to the yellow circle.

"There's also a Strawberry Moon. It was back in June to celebrate strawberry season. Some cultures call it the Rose Moon, though, while others call it a Hot Moon because it marks the beginning of summer."

Still watching the sky, Scarlett speaks. "My father called me

Strawberry when I was little." Her tone softens around the memory.

"Have you spoken to them?"

She squints at the sky. "I haven't. And I don't expect to, but I'm okay with it." Her head rolls to face me again. "As long as I have your family, Bull, that's all I'll need. Your brothers are like the siblings I never had, and your father has been kinder to me in a matter of days than my parents have in my entire life."

"They aren't saints," I remind her but smiling at her comfort with my kin.

"No, but they're real. They're not putting on a façade like my parents. Not asking me to play a charade."

I nod to agree and decide I don't want to discuss her parents. "Speaking of wolves, February was the Wolf Moon month."

"Really? What moon was in March?"

"A Worm Moon."

"Worms?"

I chuckle. "We prefer Sap Moon in these parts as it's the time to tap trees for sap."

"I think it should be renamed sperm moon." She giggles at herself.

"Why?" I laugh.

"Because that's when you got me pregnant."

I laugh harder. She's really on a roll tonight. "Well, the Egg Moon is actually in April, but that month is also called the Pink Moon for wildflowers or sprouting grass."

"Sprout has a moon." Scarlett smiles. "I like that as that's my birth month, though." Guilt hits me that the month of April I hadn't known Scarlett was still in Vermont, and I missed her birthday.

"As an October baby, my moon is the Hunter Moon. It's the preferred month for hunting. It's a particularly bright moon that month."

Scarlett still watches me as I describe these moon names, absorbing all I tell her. "So, you're a hunter?"

"I've been known to go out on occasion, but it's been a while."

Scarlett perches up on an elbow, glancing down on me. "No, you're a hunter. You go after what you want." Her eyes meet mine, trying to tell me something, but she doesn't explain what she sees.

"I have something for you," she says as she bites her lower lip. Her face nearly glows with excitement.

"What?" I tease, finding the gleam in her eyes contagious. She pulls two envelopes from her dress pocket, and I wonder how I missed those inside her clothing. She holds them both upright. One is pink and one is blue.

"Pick one."

"Is this a test?" I question, playing along with her. We've been referring to Sprout as him, but he could just as easily be a she. For a moment, I picture waves of red curls running through this field, giggling as I chase a little one in cowboy boots and ruffles to the fort off in the trees. I'll need to reinforce that thing before any child of mine climbs up to the platform. Snatching the pink one from her fingers, I ask, "Are you trying to tell me something with these?"

"Yes." Her voice drops a little, and I stare up at her.

"Did you find out about the baby's sex?" We had agreed to wait unless it was obvious with her next ultrasound. However, the doctor warned the amniocentesis test would tell us the DNA of our baby, thus revealing the gender.

"Like a gender reveal? No, this isn't something like that." She smiles to reassure me.

"But you know I'd be just as happy with a little girl as I would a boy," I say. She smiles larger.

"I know, Bull."

"As long as he or she is healthy, that's all I really want." And if the baby isn't perfect by some societal imposed standard, Scarlett and I will love Sprout no less.

"I know, honey." She nods at the envelope in my hand. Opening it, I pull out a thick set of folded papers. The top line reads divorce decree. My eyes blur as I attempt to read the remainder of the page.

"What is this?" I ask with a shaky voice, although I should recognize it. I have one of these myself with Jennifer.

"It's my divorce. It's over with Shelton." I drop the papers and sit up, forcing her back and kissing her hard. Our mouths fuse, and my tongue surges forward. I don't think I realized how relieved I'd be once her divorce was final. It's over. She's really free of him. She's free to be mine.

The thought pulls me back from her, although I still grin a goofy smile of relief.

"And what's in the other envelope?" My voice shakes as I think I know what's inside.

Scarlett holds it to her chest while I perch over her, balancing on an elbow to keep my weight off her.

"No matter what it says in here, you're Sprout's father. In my heart. In his heart. You will be his dad." She tips the envelope at me. "I haven't opened it."

Nodding, I take the slim form from her and peel back the flap. My heart races as I pull a paper from the envelope and open it next. Again, my vision blurs as I scan the numbers and the explanation until I find what I need.

A match.

We match.

Scarlett's brows pinch in concern as I don't speak a moment, staring down at the words once more. More relief floods my body, and I'm ready to howl at the moon myself.

"Just ki—" The word cuts off as my mouth falls on hers once again, drawing in her breath to feed my lungs. I hadn't realized I'd been holding mine with every motion of removing the page until I read what I wanted to read. Not that it mattered. No lab result would change how I feel inside for a child not even officially born yet, but it's still a relief to know Sprout belongs to me.

Scarlett and Sprout are both mine.

23

WORKING MOTHERS WORK

SCARLETT

As July bleeds into August, I reach six months and the start of my third trimester. When I take my monthly urine sample and the gestational diabetes test, I almost fail both. Bull couldn't attend this visit with me as he had an auction to attend that only happened on this day. I would have rescheduled myself, but my visits are on a regimented calendar. I told him not to worry about missing this one. The tests were routine and he wouldn't miss anything, like our second ultrasound, which we attended together last week. Measurements of the baby in utero during the ultrasounds determined I'm on schedule for the second week in December due date.

"I'm so fat. Like everywhere," I groan.

"I am detecting an increase of protein in your urine sample," the doctor informs me.

Cringing, I ask, "What does that mean?"

"It means you might have preeclampsia." I've been reading up on all things pregnancy over thirty-five, and preeclampsia is a possible risk, but the odds seemed so low.

"How do I get rid of it?" I ask as if it's a common cold.

"Preeclampsia is basically high blood pressure during pregnancy. If you continue to take care of yourself, it will go away once the baby is born. In the meantime, keep eating healthy, lots of fluids, and exercise but also rest more. Are you still working at the Busy Bean Café?"

"Yes."

"Do you stand all day?" Her brows hitch, hinting that she knows I do.

"Typically. We're busy, but I can take breaks."

"You need more than a break, Scarlett. You need to sit and elevate your feet."

"Are you suggesting bed rest?" I've read about that too, and I'd go stir-crazy confined to a bed for months.

"Not yet, but if it comes to that, I will prescribe it. I'm not trying to hammer home your age, but you need to take extra precautions."

"Are you recommending I quit my job?"

"I'd never recommend such a thing, but I do think you need reduced hours. Less standing time."

Audrey and Zara would accommodate anything I need, but a stool in the middle of our active counter area would be in the way. Even in the kitchen, a stool wouldn't be ideal to sit on in the flow of baking.

"I'll need to think about a few things."

"Scarlett, this is important for the well-being of the baby and yourself." A comforting hand comes to my arm, and deep down, I know what I need to do.

Tears pour down my face as Bull enters the house that evening. I'd been watching a movie I shouldn't be watching, and a woman just lost her baby.

"Scarlett? Oh my God, are you hurt?" Bull falls to his knees before me as I lean back on the couch. I'm so big I don't sit. I tip.

His eyes roam my body as his hands rub down my arms and scan my belly, looking for damage. "What happened?"

"I need to quit my job," I blubber, though, leaving the Bean isn't the worst of my worries.

"What? Why?"

I explain the concerns of preeclampsia *and my age*. "It always comes down to my fricking age."

"You aren't old," Bull admonishes, holding both my hands between his.

"I know, right? Forty is supposed to be the new twenty. Raised libido. Zero fucks given. How can I be this fragile? I take care of myself. I used to work out every day." Since coming to Vermont, I hadn't been as regimented, mainly because I didn't have Shelton reminding me to exercise, citing it was good for my heart as well as those nasty fat cells developing *as I age*. It was a polite way of saying I'd be overweight one day if I didn't keep up the routine.

Bull stares at me as if I have two heads. I'm uncomfortable as I move into the final stages of pregnancy. My body is bigger than it has ever been. I'm swollen. I'm tired, and I'm crabby.

"I can't even bend my fingers." I try to squeeze them into fists to prove my point, but it feels as if my skin is stretching. Bull takes my hands, lifting them for his lips and kissing over my puffy knuckles.

"You're beautiful," he says. I chuckle through the tears. "I'm sure Audrey and Zara could make accommodations for you, but I've also been thinking about this. You don't need to work, Scarlett."

"But I've always worked." Bull nods, understanding what I mean. I haven't done manual labor like him every day, but I've always had a job. I'd been working since I was sixteen.

"Would it be wrong to just be a mother?" His voice softens as he asks, and the question reminds me of a conversation with Rita.

Perhaps motherhood is your next great adventure. Your new purpose.

I stare at Bull as if *he* has two heads. "You sound like Rita."

"I've always liked that woman." He grins. "And you don't

221

have to work outside the home, Scarlett. You could stay here and be a mom. It's a different kind of work, I know, but it's still work."

I've often heard motherhood referred to as a thankless job, and I'm well aware that it's completely unpaid monetarily. The rewards are in the little things. Hugs and handholding. Home-made presents and contagious laughter.

"But . . ." I hadn't considered it, which is what I remember thinking when Rita mentioned it. I had friends who worked outside their home because they knew they'd be a better mother if they worked rather than stayed home with their children. I also knew women who *had* to work because the second income or only family income rested on them. Plenty of families made a choice to allow for one parent, typically the mother, to remain home. *Was that the future for me?* "I don't want to be an imposition."

"Scarlett, not this again. You're not a fucking imposition. You're my—" Bull cuts himself short. His hands release mine and brace on the edge of the couch, curling into the cushions on either side of my legs. He turns his face away from me.

"I'm your what?" I ask. The first word that comes to mind is wife, but Bull would never call me that. We aren't married and, according to him, never will be.

"What am I to you?" We haven't put labels on ourselves like boyfriend or girlfriend, and I've felt a little silly suggesting such a thing. We aren't teens. But what do two people living together, raising a child, who aren't defined as a couple, call themselves?

"You're everything to me," Bull says, twisting to face me again.

"But what does that mean?" My voice strains. If we never marry, will we just continue to play house? I've also known people who live together, never marrying for whatever reason, but I don't understand it. I know it's only a legal document. It doesn't mean a couple is any less committed to one another, but maybe I am old—old-fashioned. I want to be married to him. Not just—

"We're partners."

Ugh. I want to scream, but instead, I struggle to sit forward, forcing him to move back. He nimbly stands, and I curse him even more at the ease of his large body while I have to scoot forward and press at the cushions to lift myself upright. Bull holds out a hand to help me, but I swat it away, irritated with *everything*.

"Where are you going?" Bull asks once I eventually stand and walk away from him.

"I need to call Audrey or Zara." Or just anyone who will listen.

"I think you made the right decision," Rita says once I call her after I've given my two weeks' notice to Zara over the phone. "This is the next great thing in your life, Scarlett. Embrace it as a gift."

As Rita doesn't have children, and it does not look as if that will be a possibility on her horizon, I should be more grateful for my position. Bull is telling me I don't need to work for financial means, and I still have savings if I feel a need to contribute. He'd never accept it, but I feel better knowing I have it.

Zara was sympathetic to my pregnancy issues. She reminded me how she needed to work out scheduling and eventually daycare as a new and single mother plus being a business partner to the birth of the Bean.

"We never have it easy as women. We want to work but feel guilty about leaving our children. When we're with our children, we worry about things at work."

"Does it go away? All that mom pressure?" I asked of her, finding sympathy from another mother with young children.

"Never," Zara teased. *"It's just a part of the territory, and I never appreciated my mother more than when I became a single mother myself."*

It's strange to think I'm technically a single mother as Bull and I are committed as parents but not a couple. We're unofficially official, I guess, but I don't like the sound of that label.

"I don't think I can stop working forever," I tell Rita.

"No one says you have to, but also no one is saying you need to return to a job outside your home."

"I don't know that I'll be good at being just a mom," I whisper. I consider my own mother and her lack of involvement in my life while placing overwhelming pressure on me. I haven't spoken to my parents since their betraying phone call. If my own mother could not be happy *for me* and support *me*, I didn't feel the need to include them in my future child's life. I'd heard stories of poor parents being excellent grandparents, but I wasn't taking the risk with mine. I had faith Harland would be all the grandparent Sprout would need. Plus, Sprout wouldn't lack love from uncles and a cousin who has already offered babysitting services.

"Honey, you'll be the wonderful person I know you to be. It's just a change. Change is difficult, but sometimes it's also for the best." Rita knows. She's having her own midlife crisis as she calls it. "Your life is never going to be the same again, though. So, I'd get used to constant change, my friend."

She's right in many ways. Every day will no longer be my own but the development of my child. The thought brings new tears, but this time they are a mix of fear and elation.

I'm going to be a mom soon.

It's a job I never knew I wanted until suddenly it was mine.

24

BIRTHDAY WISHES

BULL

As fall blooms into a kaleidoscope of colors, I point out the Engagement Tree to Scarlett one afternoon in October. We are two months out from her due date. The brilliant red color isn't lost among the autumn spectacular. The heart of this land beats bright as does my heart for Scarlett.

"We should have a picnic up there one afternoon," Scarlett suggests, but I shrug off the idea. It isn't that I don't want to eat under the tree and spend a lazy day with her, but I don't trust myself near that tree. Each passing day with Scarlett digs deeper into my feelings for her. I want to marry her. I want the statement of making her mine, but it's the last thing I can ask of her, and Scarlett's made no hint of marrying again.

After her ex-husband's adultery and the disloyalty added to the wound with her parents, marriage seems like the furthest thing from Scarlett's mind. She's grappling enough with mother-hood—a job she's determined to do well now that she's left the Busy Bean. She's also taken a more vested interest in the dairy.

"So what's on the docket today?" she asks.

"Insemination," I reply without a thought. Scarlett sputters her

225

coffee as we stand near the counter. I try to ignore how she looks barefoot in my kitchen. The suggestion of her being here all the time would toss me back in the 1950s, but she does look good, all sleepy and hair mussed up in another pair of flannel pajamas tucked under her belly and one of my T-shirts covering her. She wasn't wearing more than that shirt this morning in the bed we share, but it's chilly down here first thing.

"Excuse me?" Her eyes rapidly blink as she lowers her coffee mug. "Are we talking cow sex?"

"Sort of. We have an insemination technician coming today to impregnate a few of those ready to birth again."

"What is an insemination technician? Like a superhero bull?"

I laugh at Scarlett's imagination. "Well, technically speaking, an excited bull could perform up to twenty times a day, which does seem like superhero status."

Her mouth falls open. "I don't know whether to applaud him or cringe. How does he even get it up twenty times a day?"

"Stroke up the inside of his thigh." Her eyes narrow in disbelief, and I reach forward, stroking my hand along the inside of her leg. Those dark eyes of hers widen, and I see I've made my point. "Ideally, we'd put a bull out to pasture and let him go at it, but we need to be selective and organized with a schedule, so the technician comes and injects those ready with semen instead."

"Uhm, and how exactly do you collect bull semen? Giant paper cups?" Scarlett laughs at her own joke, and I chuckle with her.

"No, it's like a giant cow condom used as he mounts a cow or an old bull."

"Gay cow sex?" Her brow lifts.

"It's a thing." I chuckle as she still doesn't believe me. "You can actually order a variety of semen specimens from a catalog. It gets expensive, like up to fifty dollars a tube."

"You're kidding me, right?" Her face is incredulous, doubting everything I say. "That's like golden semen."

"Yep."

Scarlett's thoughtful a second. "So if I came up behind you—" She circles around me and places her hand between my legs. "And stroke up like this." Her fingers drag up the inside of my thigh, but the added pressure does the trick. "Does that get you ready?"

"Are you comparing me to a cow?" I tease of her insistence that she's compared to one often. I'm also struggling with how well her touching me like that worked.

"The name does fit," she teases.

"Technically, it's Bull, so I'm not a cow."

"Hmm…yes, you are. All bull." Her hand continues working up and down the inside of my thigh as she stands behind me.

"Scarlett, don't be starting something we can't finish," I warn her as I need to go soon. Before the technician arrives in the afternoon, I need to get to a final cut of our feed pastures, which will get us through winter.

"Who says we can't finish?" Her hand slips farther between my thighs, and she cups me, gripping my balls through my jeans.

"Jesus," I hiss.

"Maybe you could make a deposit in me?" Something is so wrong about what she's said, but her sultry voice is turning me on just as much as her hands massaging me through the denim.

"I already did that, sweetheart." Seven months ago, again last night, and all the days ending in day between, but Scarlett is insatiable, and I'm not complaining. Spinning around her, I switch positions with her and lift Scarlett's hands, securing them to the edge of the kitchen counter. "Want to know what it would be like in the pasture?"

"Now you *are* comparing me to a cow," she says, but when I hastily tug down her flannels to find her not wearing underwear beneath them, her laughter stops. My hand skims up her inner thigh as I stand behind her. "Are you ready for me?"

She doesn't disappoint as my fingers meet wetness. She's practically dripping. "God, I love how quickly you respond to me." Two fingers dive into her, pressing forward on a rush before pulling back in retreat. Scarlett chases my fingers, eager to keep me inside her. Her fingers clutch at the counter as her backside stretches toward me. Thrusting my fingers inward again, Scarlett grunts. Her back arches, and her arms stiffen.

"Bull," she hums, but I'm already working on opening my jeans. Button undone. Zipper down. I shove at the sides of my pants, lowering them enough to spring free.

"This is how it happens," I say to her, lining myself up, coating the tip through her slick folds. "One of the most natural acts in nature."

"If you're comparing us to farm animals . . ." Her breath catches as I surge forward, filling her. Her elbows bend, but her hands keep her from colliding with the cabinets. She's bent over and braced while I pull back and rush forward again.

"We are animals, Scarlett. Wild and reckless and crazy about each other."

"Crazy," she mutters, adding that little noise she makes that lets me know how thrilled she is with what I'm doing to her. I wish I could make a sound to let her know how happy she makes me. As our skin slaps and the suction sound slurps, I realize this is our harmony, our rhythm, and our music. This is the song that Scarlett and I sing, and I want to belt it from the mountains around us. I want the world to know how I feel about her.

"God, Scarlett, I love . . . being with you." Scarlett dips forward, her head lower between her outstretched arms as she groans and stills. Her knees give, and the telltale signs of her breaking around me occur. My fingers dig into her hips, slamming into her two more times before I find my own release. Sated, I slip my hands up her back and along her arms, entwining my fingers with hers. With erratic breaths, my forehead lowers to her back.

"Got nineteen more rounds in you to live up to that namesake?" she teases of me. At least, I hope she's teasing me.

"Any day that ends in day, I'm good to go."

Scarlett laughs. Slowly, I stand and slip out of her, reaching for the towel draped over the sink before bringing it between her legs. With a hand on one hip, I guide her to stand.

"I don't think I need it twenty times in a day," she says. "But I'm happy to do it every day ending in day with you. Especially on your birthday."

Scarlett turns to face me, her flannel pants still down at her ankles. "And I love . . . being with you, too." She smiles up at me, and I'm curious if the repetition, and pause of my words, was intentional. Could she mean something more? Could she want something else with me? It's more than sex once a day with Scarlett. It's everything about her that I love. As archaic as it sounds, I love the way she looks in my kitchen. The scent of her lingering in the bed we share. The eagerness with which she faces each day on this farm. Admittedly, this is one of the strangest conversations I've ever had, and I'd do it every day, ending in day, as long as we could do it forever.

"Happy Birthday, honey," she says. Tipping up on her toes, she kisses me long and lazily as if we have the rest of the day to celebrate, which we don't.

"I'll see you tonight," I promise her.

"I'll be here waiting on you."

I love the thought. I love that she stuck around—staying power, as she called it.

"You never told me what you'd like for your birthday," she teases, wrapping her arms around my neck, making me linger just a little longer. Can I tell her the truth? The thing I want most is for her to marry me. I want her to be my wife, yet even thinking about it makes me edgy. Proposing to her would ruin everything we have that's going so well.

"You don't have to get me anything, sweetheart. I already have all I ever wanted." My hand falls to her belly before I lean down for a kiss on her covered skin. The baby kicks back as if it felt my touch.

"Sprout can hear you," she whispers as I stand upright but still cover her swollen stomach.

"Oh, yeah?"

"Yeah. Say something to my belly."

Lowering again, I lift her shirt to make contact with her extended stomach. Pressing my lips to her skin, I feel a little silly, but I speak. "Hey, baby. I can't wait for your birthday. I'm gonna love you like crazy."

A little nudge at my face against her tummy has me standing quickly again. Scarlett laughs at my widened eyes. "He knows you're his daddy and you're waiting on him."

Jesus. My eyes burn. My nose prickles. Every birthday wish I've ever had is standing right in this kitchen, and I love it. I love them both, but I'll keep that sentiment on lockdown. I won't risk giving it up.

"So birthday," she interrupts my thoughts. "We'll just be having a family dinner at the main house and then return here.

"Maybe you can be my cake?" I tease, and Scarlett laughs.

"You like cake?" she teases, slipping her arms down to my chest.

"I love Scarlett cake."

Her breath catches, and I realize how close I came to slipping up.

"If I say I love Bull cake, that just sounds wrong somehow." She chuckles, dismissing the panic I'm certain has spread across my face.

"Well, it's better than liking Bull's stick," I state.

"Is that something related back to the insemination expert? Because if it is, I'm definitely liking Bull's stick."

"Scarlett, you're crazy." I laugh.

"And that's what you love about me." Her eyes sparkle, waiting me out to confirm or deny her words. Instead, I just kiss her again to distract her from the fact that as much as I want to confirm my emotions, I'll deny them in order to keep her here.

That night at the family dinner, a discussion about the Bottom farm next door comes up.

"So let me get this straight. They are sheep farmers, but they want to share the land," Scarlett asks.

"Our back pastures butts up against theirs, and they want to expand. They thought we could share the space," Dad explains.

"Well, Redd wanted to share the field," I remind my family.

"Was this the same field that . . ." Scarlett's voice drifts, leaving the implication clear. It's the same field that flooded, where I was captured on film. Her face grimaces.

"Anyway, Redd's father, Harry, passed away years ago and—"

"Wait?" Scarlett holds up a hand, a chuckle already filling her voice. "His name was not really Harry." She pauses for clarification. "Harry Bottom?"

"Yes," Dad answers in all seriousness, but Scarlett's already giggling, and Blade's grin begins to grow.

"Harry Bottom," Scarlett repeats, looking at my father, who doesn't crack a smile. He only nods. "Harry Bottom had a son named Redd Bottom."

Scarlett snorts, and it finally registers with Dad. "After years of working to keep a straight face over that name, I get it, but Harry was a good man. His son, I cannot say the same of."

"Because Redd Bottom is an ass," Canyon mutters, and Scarlett loses all control. She's laughing so hard tears fill her eyes. She's holding her belly, and the sound coming from her is infectious. Blade starts laughing next.

"Okay, settle down," Dad says, finally giving in to the smile curling his lips.

"Harland, if you tell me he has another son named Prickly or Round or something like that, I'm going to have to excuse myself." Scarlett's already told me the baby presses on her bladder, and some days, she embarrassingly can't hold it all back if she coughs or laughs. Explaining this fun fact, which was more than I needed to know about her, sent her into tears.

"He actually has a daughter," Harland explains. "Her name is Cherry."

"No," Scarlett says, dragging out the word.

"Kid you not," Dad says again, and Scarlett's laughing uncontrollably once more, but Blade isn't catching on.

"What's so funny about that? Cherry is sweet," Blade defends, and Scarlett can't even breathe.

"I bet she is," Canyon adds, narrowing his eyes at Blade. Scarlett presses off the table, excusing herself as she holds her belly.

"Anyway," Dad says, still smiling at the laughter following Scarlett like a comet tail. "We need to shore up those fences so his damn sheep don't escape onto our land again. They'll tear up that field with their hooves. And loose sheep just beg for predators to come hunting on our property."

Dad doesn't need to remind me. Scarlett returns within seconds, still wiping at her eyes.

"Oh my. I needed that laugh." She snorts once more, and Canyon shakes his head at my . . . *girl*. It seems silly to call a grown woman my girl but calling her my woman sounds a bit harsh. Girlfriend seems like we're teens, and woman-friend sounds worse. There's only one label I want for Scarlett, but she won't be getting it.

"Okay, boys. Carly. Joey. I have a special cake for Bull back at the house, so we should be heading out," Scarlett says in her take-charge voice. Her face gives nothing away, but we both know the cake she's referencing is her own body.

"You baked?" Carly teases.

"Of course not. I stopped at a bakery in Colebury." Scarlett winks at me, and I stand to thank the family for the presents they'd given me. A new belt from my father. A gift card from Canyon and Joey. A book about the moon from Blade. Carly makes good food, and that's all I've ever needed from her.

"What's this?" I ask Scarlett the following evening. Holding out her phone, I glance up at her. The screen lit up while she was in the bathroom, and I caught a glance of the notification.

"What's what?" she snaps, matching my sharp tone. She's defensive somedays and then quick to apologize, explaining the pregnancy weighs on her. She's been cooped up since leaving the Busy Bean back in August, and while she's adjusting to farm life as a city girl, some days are a struggle.

She's only seven weeks from her due date and growing incredibly uncomfortable. Relegated to more rest than play, she's coming out of her skin.

As she steps up to me, I turn her phone so the screen faces her. Reaching out for it, she tugs the device from my hands and stares at the portion of a notification presented on the home page

Call me about the opportunity to . . . The partial message is from her former boss, Lex.

"What does this mean?" My tone is harsh, although I don't mean it to be. I'm on edge myself lately. It's getting harder and harder to fight my feelings, especially after a wild night like last night where we celebrated my birthday in our own manner, and then Scarlett presented me with a telescope to see the moon.

It's a Celestron brand PowerSeeker worth almost four hundred dollars.

"I had a telescope as I kid, but I haven't used it in ages," I'd told her.

"Well, it's time to start moon gazing again. You'll need to teach Sprout everything," she'd said. I explain to her how the moon dictates almost as much as the sun for farming, and as Sprout is the future of this land, she wants him to know everything.

"It means you should ask for more information before snooping on my phone," she sasses back, and while most days I love it, I don't appreciate it today.

"I thought that's what I was doing. I'm asking *what does this mean*?" Anger fills my voice. "Are you looking for another job?" The thought hits me like a whack-a-mole machine.

How could she do this to us? Isn't what *we* have enough? I

thought we'd gotten to a point where we were settled into who we are and who we will be as Sprout's parents. We'd come to an agreement that Scarlett would stay home and mother our child. It's a big change for her, I understand, but she won't be alone. It takes a village, and she'll have the entire family helping her with our baby. How could I be so stupid? Of course, she wouldn't be happy just being a mother. The farm would never be enough for her.

"And what if I did want another job working someday?" *Them's fighting words* in her tone, and I don't blame her. I'm looking for a fight for some reason.

"Reporting again?" I sneer as I wave out at her phone. My voice rises. With my broad shoulders set, I glare at her. "We made promises to each other." She wasn't going to work for them again, but what have I promised her? I'm here for her day in and day out. What more could she want from me?

As she stares up at me, Scarlett's face blanches, reading the questions in my own expression. I just want her to tell me the truth. Why is her former boss contacting her? What does she want with them? Obviously, a job, more opportunity, a return to the city life.

"I'm not . . ." she quietly admits. "I just . . . have something to discuss with him."

"What?" I snap.

We've been together all these months. I don't have a reason to feel the way I'm suddenly feeling, but still, I can't seem to help it. My chest constricts, and suspicions race.

"It's nothing. It's not a job or anything like that," she states. What else could her former boss offer her, though? Turning away from me, she stares outside the window.

"Is being here not enough?" Scarlett flinches as if the words cut. I was so close to opening up to her, telling her how I felt. We made love last night before the fireplace in the coolness of an October evening and in celebration of my birthday. I want to slap myself in relief that I hadn't told her how I feel. I'm grateful I haven't admitted I love her, so at least I can keep my dignity if she decides to leave.

"You know that's not it. I asked you to have faith in me. Have I not proven myself to you?" Frustration fills her voice.

Now would be the time for me to offer her reassurance. Perhaps if I opened up, she'd know the truth. I love her, and I don't want her to go anywhere. We can find her other work in Vermont. She can return to the Busy Bean if she wants, or whatever she feels she needs to do to keep her here.

Instead, my feelings seize up. My mouth opens but quickly shuts. Without another word, I turn on my heels and head to the barn.

25

INVESTIGATIVE REPORTS

SCARLETT

I'm so sorry Bull misunderstood my text, but I can't tell him yet what I've been doing. Deep down, I still felt sick about the Bovine Bridegroom scandal and wanted to make things right by Bull and his family. Mainly, I wanted Bull to know how the network got such a story in the first place. What drew our attention to it? Who passed it on to us? Lex wasn't as helpful as I thought he could be, but when I reminded him I could sue the network for age discrimination, he was willing to give me the favor he owed me.

"We can have a crew there in two days. In and out."

"Perfect." It had to work.

"You know, we really do miss you around here," Lex stated, his voice dropping just enough I might believe he's sincere.

"Funny, I haven't missed you," I teased.

"You'll always miss me, Red," he joked. I worked with the man for twenty years. He was my work-husband as labels go, yet he dumped me as easily as my true-husband did.

"I appreciate this, Lex."

"Anything for you," he lied.

No, I'd be doing everything for Bull.

Two days after his birthday, Bull was still upset with me. He used the barn as an excuse to rise early and work late, falling into our shared bed but not drawing me into him as he always did. I hated it, and I slept terribly. Shelton and I didn't sleep pressed up against one another but rather on our own sides of the bed. Bull liked to be right in the middle with me tucked into him.

I missed Bull. I missed our night's cuddling and his hand stroking over my belly, speaking to Sprout with his touch.

We have plans to attend a fall party at Speakeasy. I was seven weeks out from having Sprout and really needed a break from the house. I wasn't quarantined to bed rest, but I did lounge around more than I ever had in my life. Keeping my feet up and my blood pressure down took work. No more sad movies, Bull warned me months ago. I read a copious number of romance novels, which really heated things up between Bull and me. Not that we needed help in that department as my pregnancy hormones were still off the charts. It's another reason I missed Bull these last two evenings.

The plan to attend the party had another purpose, one which includes the fact Canyon will be playing his guitar this evening as a part of the entertainment. I was hedging bets that the place would be busy, filled with locals wishing to support the party. It was something I was counting on happening. Begrudgingly, Bull agreed to still go in support of his brother. He'd hardly been able to look at me as I walked around in just a towel, not even feeling remotely sexy but still trying to draw his attention to me as we used to do to one another when I first moved in.

While I didn't doubt Bull's feelings for me, I was suddenly doubting his feelings about me living with him. I didn't want to lack confidence in our situation. All would be revealed soon enough, but the silent treatment unnerved me. Maybe I was making a huge mistake.

Speakeasy is another bar located on the old gin mill property where the new Gin Mill bar exists. The Busy Bean Café also sits on the same land. The microbrewery is another combination of Rossi and Shipley with Zara's brother, Alec, being part owner and Griff Shipley, Audrey's husband, being part investor. The large open layout houses a viewing window of brew tubs to the left with a giant oval bar in the center of the plank wood floors. Exposed brick and wrought-iron chandeliers give the place a rustic vibe. A patio runs the expanse of the back of the building, overlooking the Winooski River.

In the corner is a small stage for entertainment, and we quickly find Canyon setting up. He was formerly in a band, but he's mellowed his tune into a singular guy with a guitar. Bull told me Canyon has always fiddled with his instrument, but living away from the main house means we don't hear him practicing. Still, sometimes, he'll take his favorite strings to the fields, and the slight echo carries to our house. Bull jokes that it's been a long time since Canyon sang before a crowd other than our milkers.

Once we find a table near the stage, I can't sit still. My foot taps. My fingers rap on the tabletop. I can't drink, but I wish I could sip some wine to calm down. Eyeing the crowd, I see it's a full house, and I nod at a few people I recognize. Bull gazes at me, noticing my jiggling fingers but not mentioning it.

Finally, I see who I'd been counting on attending the party. To my surprise, though, he has Louisa Miller on his arm. After putting Redd in his place a few months back, I realize things could go one of two ways. Redd could ignore Bull because he'd been schooled by a woman, or he could be pissed off that a woman schooled him before fellow farmers. I was counting on the latter and was lucky to find Redd Bottom was so easy to predict.

"Well, what do we have here? Farmer in the dell and . . . a bun in the oven? Did he finally take a wife?" Bull glares up at his nemesis, and I reach for his forearm. I hate that he bristles under my touch, but I keep my hand there as both a way to steady him and myself. I need Redd to stick around a bit.

"Not yet," I tease while adding some sassy. "I'm thinking of asking him."

Bull's head pops up, and his entire forehead furrows. Unable to meet his eyes at my suggestion, I focus on Redd instead and Louisa glancing over her shoulder, feeling uncomfortable near our table.

"Don't want to jinx the bull. Maybe he'll be the one to run for the hills this time," Redd mocks.

Before I know what's happening, Bull is standing to his full height. Chest out, arms at his side in fists, his jaw clenches. I can't stand as quickly as him, and while I'm struggling to get upright, preparing to place myself between two large men, Blade walks in with Clayton behind him.

"I might have swollen ankles and fat feet, but I'd still chase him." This comment doesn't even tip Bull's head in my direction, but his eyes shift my way.

"What's going on here?" Blade asks, meeting his brother's gaze and noting the stature of both men. I wait on Bull to answer, but Redd interjects.

"Nothing." His lips purse. "We're stepping out for some fresh air as it smells like bullshit in here." Redd wraps his arm around Louisa's neck, nearly choking her as he tugs her into his side.

"Better than smelling like a wolf in sheep's clothing," I add. Redd's brows pinch like I'm one strange bird before he tugs Louisa behind him, and they head for the patio.

"What was that?" Blade questions, watching Redd walk away before looking at his brother. "You feeling alright?"

Blade must know what I've already surmised. Bull is not one to fight. Not when it comes to juvenile, immature, full-grown adults.

"Yeah. I'm fine," he lies, lowering back to his chair. I want to return my hand to his arm, but the vibe coming off him says don't touch him. He addresses his brother and his friend instead. "Take a seat."

Bull nods to the other two chairs at our table, and the men join us.

"And look at you all feisty with her sheep's clothing comment," Blade teases.

"Too much?" I ask, as I often have in the past. I've been known to be over the top at times. It's one way a woman could make it in a man's business world.

Thankfully, Canyon walks onto the stage and introduces himself.

"Thanks for coming out tonight. I'm Canyon Eaton."

"You're Canyon Blaze," someone shouts from the back, and Canyon sits up taller at the recognition of his former stage name.

"Now, I'm just Canyon." He smiles sheepishly, and I see the rock star behind the smile. The man who wooed groupies and got one pregnant on his road to success. He strums at this guitar and introduces the song over a few practice chords. "This one's a favorite called 'Fools Rush In.'"

My neck cranes as I glance up at the side of Bull's face. He slowly shakes his head with only the hint of a grin.

"Dammit," he mutters as Canyon breaks into the opening line of Elvis Presley's famous song. My hand is covered by Bull's.

"Want to dance?"

I glance around as there isn't really a dance floor. "Here?" I question. There's hardly space between tables, and I'm almost double my size.

"Right here," Bull suggests. He stands, and I follow, wrapping my hand into his as his arm comes around my waist. I need to stand almost sideways to him, but he's somehow still tucked me into him. We listen to the harmony about fools rushing into love and how it can't be helped, and the song is the theme for Bull and me. We remain quiet as Bull sways me back and forth, and my cheek rests near his heart, which races wildly in his chest.

My eyes scan the room again, finding another pair of men I recognize, but I close my eyes to them, swallowing up this moment before all hell breaks loose.

When the song ends, I glance up at Bull.

"Thank you," I whisper, and his brow furrows once more.

"For what?" he says.

"For loving me." He hasn't said it to me. He might never admit it, but I want him to know that no matter how he labels it, this is love. What he's done for me, how he treats me, who he is, has to be love.

"Scarlett, I—"

"I need some air." Immediately, I sense I've made a mistake and excuse myself.

I step out to the patio where propane heaters warm the area, lessening the October chill. I approach the railing, looking out over the river. It feels ironic that I'm standing here, facing the same flowing water where I broke the news to Bull that I was pregnant. Slowly, I scan the surrounding patio finding the two men I recognized inside taking a seat at a table in the corner, closer to a space heater. Through the opening of the door, I can hear Canyon crooning through another song. This one I don't recognize as well.

The air remains cool, but pregnancy weight keeps me warm as I wait out one more song.

Come on, I mutter to myself, counting once again on a foolish man in the bar. Keeping my back to the entrance, I tap my fingers on the railing as the music softly lulls out to the patio.

"With a name like Scarlett, you and I are better suited for one another." Tipping back, I make eye contact with the men across the patio. Just want to make certain someone has me in their sights as I spar with this man.

"Redd." I chuckle softly but don't finish my giggle before the entrance door to the main bar opens, and Bull stalks toward me.

"Get out of here, Redd," Bull demands, and the sheepherder turned woodcarver chuckles.

"Feeling threatened?" he teases.

"Bull would never need to feel that way," I state, catching Bull's eyes finally. "He knows I have staying power."

Redd huffs and turns on his heels, and I reach out for Bull's wrist. "But Redd, I'm curious if you've ever heard of Lex Steinman." Redd stills and turns back to face me. In the dark of the night, only the fire lamps illuminate the space plus a dim outdoor light. Still, the pinch of Redd's face is evident.

"Can't say that I have?"

"Scarlett," Bull hisses beside me, but I squeeze tighter at his wrist.

"What about MoosHaveRights2? Ever hear of that group?" I question. Redd rolls his head back a bit and glares at me.

"Everyone's heard of the group. What are you going on about?" he questions.

"Don't speak to Scarlett like that," Bull warns, and everything in his voice drips malice. I've never heard him so gruff, and it's a bit titillating while scary at the same time.

"Redd, when was the last time you were on Eaton property?"

"Scarlett," Bull hisses once more.

"Say that back field."

Redd seethes.

"The field you want to share with the Eatons."

Bull doesn't comment.

"The one you stole onto with a MoosHaveRights2 member and planted that hellish story about Bull and his cows."

Bull remains silent, but Redd nearly vibrates with anger. His fists clench.

"That's private property you stepped on. Invaded. And took illegal films on without proper consent. You could go to jail." Redd's shoulders slowly lower. "There's also defamation of character, slander, and libel."

"I didn't report that shit. The network who bought the story did." Legally or not, we didn't always buy our stories. We sometimes just took the films directly from the internet like everyone else. Somehow, I don't think Redd is smart enough to know that.

"But the network wouldn't have seen the story if you hadn't taken illegal action with a known animal activist group, putting them in question as well."

"It was only supposed to be local."

Bull gasps, and I slowly smile.

"What the hell did you do?" Bull demands.

"Your old man is so stubborn. He won't give us a share of the land although we're willing to pay."

"We won't give you a share of the land despite the money because your sheep would only tear up the land, something *your* old man knew, and that's why he never asked us for it. Clean up your own fields."

Redd glares deep daggers of hatred at Bull.

"A wolf in sheep's clothing smells worse than bullshit," I state again, and Redd snaps at me.

"You're the one who reported the story."

"And you're the one who just admitted it. On camera." I point in the direction of Glenn and Robert, our old camera crew. "Smile for the camera, Redd."

His head turns from the men at the corner table to me. "That's not legal. I didn't give my consent to be filmed."

"Didn't give that opportunity to the Eatons, either, did you, Redd?"

"You son of a bitch." Blade Eaton has been standing off to the side, behind Redd, listening in, but he steps forward until his eldest brother catches him. "I'll shear you myself, you fucking red ass."

Redd squints at Blade. "I'm so scared."

"You should be. When KTEL's *Insider* airs that video with you admitting your fault in framing an innocent family all for a piece of land, I don't think anyone's going to be interested in business practices with a cheat."

"You don't know what you're talking about," Redd snaps.

"Try me. Think that story hurt the Eatons? I'll bury your farm." The old Scarlett reigns as I seethe at Redd.

Blade still struggles under Bull's hands, and Canyon joins us on the patio.

"What's going on out here?" he questions, eyeing his eldest brother holding back his youngest and me facing off with their neighbor.

"Just setting the record straight," I tell him. "Meet the culprit who set up your family for ruin."

Without a second of thought, Canyon pops Redd in the nose, and a bone cracks. Blood seeps from his nose.

"You-un-ow-itch." His hand covers his face. Bull reaches for a napkin from a table, unrolling the silverware inside.

"Here." He tosses the napkin at Redd in a final act of decency from this family before Redd helps himself off the patio.

Canyon shakes out his hand.

"Shit. I didn't know you had that in you," Blade teases of the middle Eaton.

"Can you still play? Do you need ice?" I step forward as Canyon glances after Redd.

"It was worth it." Gazing down at his hand, he squeezes it into a fist and back to sprawled fingers. "I'll be okay."

"Aren't you Canyon Blaze?" We all look up at Glenn, the cameraman. "I'm a huge fan."

"Thanks," Canyon says as the two start a conversation about Canyon's former career.

Finally, I risk a look up at Bull.

"What did you do?" he asks as if his emotions are hardly contained. Uncertain if he's upset or just stunned, I rush to answer.

"I started investigating Redd after a few of the things you said about his family, their property, and his desire for that land. Lex finally got back to me the other night. That's the text message you saw."

Bull's eyes widen. "Scarlett—"

Placing my hand on his chest, I stop him. "I just wanted to know the truth for you. Lex owed me this, and he sent Glenn and Robert to film everything."

Bull looks over at the two men, but only Robert waves as Glenn is still starstruck by Canyon.

"What were you planning to do with what you recorded?" Bull's cautious asking still hints at a vibration of doubt.

"That's up to you. *Insider* is happy to air a retraction, explaining the facts behind the fiction created. I'm willing to report it myself."

"But—"

"Or," I cut him off. "We can keep the truth to ourselves, but just knowing the truth should feel better, right? I did this in hopes you'd have answers."

I hold my breath as Bull could easily say I did this for myself. He didn't ask for a retraction. He didn't ask for the truth, but I wanted him to know that it was someone in his own backyard who tried to damage his family and their reputation. If he wants recourse, he has the means. If he wants a retraction, we have the confession.

"He isn't worth it," Blade speaks up beside his brother. "I think he's had fair warning. One more slipup and he's over."

Bull nods, still looking at me. "You did this for me, didn't you?"

"I did."

"And you weren't planning to take a new job?"

"No, Bull. I'm right where I belong."

Bull scrubs a hand down his face, relief washing over him, but then something else fills his expression.

"Jesus, Scarlett. I'm so sorry. Why didn't you say something sooner?"

"I wanted to catch Redd and the truth. I'm a reporter. That's what I strived to go after."

"You're a gossipmonger," Blade interjects. "But damn, I'm glad you had the skills this time."

I softly chuckle.

"Thanks, Scarlett." Blade's gratitude surprises me, and he steps forward to give me a hug. Canyon turns to me next.

"I need to get back in there, but I always knew I liked you, Scarlett." He winks at me before turning back for the entrance, Glenn on his heels.

"We'll send you all the footage," Robert says next, stepping up to me.

"It's your choice, Bull." This time it's up to him if we report on his family, making it right, or if what's been done is good enough.

"I think you've done enough," Bull says, his voice still edgy, and Robert steps away next.

"I'm sorry, Bull. I thought I was—" My words are cut off as I'm tugged to him and kissed hard and fast. His tongue comes forward, claiming my mouth, and I'm too stunned to respond at first.

"Kiss me, sweetheart," he mutters against my lips, and I give in to his request. I'll give in to anything he asks of me.

Pulling away rather quickly, Bull rests his forehead against mine. "What am I going to do with you, sweetheart?"

I can think of several things, starting with asking me to marry him, but I bite my tongue on that one.

"How about taking me to bed, partner?"

Bull chuckles before leaning back and gazing into my eyes. "I thought you'd never ask."

26

SURPRISE, BABY

BULL

It's two weeks before Scarlett is due. Snow is falling, and a storm is on its way. The clouds are heavy, and I feel like I'm standing on a precipice with Scarlett. I need to tell her how I feel despite the risk. Despite the fact I know admitting I love her might jinx everything, I need her to know I want her forever.

After the incident with Redd back before Halloween, Scarlett told me more details, including how she threatened Lex for help but assured me she was never going back to work in the industry again.

"That was my last official report, even if it never makes the news."

On that night in October, I'd felt a mix of emotions. I was so angry, thinking she was considering a job with that gossip rag and so upset she hadn't talked to me about it. I shut her out for two days, wallowing in my fears that she was leaving me for bigger and better. It was easiest to jump to conclusions instead of accepting Scarlett wouldn't do that to me, and we talked about it later that night.

"I hate that you doubted me," Scarlett softly said as we lay on our bed. The one we hadn't shared in the manner I like to share it for two full nights.

"I hate that I doubted you," I admitted to her.

"Why would you do that?"

"It just seems more believable you'd rather leave than stay. Back to city life. Back to the flashy job."

"Bull, have I given you the impression I want to go?" she questioned, keeping her eyes lowered while her finger ran along my collar.

"No." No, she hadn't, so I shouldn't have been pushing her away, which was what I was starting to think I was doing. Was I forcing her to leave because I wasn't giving her a reason to stay? I wasn't considering I was enough. Or the farm. Or my family. But Scarlett had not been the one doing that to me. I'd been doing that to myself.

And still, I didn't tell her I loved her. I didn't ask her to marry me because I did not want to lose her.

We celebrated Thanksgiving with much gratitude this year as we are thankful for Scarlett and the anticipation of Sprout's birth.

I'd been off to the tractor supply shop for a plow part, hoping to return before the heaviest snow fell. That damn tractor needs a new wedge for the small plow. We really need to replace the thing next spring, but replacing farm equipment is expensive. Being a farmer, one learns to be thrifty, and I've been putting away my own money for a while, saving up for the likes of someone like Scarlett. *A certain someone.*

As I pull up to the dairy barn while the day grows dark early, Blade exits the building and stops short when he sees me getting out of my truck.

"What are you doing here?" he asks, staring at me before looking over my shoulder at my truck.

"What do you mean, what am I doing here? I'm working." I snap, stepping toward my brother, who blocks my way. "Blade, move."

"Where's Scarlett?" His eyes widen, searching my face.

"Home." Stepping right, Blade follows again, blocking my path. "Dammit, Blade."

"Didn't Scarlett call you?" Blade questions, his voice a drop of concern.

"Why would she call me?" Instantly, the hairs on the back of my neck prickle. I reach for my phone in my pocket to find a text I'd missed. She'd contacted me an hour ago.

Meet me at the Engagement Tree at five.

My eyes drift to the time. It's five thirteen. On top of that, it's pitch-black out, and the snow is coming down heavy. Instantly, I dial her number, but it goes to voicemail.

"What's going on?" I ask, my stomach flipping as there's no way Scarlett could have gotten to that old tree. There's no discernible driving path leading to it, and walking would have been dangerous in her condition plus with the weather. "What did you *do*?"

"I'm not supposed to tell you."

"Blade, you have half a second to speak."

"It's a secret. A surprise."

"It's also fucking snowy and she's pregnant," I remind him.

"She's at the tree waiting for you."

"I'm thirteen minutes late," I snap. She had to have left when I didn't show. "Why is she there?"

"I can't say, but she's probably still there. She couldn't leave."

I press her number again on my phone, waiting on her response, and see red despite the whiteness swirling around us. She doesn't answer again. "What do you mean she can't leave?"

Blade swallows. "Well, the generator is kind of connected to the tree from the back of the truck and—"

"What the fuck?" I snap, swiping my cap off my head and running gloved fingers over my hair. "I need to get up there. Where's your truck?" The plow is on the front of Blade's truck as he was given the responsibility to clear the drive and the lane in my absence. Blade's head turns, looking away from me. "I need the plow to get up there."

"Well, it's . . . actually . . . it's already there."

"What?" I bark again. Glancing down at my phone, I press her number one more time with no success, as Blade explains. "I plowed a path for her and left the truck."

"You left a pregnant woman in a snowstorm?" I glare at my brother, completely flabbergasted by this action.

"She said she'd be fine. You'd be there soon enough, and everything would be better."

Hissing his name, I turn for my truck. "Get in," I snap over my shoulder, demanding he come with me because if I get stuck, I'm going to need his help to get out of the rut. Blade follows my quick pace, climbing into my truck at the same time I do.

"Start talking," I demand, wanting to know just what the hell Scarlett intended to do with a generator, a plow truck, and that old tree.

"No way. She'd have my balls if I tell you anything."

"I'm going to have your balls if you don't talk."

"No offense, Bull, but I'm more afraid of Scarlett." I'd chuckle at his response if I wasn't so angry as well as anxious. This is not a good scenario. With Scarlett due in two weeks, I can't believe she'd put the baby at risk. I can't believe she'd do something to herself.

Too upset to consider all the bad things that could happen to her, I peel down the lane, the truck fishtailing a bit on the freshly fallen snow.

"If anything happens to her—" I hiss.

"Nothing's going to happen." Suddenly, he doesn't sound so sure as the truck struggles for traction on the slowly mounting snowfall.

"Blade," I growl. He doesn't answer, tipping his head into his hand as his arm perches on the passenger door. As we turn in the direction of the tree, lights illuminate the dark up ahead. "What the hell?"

Risking a quick glance at Blade, he smiles to himself.

"It's a surprise," he whispers, and before me, it certainly is.

27

BIRTH PLANS

SCARLETT

I'd been sitting in the warm truck ever since Blade left me. The plan was for him to plow the path, and I'd follow in my car, which he'd drive back to the house. But as time passed, and Bull wasn't answering my text, I stepped out of the truck to pace. It's cold, but I'm sweating with nerves. I'm also cramping a bit, and the doctor had told me walking can rid me of false contractions. I'm two weeks away from my due date, and my hand rubs over my tightening belly.

"Whoa," I gasp, bending forward at my waist at the sharp pain. This isn't like the time I was dehydrated and stressed over my parents, although I've certainly been stressed for the past forty-eight hours. There have been moments I've wondered if what I was doing was too much.

Bull certainly had doubts about us, and I hated that I played into them just a little bit back in October to get some answers for him. That night, I learned that despite my grand gesture, Bull wasn't going to take action unless my gesture was even grander. Like the grandest gesture I could pull off, and I really wanted to pull this off. I'd noticed that every time I mentioned the Engagement Tree, Bull refused to confirm going back to it. I'd suggest picnics or date nights moon gazing, and he'd always shrug, brushing me off with a maybe. Then he'd never mention it again. The tree scared him or I did, and I couldn't figure out why until I put two and two together. Or rather, Bull's fear of two and two, leaving only one person standing under the tree.

Now, I was in the same position. I'm afraid I'm about to fall flat on my face, and Bull isn't going to show because of the tree. Putting myself out there in a way I never have, this could either be glorious or the biggest mistake of my life.

"Wow," I grit through clenched teeth, stopping next to the truck to hold the side as another wallop of pain rushes through me. The snow is falling pretty heavy, but surprisingly, I'm not freezing. A chill seeps through my jeans, but I'm still warm enough.

It's all the baby heat, I tell myself. I've been exceptionally hot during pregnancy, hardly needing a coat some days despite the colder temperatures. It could be the elevated blood pressure, although I have the preeclampsia under control. Or so I think when another stab of pain bends me forward for my knees, which I can't reach.

"Settle down, Sprout," I demand, keeping a hand on the side of the truck as I slip with my first step in the freshly fallen snow. Using the edge as a guide, I return to pacing a few times before opening the truck door and reaching for my phone in the cup holder. The engine still runs as does the gas generator. Blade was hesitant to leave the machinery in the bed of the truck but being full of gas, it was too heavy to move alone.

"Don't leave," he warned me, as the generator is connected to the power cord, leading to the lights, which illuminate the tree. Blade did a beautiful job of hanging Edison bulbs on an outdoor lighting string through the lower branches of the tree. I really wanted to picnic here, despite the cold temp, covering up under heaps of blankets in the back of the truck, but the snowfall worries me. And the generator is louder than I predicted. Bull and I wouldn't be able to talk, and I have so much to say.

Another whammy of pain rushes over my middle, causing it to harden, and I pause, unable to move under the shooting rush. Standing still, I hold my phone. Five twenty-two.

At what time do you call defeat? It's been twenty-two minutes since he was supposed to be here, and he hasn't shown. He didn't even respond to my text.

"This was all a mistake." I don't know what I was thinking. Actually, I do know what I was thinking, what I was hoping would happen, but Bull isn't coming. I went too far.

Pulling my phone from my pocket, I struggle to remove my gloves, fumbling my phone before cold fingers press at the screen for Bull's number. As I wait for the phone to ring, I pull back the silent device when no dial tone occurs.

No service.

"Frick," I hiss aloud. Stepping toward the tailgate, I'm wondering if I can simply unplug the lights. Blade explained how there's a switch on the side of the generator to cut the power, but he also mentioned Bull would know how to take care of everything.

Bull, who didn't show.

Once I reach the end of the truck, I realize the tailgate is not lowered. I'd have to climb up on the bumper to hitch my legs over the barrier to enter the bed and flip the switch.

Unfortunately, I can't lift my leg. To angle my leg to the left, bending my knee around my belly and awkwardly trying to position my foot on the bumper, another shot of pain rips up my middle, and I bend forward instead, gripping the metal bumper as I scream.

"Scarlett?!"

My name is an echo in the whirling wind, and I straighten as best I can, holding onto the edge of the truck to round the corner of it. With the generator so loud, I hadn't heard the approach of another vehicle.

"Bull," I whisper. Rushing to me, his hands grip my shoulders.

"What the hell are you doing out here?"

"You came," I say through clenched teeth, holding my belly with one hand while my other curls around the edge of the truck.

"I told you once, I'd always find you. I'm sorry I'm late, but what is all this?" His eyes lift for the lights circling the tree and highlighting the trunk.

"I wanted to ask you something, but *oh God* . . ." I groan, my knees bending under the weight of the contraction. Bull's eyes focus back on me as we wait out the tightening in my belly. Once it subsides, I try to speak again, no longer able to remember all I wanted to say.

"This is really important," I begin, but the words are strained as my stomach clenches once more.

"Just relax," Bull says, ignoring me as he lifts his gloved hand for his teeth and bites at the leather. With his left hand free, he reaches into his pocket, and it reminds me the item I need is still sitting in the cup holder. Bull holds his phone, watching me.

"I need to ask you something," I grit out.

"Scarlett, are those contractions coming sooner than five minutes?"

I shake my head. "It's just Braxton Hicks. I'm not going into labor," I say, but the second I speak, reality hits me. *Could I be going into labor early?* I'm two weeks early.

"Sweetheart?" Bull questions, holding his phone as he looks at the screen.

"Maybe," I say of the timing and moan again as my knees give out a bit. Bull catches me under my arms and yells over his shoulder. "Blade!"

What? *No.* We need to be here alone.

"Bull, I have to ask you something," I strain through the pain.

"We need to get you to the hospital," Bull says, searching around our feet as his brother approaches. "This snow is really piling up, though."

"What's going on?" Blade asks.

"We need an ambulance," Bull states, but I'm shaking my head. I need to get this out. I need to say what I have to say *before* the baby gets here. "There's no phone service. Radio the house."

Blade races back to Bull's truck. Bull told me they started using two-way radios for occasions just like this when conditions interrupted phone service. Bull picks me up, and I hiss as he carries me to the cab of Blade's truck. Setting me back on my feet, he opens the driver's side door and demands I get in.

Blade returns with the radio, and we hear Canyon snap through the device. "Having a blizzard here."

"Scarlett's having a baby," Bull barks over his shoulder.

"Frick," I groan, clutching at my waist.

"Fuck," Bull adds stronger. "We need to get her out of here."

"No," I yell through the pain. "I need to—"

"It can wait," Bull demands, his voice harsher than it's ever been toward me.

"Lay down in the back," he commands as he shifts me so he can tug the front seat forward, and I scramble to the back. Groaning once more, I begin to shake uncontrollably.

"What the fuck?" Blade mutters just outside the door as I lower for the seat.

"I think she's gonna have the baby right here," Bull says over his shoulder, climbing in after me.

"I am not having this baby in the back seat of a truck."

"It'd be appropriate if that's where it was conceived," Blade states, and Bull and I both yell for the youngest Eaton to shut up.

"Scarlett, I don't think we have a choice. An ambulance is on the way, but it could take half an hour or more. If you need to push, you've got to tell me."

"Why?" I moan.

"Because I'll have to deliver the baby. I've delivered hundreds of calves. I can do this." I'm not certain if Bull's trying to talk himself into it or convince me, but the idea of him delivering our child in the back seat does not sit well with me.

"Are you comparing me to a cow?"

"Dammit, woman. You aren't a cow. You're the woman I love, and we need to do this." The words hang in the air as Bull's eyes leap up for mine, and he freezes, hovering over me.

"You love me?"

His eyes close, and a painful expression crosses his face. "I didn't mean for that to come out like that." His voice softens.

"So you don't love me?" I whine as another contraction claws at my belly. I twist under pressure, and Bull stays quiet as I ride out the clenching.

"It's not that I don't love you—"

"You don't have to make it sound like you're doing me a favor. I get it. I asked you to be here at five, and you didn't show."

"I hadn't seen your text until I got back from the tractor supply store, and don't turn this around on me. What the hell were you doing up here?" he snaps again.

"I wanted to tell you I loved you," I bark through another wave of pain. My head tips up as I yell at him, but it falls back as the wave crests, and I clutch at my belly. Tears rush from my eyes. A gush of warmth flows between my legs. I curse my weakened bladder. "Frick. I just wet myself."

"Ah, Scarlett, sweetheart, your water broke."

"No," I yell. "That means the baby is coming."

Risking a glance at Bull as I feel like I'm in the most vulnerable position I've ever been in, I find him smiling at me.

"What?" I snap, sticky and wet as the cold is catching up to me.

"The baby is coming," Bull slowly repeats, his voice soft and sweet as his hand comes to my ankle. He's unlacing my boots. "Maybe we should get you out of the wet things."

"No," I hiss again, but my body jackknives, and I clench my teeth as I groan through the pain.

"Okay, sweetheart. Breathe for me." Bull repeats the breathing technique he used with me in the baby store when I had the panic attack last summer. Breathing with Bull calmed all my fears then. He was with me. I was safe. He wouldn't let anything happen to me. I follow his lead as he shifts, looking over the front seat and finding the stack of blankets I brought.

He snags one and pulls it into the cramped space we occupy. Then he removes my boots and slips down my jeans. The cold rushes up my legs, but Bull has one thick sleeping bag under me and wrapped around my legs before another wallop of pain hits.

"What can I do?" Blade mutters from where he stands just outside the slightly open door.

"Get in here and close that door," Bull commands.

"I'm not coming in there and listening to her scream."

"Get in here and help me," Bull demands, struggling as he keeps his hand on my knee while reaching over the front seat. "Thank God there are so many blankets in here. Ready to tell me why?"

My mouth opens, but another wave of pain hits me, and I turn for the back of the front seat, screaming through the pain.

"I'm out," Blade states. "I'll check on the ambulance status." Blade slams the driver's door closed, enveloping Bull and me in darkness minus the lights streaming through the back window from the Engagement Tree. That beautiful tree. My moment is ruined.

"I'm so sorry, Bull," I whimper, tears leaking down my face.

"Why are you sorry, sweetheart?"

"I wanted to do it right. I wanted you to know I love you."

"You love me?" he chokes.

"I do," I groan as another wave hits me.

"Breathe," he whispers to me, and I try, I really do, but the pain is more than anything I've ever felt. Bull stretches his body over the front seat before turning his head to look at me. "There's a picnic basket on the floor."

Yep. I had it all planned. The picnic in the bed of the truck. The warm blankets. The . . .

"What's this?" Bull holds up the small black box and more tears blur my vision. I've messed this all up. Screwup Scarlett. It's not going to get any worse than this.

"I wanted to— *Ahhhhh*." I scream. Bull settles back to the seat as best he can. He barely fits where he's wedged his body, and his hands come to my knees again, watching me through the pain. His fingers clutch at the box balanced on my knee.

"Scarlett, just hang on, sweetheart." He encourages. "You're doing great."

"I screwed up," I yell through the subsiding wave.

"Nothing's screwed up," Bull says.

"I had it all planned. The tree. The dinner. The ring."

Bull stiffens.

"I just wanted to do this right."

"Do what right?" he quietly asks.

"Ask you to marry me."

Bull doesn't move. I'm not certain he's even breathing, but I'm huffing and puffing, trying to make it through the pain. "Bull, I need to push."

My knees bend upward, and I shift my tired body. Bull slips the ring box into his coat pocket, and he loosens the sleeping bag around my legs.

Shifting up on my elbows, I bear down, screaming through the pain as the driver's side door opens and just as quickly closes. When the pain stops for just a second, my head falls back.

"You've got this, Scarlett," Bull says, lifting his arm and pounding his fist on the driver's side window. Blade opens the door again.

"I'm not looking. I don't see anything," Blade yells.

"Where's that fucking ambulance?"

"They're struggling through the snow but still on their way."

"The baby is coming," Bull yells.

"So is winter," Blade jokes.

"Are you referencing *Game of Thrones*?" I snap.

"Yeah, have you seen it?" Blade says, shifting so his head pops into view, but just as quickly, his face disappears again.

"Busy here," Bull hisses.

"Never mind," Blade states, closing the door once more.

"Bull, I don't think I can do this," I whimper.

"Marry me?" Bull questions, his voice full of incredulous hurt.

"Have the baby," I cry, rolling my head side to side.

"You can, Scarlett. You're strong. You can do this." While I want to yell at him that I don't need a fricking cheerleader, another wave hits me, and I sit upward, knees to my shoulders, clenching. I don't even hear what Bull says to me. The next thing I know, my jacket is opening, and Bull is unbuttoning the cute new flannel shirt I bought for this occasion. The proposing occasion, not the birthing scene, which is happening in the back of a fricking pickup truck.

"When Sprout comes out, he's going to need skin-to-skin contact, Scarlett. He'll need your warmth until we get you to a hospital."

While I agree, I shake my head because I'm so tired. It hurts so much. Another wave of pain rips through me. For a moment, I feel like I'm outside of myself. My eyes roll back. My heart races, flooding all sound in my ears.

A rush. A gush. And then the cry of a newborn.

"He's so beautiful," Bull says, his voice full of liquid, but I only nod as something warm and slimy is placed over my skin, and red lights filter through the steam-filled windows.

"The answer is yes, Scarlett," Bull says before the driver's door is opened and a blast of cold air hits me.

"Yes," I whisper, not remembering the question as my lips find the head of a little being on my chest.

28

FAMILY NAMES

BULL

The adrenaline high of the past few hours churns with emotion.

My baby born.

My woman admits she loves me.

My sweetheart asks me to marry her.

As we sit in the hospital, the final moments come back to me. I delivered my own child as the ambulance arrived. Scarlett was dead tired, but she'd produced a beautiful baby boy.

Blade sits next to me in the waiting room, his head tipped back and his mouth hanging open as he snores. My brother has already told me he might be scarred for life witnessing Scarlett squeezing out a tiny human. I didn't want to remind him it's no different than birthing a cow. Scarlett would hate the comparison.

We've been told to wait out here as mother and baby are checked out due to the conditions of delivery. A cold night. The back seat of my brother's barely clean truck.

I ask myself again what Scarlett thought she was doing up there.

I wanted to ask you to marry me.

She couldn't have been serious, but I glance down at my finger staring at the titanium band on my third finger.

"Mr. Eaton. You can see your wife now." I don't correct the nurse as I jump from my waiting room seat and hastily follow her. Stepping into the hospital room, Scarlett is sitting upright, holding a baby to her breast who eagerly eats.

"He's starving," she says, staring down at the infant while her finger coasts over his cheek. While my eyes are drawn to her touch on the baby, I go for Scarlett first. My hands cup her cheeks, and I turn her face to me.

"You are so beautiful," I tell her, holding her eyes. "He is beautiful." Before she can respond, my mouth meets hers, taking her lips slow and sweet. When I pull back, Scarlett's eyes remain closed a second longer, and I rub my nose against hers before I lean over her, watching Sprout suckle.

"We need a name," I whisper, not wanting to disturb him. We discussed names and agreed on Eleanor Rose for my mother if we had a girl but hadn't narrowed down the male names even though we were more certain of a boy.

"Harland Bull Eaton the fourth. We can call him Harley."

"Harley Eaton." I nod to agree with the name, and Sprout pulls free of his mother, looking up at me as though I interrupted him.

"Say hello to Daddy," Scarlett coos.

I'm a father. This beautiful woman gave me a child, but she's also filled my heart with her love.

"I'm going to have a hard time not calling him Sprout."

Scarlett looks up at me. "We can pick another name."

Our eyes meet. "No. I love what you suggested, but we'll call him Sprout as a nickname while he's still little."

"I like that," Scarlett admits turning back to the baby. "Want to hold him?"

"You know I do," I say, reaching out with grabby hands for my son. "And while I'm holding him, I want you to explain everything to me." Tucking Sprout into my left arm, I take a finger to his cheek, stroking his soft cheek. His dark blue eyes match mine although they could change color. Most newborns have blue eyes.

Scarlett sighs.

"It's best to start at the beginning," I state to the baby but addressing Scarlett. The statement feels very déjà vu. Our son is the reason for everything. Then I realize that isn't true. Scarlett and I had an instant attraction, and we both agreed to keep it to one night in hopes of setting us both to rights. We never could have predicted setting us to rights meant bringing us together. I glance over at her. "What were you thinking in a snowstorm?"

Scarlett shrugs. "I'm wanted to surprise you. I knew you'd never ask me to marry you, so I wanted to ask you." Her dark eyes express a mix of emotions.

I lower for the edge of the mattress. "Tell me what you had planned."

Scarlett shakes her head, lowering her eyes. "I screwed it all up."

"I want to know. Let me see it in my head."

"I had the lights on the tree. That beautiful tree that's so special to you. And a picnic dinner for the back of the truck and blankets and the—" She stops short as her eyes land on my left hand, holding a sleeping babe in my arm.

"Keep going," I whisper, wanting all the details of how it could have been.

"And a ring."

"This ring." I tilt my hand upward as best I can, flashing her the backs of my fingers.

"Yes," she says, staring at the band surrounding the base of my third finger.

"I think that's my word. *Yes.*"

Her head tips up, wide dark eyes staring at me.

"How would you have asked, other than screaming at me while you were in labor?" I smile to show I'm teasing her.

"You once said you'd do anything for me. Anything means marrying me. I know you're against it, but I thought it was worth a shot to ask. I wanted you to know that a woman really wants you, wants to love you, but not just any woman. Me. I want to marry you. I want to love you. I do love you."

"You said that part while you were yelling," I remind her. "And I love you, too, sweetheart." The relief in telling her is like air being let out of a balloon. It's not deflating but weightlifting and freeing. Hesitantly, she smiles at me.

"I'm pretty sure I fell in love with you one night, and it's grown every day ending in day."

Scarlett giggles. "Every day." She nods at Sprout. "We have a lot of days ahead of us."

"We have years," I say, wiggling my finger at her. "Ask me."

"Here? Don't you think I've botched it up enough?"

"I think it's been perfect."

Scarlett straightens the blanket over her waist. Combs her fingers through her hair, which is marked by the hat she wore, flattening the top while the ends against her neck curl. She's never looked more beautiful.

"Bull Eaton, I'd really like to be your wife. Will you marry me?"

Leaning forward, I keep the baby tucked to my chest as I kiss her and blink back the liquid in my eyes. "I would love to be your husband, Scarlett Russell." Our lips meet again for a minute before Scarlett pulls back, swiping at her own eyes.

"Why now?" I ask, still curious how she could think proposing at the Engagement Tree during a snowstorm was wise.

"I wanted to ask you before the baby was born. I wanted it to be that you chose me *for me*, not just the baby. And I wanted you to know, I chose you for you, not just because of Sprout."

"I'll always want you, sweetheart. You because you're you," I say, smiling at her.

"And you're you," she says back before cupping her hand over the head of our sleeping son.

"And he's ours," I whisper.

"Ours." Scarlett holds up a finger. "But if you say partners—"

"You don't like partners? What's wrong with that word?"

"It's too business-y sounding. I like husband and wife better. Mom and dad work, too."

Leaning forward, I kiss her again before standing and placing Sprout in the baby bassinet provided. I don't want to set him down, but I want to hold my future wife even more. Climbing up next to her, she rolls to her side, and I scoop her into my chest.

"How about if we just call us a family?" I say into her hair, and Scarlett snuggles closer to me, wrapping her arms over mine around her body.

"I like the sound of that. Family."

EPILOGUE

SCARLETT

Five months later

It's a beautiful May day. The sun is shining. A slight breeze warms the air, and Bull and I are under the Engagement Tree. Last night, our five-month-old slept through the night for the first time, and we both feel a little stunned by a good night's sleep.

"We need to celebrate," Bull suggested, so we drove here. I watch as Bull carves our initials into the sacred family tree. B.E. + S.R. A heart surrounds the initials once he's done.

Bull's wearing my ring, and I'm wearing his mother's engagement ring with a wedding band Bull purchased. It's the first diamond he'd ever given a woman, and we were married at Christmas in a small ceremony by a family friend priest in Colebury.

Bull sits next to me, stretching out his legs on the blanket. A picnic basket rests in the corner, but for now, we're just enjoying the sound of a light breeze and the rustle of the leaves overhead.

That night at the Gin Mill changed everything for me, and like Rita said, change is scary but sometimes necessary. The Busy Bean Café needs that on their chalkboard beams.

As my red curls blow in the wind, Bull scoops a section over my ear.

"I love you," he says so easily, telling me every day that ends in day.

"I love you, too," I say before leaning in to kiss him. Harley sleeps in his car seat at the other corner of the blanket, and Bull and I stay quiet. We're quieter when we make love. We take time to savor those rare moments between duties on the dairy and raising our son. I've embraced motherhood. At forty-three now, I lived a full life with a career, but I'm living my best life as a stay-at-home mom. It's not the most glamorous job. In fact, most days, it's full of shitty diapers, spit-up shirts, and leaky breasts, but I wouldn't change a thing.

"What're you thinking about, sweetheart?" Bull says, breaking me from a stare at our son in the car seat.

"I'm thinking about that first night," I say, which isn't a hundred percent true. "How I would never have thought it'd bring me here." I look up at the budding foliage.

"Still like it here?" Bull asks, picking at the blanket before him.

"I love everything about Vermont, and you, of course." He looks at me, and I smile.

"I think we need a return visit to that room in the Green Rocks," Bull says, watching me.

"Why?" I giggle.

"Sprout needs a sister."

My mouth falls open. "Oh, he does, does he?"

"Yep, he told me." Bull scoots closer to me, wrapping his arm over my waist and tugging my middle, so I fall to my back next to him. Perched up on an elbow, Bull looks down at me. His hand coasts along my side, rubbing over my hip.

"Really? What did he say?"

"He said, can't get it up twenty times a day, old man, but you can at least get it up once a day ending in day, so get after it."

I laugh and then cover my mouth, afraid to wake Harley. "He did not say that," I mumble through my fingers.

"He said take her to bed, partner," Bull continues, leaning in to kiss my neck.

"Bull," I whisper to him.

"He said love her the rest of your life."

"I plan to do that to you," I tell him.

"Same, sweetheart. Now, about that baby-making . . ." His hand comes to my dress, lifting the hem for the promised land, and soon enough, he'll be buried in me, which is exactly where I want him to be all the days ending in day, and the nights, too.

THE
END

ACKNOWLEDGMENTS

(L)ittle (B)its of Gratitude

First and foremost, I want to thank Sarina Bowen for the World of True North. As a reader, it's a series I loved! And as a writer, I'm honored to be included in this wonderful adventure in Vermont. Heart Eyes Press also comes with a team: Natasha, Jenn, and Jane, who tackle all of us, rope us in and keep things going smoothly. Also a shout out to my fellow writers in the Busy Bean Café. It's been a mouthwatering blast to work with you.

As always, I need to thank Melissa, not only for her patience but her knowledge as this city girl knows very little about dairy farms. Yet, in writing this story I recalled how the father of one of my best friends as a teenager ran a major dairy farm for Michigan State University. As that was eons ago, the memories had faded.

Thanks also to Jenny and Karen for eagle eyes in edits and proofing. You make my words prettier . . . or is it, more pretty?

Thank you always to the wonderful ladies (and a few gentlemen) in Loving L.B. on Facebook. Your laughter and inspiration keeps me going . . . as well as your love of a sexy silver fox.

And finally, to my family: Mr. Dunbar, who is not a farmer, and our four sprouts who are now adults: MD, MK, JR and A.

Here's to 2021. We survived quarantine and 2020 together, and I still love you most because you're you.

Made in the USA
Las Vegas, NV
01 March 2021

18864520R00154